ALIVE ON THE INSIDE

D1367242

ALIVE ON THE INSIDE

…Torturo shook his hand, his grip firm, but he lingered just a second too long, as if reluctant to let go. "Hello, Nicholas."

Nick, lost in the large changeable hazel eyes, almost lingering himself, barely noticed the delay in the grip. "I'll definitely hike out. Probably not tonight. I work late. But tomorrow."

Torturo smiled a dazzling smile and produced four red pieces of pasteboard. "I'll see you tonight." Nick wondered privately if he realized that sounded more like a date than a show. At least everyone else was out to lunch and he was minding the store alone.

Nick looked at the free passes Torturo was offering. "I only need one."

"We're here four nights, or share them with your friends."

Nick smiled. "Maybe I should bring my fiancée."

Torturo's smile widened. "The more the merrier," he said, so cheerfully, Nick wondered if he'd imagined the flirting.

"Thank you. Would you like to approve placement?" He hung a couple of the posters in the front windows and one on the bulletin board beside his desk.

"That's perfect." Torturo's smile still looked inviting. "Thank you, Nicholas." This time, he held out his hand to shake. When Nick took it, once again, Torturo lingered too long and parted with something that was almost a caress of the back of Nick's hand.

"You're very welcome." He tapped the passes. "And thank you."

Torturo shot him a quick backward glance at the door and Nick smiled. He watched the performer ride off and looked more closely at the passes. Good for one admission to general show or adult show. He wondered what that meant…

ALSO BY ANGELIA SPARROW & NAOMI BROOKS

The Curse Of The Pharaoh's Manicurists

ALIVE ON THE INSIDE

BY

ANGELIA SPARROW &
NAOMI BROOKS

AMBER QUILL PRESS, LLC
http://www.amberquill.com

ALIVE ON THE INSIDE
AN AMBER QUILL PRESS BOOK

Amber Quill Press, LLC
http://www.amberquill.com

Layout and Formatting provided by: ElementalAlchemy.com

PUBLISHED IN THE UNITED STATES OF AMERICA

Welcome to the funhouse of our minds.
There is a lot to see here, so step right this way. Mind the
geography of Peculiar, we've taken a few liberties.

First, we owe thanks to Ray Bradbury, the late
Tom Reamy and Bryan D. Smith for their inspiration, and
to Bryan and Brian Keene for good advice.

We owe special thanks to the following people:

The Raymore Peculiar Class of 1986 for
volunteering to die hideous deaths as needed.

Harrisonville Girl Scout Troop 119, of which Angelia
was an honorary member. (Love y'all—A.)

Kiwi Carlisle for letting us borrow her dream of the
Peculiar Tea Shoppe and correcting the Tarot reading.

Our early readers: David Tyler, David Kopfer,
John Lucas, Drew Wallace, Kiwi (again) and Cat Grant.
Every one of you contributed on this.

The Memphis NaNoWriMo support group and
Word Catchers writers' group

Extra thanks to Trace Edward Zaber for encouraging us
to submit this and doing the wonderful cover,
and to Catherine Snodgrass, our editor.

This book is dedicated to the memory of Clyde Montgomery,
who did not get a hideous fictional death as he requested, but for
whom Death did indeed come calling in the fall of 2009.

Now, get comfortable. The show is about to begin.

—Angelia and Naomi

<u>FOREWORD</u>

There had always been a Phantasmagoria.

Somewhere, in the dim, dead remains of the past, it began with a juggler in Babylon or a dancer in Crete, a snake charmer in Memphis or an acrobat in Palmyra. One by one, they came together and the Phantasmagoria took on its own life.

It watched the pyramids rise and Troy fall. It entertained as Alexander swept east and the Visigoths swept west. The dead carts rolled and the Renaissance revitalized Europe. And always, the Phantasmagoria was there.

The acts came and went, dwarfs and dancers, giants and storytellers, freaks and fortunetellers, but the Show continued on.

The Enlightenment and Industry brought new techniques to the ancient Show and the Phantasmagoria carried these, as well as knowledge and disease wherever it traveled. To India, to learn the secrets of the fakirs and China where pretty girls touched the tops of their heads with the soles of their feet. To Russia, amid fire-eaters and fortunetellers, and into Africa, where men grew tall as trees.

In America, the railroad sped the travel and the Phantasmagoria learned and created anew the vaudeville show and traveling carnival. Times changed and the Phantasmagoria roared through the twenties, horrified through the fifties, and endured the arrival of movies and television.

But always, there was the Show.

Always, there was the Phantasmagoria.

PROLOGUE

Hitchcock, Oklahoma
August 12, 1925

Jacob Plum settled the outhouse over the new hole. There. Perfect. Mama wouldn't complain at all. She'd been after him to dig a new one for a week now.

"Move the backhouse every three years," he could hear her saying just that morning as he'd finished washing the dishes. Mama didn't get up much anymore. She didn't walk too well after the last baby had slid out of her much too early, a raw-looking thing not able to live. She'd almost bled to death.

So these days, Jacob handled the cooking and washing up and what little housecleaning got done. He was the only child, too big by far to have been born of the petite woman. None of the next babies had lived to draw breath. And the doctor said another would kill Mama.

He sat down in the shade of the big cottonwood tree and ate a peach, letting the light breeze cool him off. He tossed the pit in the old privy hole, knowing it would grow very fast. The whole back yard was a peach orchard now, with eight trees. He had just planted the ninth. That, too, was perfect, three lines of three.

His life had always been threes. Mother, father, and son. Work, eat, and pray. Home, church, and school. Apples, peaches, and pears. Cows, chickens, and pigs. Peas, beans, and corn. Nothing ever changed and everything came in threes.

He got up and shoveled the dirt from the new hole into the old one. He took one last glance down the hole as he tossed the first shovelful in. Damned waste of a good pair of overalls, he thought as the dirt rattled down on his father's body.

When the hole was full, he went to the barn. The pitchfork needed cleaning, too. He washed it out in the creek up in the pasture and thrust it into the ground. Dirt and hay soaked up the old man's blood.

Jacob just prayed he hadn't gotten much on him. Daddy had been making him stand in for his mama since she got sick and Jacob had finally gotten big enough to fix the problem. He went to the pump to wash before supper, making sure to get his back and the blood from his shirt before it set.

He walked back to the house, his afternoon's work complete, whistling "For he's a jolly good fellow," in honor of his sixteenth birthday.

CHAPTER 1

NICK

Nick Harper would be the first to say that he had a nice life, much better than he deserved. He smiled at that thought as he parked the little blue Dodge Laser, a perk of working for his uncle's dealership, in the drive of his duplex and picked up the *Cass County Democrat* from the lawn. He had plenty of time to read the paper and have a bite of dinner before Bible study.

With fall coming, his life got busy again. Next week was the first Cub Scout meeting. His nephew was a Webelo this year, which meant the fun stuff like camping and fire-building would really be starting.

He stubbed his toe on the bowling bag as he came in, because he leaned out the door to grab the mail instead of watching where he was going. Nick put the ball away, feeling guilty. It wouldn't do for Lisa to find out from nosy neighbors that he was a slob who didn't put his bowling ball away between Monday League night and Wednesday. Nick popped a TV dinner in the oven and sat down at the kitchen table with his mail.

Bills and more bills to drain his poor little checking account. Again, he was glad his small student loan was paid off. His savings account was full enough to put a down payment on a house. But doing that would leave him without a cushion and that, he told himself, was why he hadn't set a date with his pretty fiancée.

Lisa made his life lovely. He couldn't wait to see her on Saturday.

He always took the afternoon off for her. The *Democrat* showed the Raymore Peculiar Panthers out training for their first football game. Maybe he'd take her out to that. He always had season tickets.

A Friday date was a treat, but Saturday was always Lisa's. He'd get off at noon and pick her up. She didn't drive. They'd go for a late lunch and run errands. Then they usually went to the park and had a picnic supper, weather permitting. They talked about everything, politics, religion, their plans, their hopes.

She was a nice girl. But Nick fought a constant battle against his own desires. He consigned any lustful thought that intruded on his mind to the mental dustbin while he indulged in some exercise or an ice cold shower and reminded himself to flee fornication.

His relationship with Lisa could be summed up by a single interaction shortly after they started dating. Lisa had sighed and smiled when she looked at Nick and tenderly told him, "You're not like other boys are." Nick had swallowed hard, blushed and pretended that he was shyly embarrassed by the statement. But, deep inside, he knew the true reason he hadn't wanted to hear her say that.

He had no television. He did not take Lisa to the movies. He read some of the newspaper, but screened the stories carefully. There could be nothing to provoke lust. Slings of the Enemy he could fight, but lust was his weakness.

He hadn't always fled from it, which he regretted. The blonde girl he'd kissed while half-drunk at an unofficial college party had offered him much more when he returned for more kisses the next evening. It hadn't been just his mouth the pretty history major had kissed that time. Nick did not dwell on that, when he could help it. He wanted to go to Lisa as pure as she was coming to him.

He glanced at the timer, once the bills were paid. He had just time for his evening chapter. He read through the Bible every year. He had since the fateful day in 1980 when he'd been born again.

He flipped to First Corinthians, the evening reading, and made a little check on the bookmark that told him which passage to read that day. He read the warning given by the example of the Israelites twice. It resonated with him, since just that day, Nick had thought about kissing Lisa. "These things happened," Nick murmured, repeating verse six, "as examples to us, that we might not desire evil things."

He held that verse in his mind as he ate dinner and went to the men's Bible study.

Nick prayed for a long time that night, confessing his weaknesses and begging God to make him holy, make him pure and to take all the desire for wickedness from him. Then he took a quick, cool shower and went to bed.

The lesson didn't take. Although he fell asleep in his narrow, single bed, he dreamed. As a child, he had dreamed vividly and often. In his teens, these had lessened and since he'd been saved, he hadn't had more than a handful that he remembered. Most of the time he woke up remembering he'd had a good dream or a bad one, but not the content.

This time, he was at a frat party, like so many he had attended during his first semester in college, before the beer got hold of him, his grades went bad and his life had gone into freefall. God had caught him then, but in his dream, things were different.

He held a cup of beer in one hand and Lisa hung on the other arm. She giggled. Lisa never giggled. Nor did she wear skirts above her knee or a crop-top that plunged to show her cleavage.

"Let's go upstairs, sweetie," she said and he drained his beer, gamely allowing her to lead him up. It was his room at this frat, although he never joined one, and she sat on the bed smiling at him. "You had your drink," Lisa said. "Now I get mine."

She reached for his belt and then his zipper.

The loud train whistle sounded like something out of an old movie rather than any diesel engine horn when it woke him. He bolted upright, coming, the unfamiliar sensation of orgasm making him spasm. His underwear and pajamas lay cooling and sticky against his groin. He peered out the window of his duplex's back bedroom. He slept back here instead of in the front bedroom, because the biker gang on down the cul-de-sac liked to race at ungodly hours.

The night-black monstrosity looked more like the Eli at Worlds of Fun than any train that had ever held him up on his way to work. It slowed, the wheels screeching on the iron rails. Definitely an artifact, he decided. Private collector or something, since that style of car had gone out in the 1900s with the Pullman sleeper. Silvery scrollwork chased itself around the cars that looked like something from the Old West.

He heard the brakes grinding and squealing as it came to a stop, the red lantern on the caboose showing just past the lumberyard a quarter mile away.

Nick got up, got fresh underwear and pajamas and went to the bathroom. He dropped his fouled clothes in a heap and stepped at once into a warm shower. He scrubbed himself all over with the washcloth.

A train. Nick's first crazy thought was a circus train. That was ridiculous. The duplexes on Sheri Lane backed against the railroad tracks, but no train had been through for seven years. He toweled off and threw his pajamas and boxers into the washer before going back to bed.

Nick glanced at the clock, two-thirteen. He lay back down. The weird train was just passing through. Nothing exciting ever happened in Peculiar, Missouri, population 1156, he thought, staring at the ceiling. The place wasn't even big enough to have its own high school, but had consolidated with Raymore back in the early sixties.

The local festival, Bushwhacker Days, never terribly impressive in recent years, was over. It seemed to be making a comeback this year. Like everyone else, he'd gone out to the parade on a sunny June morning. He'd cheered the clowns, the horse units, the high school marching band, the Shriners with their little cars from down in Harrisonville, a little girls' drill team stepping to "Yellow Rose of Texas."

There had been booths all over Peculiar Park and a little carnival Midway for the first time in years. He remembered when he was a kid, the talk that one of the carnies had raped a local girl, so the city fathers had gutted the festival.

There was nothing else until Homecoming in October. He supposed he'd go. He'd been a mellophone player in the marching band for four years and still enjoyed watching football enough that he bought a season pass every year since he'd graduated back in '78.

He had to work in the morning. He lay quietly, meditating on his favorite Bible verse, trying to ignore the dream-vision of Lisa dressed scandalously and offering him lewd acts that Lisa would never perform. He slept again, with no dreams.

*   *   *

The double bell of his alarm rattled him awake. He turned it off and slogged to the shower. He read the *Kansas City Star*, carefully sticking to politics and avoiding any of the sexual violence stories, while eating his toast. The school bus went by outside. The loud wailing from the front yard told him that little Jenny in 201B had missed the kindergarten bus again, probably because their Saint Bernard was sitting on her again.

A few minutes later, he climbed into his brand-new Laser and headed for work. Every boy on Shari Lane envied the little electric-blue sports car, but Nick knew it was woefully underpowered and the T-top leaked in the rain. The one time he'd accidentally had it up past seventy, the mirrors had fluttered in the wind. He hoped for a LeBaron next year.

He pulled into the dealership with ten minutes to spare, as always. He took a minute to check his yellow silk power tie and then headed for his desk. There wouldn't be anyone in today. They'd sold four cars in August, all used. The economy was picking up, thanks to Reagan, but Nick wished it would move faster. He needed the commissions.

The delivery of the new Apple IIcs caused a bit of excitement. Nick spent most of the morning trying to get his set up. He opened the manual and followed it diligently, step-by-step, until a little green cursor glowed on the black screen.

Now he had a computer. What he was going to do with it, he had no idea. Someone would explain it, eventually. He went back to filling out clearance pricing forms. The new 1986 models had just come out, so they had to move the '85s.

When the paperwork was done, he doodled a little on a notepad and had another cup of coffee to kill the last forty-five minutes before lunch. Maybe on Saturday, he could steal a kiss from Lisa. Nick wrenched his thoughts away from that track. He never thought about sex, not if he could help it. That dream. It kept getting to him.

He'd take her out Saturday. They'd go up to Truman Corners, have dinner at Ponderosa and window shop some at the stores. Unless she wanted to go walk around Bannister Mall and then to Bennigan's. Lisa was addicted to their Death by Chocolate dessert.

He kept telling her that they'd get married when he could afford a down payment on a house. He had enough, but he wanted an emergency fund, too. He'd seen folks out of work the last six years and was determined that he wouldn't take a nothing job just to eat and that his wife wouldn't have to work.

Nick shied from the real reason he kept putting off the wedding, despite being twenty-five. He loved Lisa, but she didn't do anything for him. Kissing her was like kissing his pillow. He knew he should be more excited about her one offer to let him feel her breasts. And she had looked at him distinctly aslant when he had refused to make out with her when they'd gotten engaged on Valentine's Day. He'd kissed her cheek and said, "I want to wait until it's all legal and we're married. It'll be better that way."

He'd marry her in a year or so. He knew that as surely as he knew the route home.

When the tall young man came in through the door, Nick was too lost in thought to notice. But when the newcomer plopped a roll of posters on his desk and gave him a smile, Nick noticed. No one wore mustaches anymore, especially little pencil-thin Errol Flynn ones. They just sported three-days' growth of beard like Indiana Jones and Don Johnson. The newcomer looked kinda like the great Flynn, too. Nick had loved old movies in his teens, before he had cleansed his life and mind.

Nick automatically smiled and went into his patter. "Good afternoon. What can I do for you? Looking for something in the way of wheels?"

The newcomer laughed, rich and throaty in a way Nick had never heard in real life, as if he were inviting the whole world to laugh along with him. "Well, it's times like these I wish I could drive. Just for the pleasure of seeing what sort of flivver you'd sell me."

Nick's eyebrows went up at the admission and the antiquated slang. "I thought everyone drove."

"Not I. I go everywhere by train, or bicycle when the train is stopped." He gestured to a well-polished old-style bike with shiny chrome and a leather seat. "But even so, I find myself needing a bit of help." He tapped the roll of posters on Nick's desk. "I have free tickets if you could put these up for your customers to see."

Nick looked them over, musing at the old-fashioned art work. "Hmm. Train. Was that you about two A.M. up in Peculiar? I live in the duplexes right there on the tracks."

"That was us. I'm sorry, did we wake you?" His thin mustache quirked as if he were about to smile. He didn't look the least bit sorry.

"I woke up. Nice train. I'll have to come out for the show." He looked up from the posters. "Been a while since I've been on a Tilt-A-Whirl."

"And you'll come to my show?" The visitor's eyes twinkled and his smile looked inviting. "It'll be worth it," he said, almost suggestively.

Nick distracted himself by looking at the poster again. "You have real freaks? Not just a so-called museum? 'Cause I got scammed out of fifty cents when I was eight. I spent ten minutes in a stuffy, smelly trailer looking at old photographs."

"All the freaks are real. I'm one of them and I'm real, aren't I? I'm Torturo, the Pain King."

Nick brought down the unruly eyebrow that tried to climb his forehead. "Nick Harper, nice to meet you." His right hand came up automatically to shake.

Torturo shook his hand, his grip firm, but he lingered just a second too long, as if reluctant to let go. "Hello, Nicholas."

Nick, lost in the large changeable hazel eyes, almost lingering himself, barely noticed the delay in the grip. "I'll definitely hike out. Probably not tonight. I work late. But tomorrow."

Torturo smiled a dazzling smile and produced four red pieces of pasteboard. "I'll see you tonight." Nick wondered privately if he realized that sounded more like a date than a show. At least everyone else was out to lunch and he was minding the store alone.

Nick looked at the free passes Torturo was offering. "I only need one."

"We're here four nights, or share them with your friends."

Nick smiled. "Maybe I should bring my fiancée."

Torturo's smile widened. "The more the merrier," he said, so cheerfully, Nick wondered if he'd imagined the flirting.

"Thank you. Would you like to approve placement?" He hung a couple of the posters in the front windows and one on the bulletin board beside his desk.

"That's perfect."

"Thank you for coming by, Mr. Torturo."

Torturo's smile still looked inviting. "Thank you, Nicholas." This time, he held out his hand to shake. When Nick took it, once again, Torturo lingered too long and parted with something that was almost a caress of the back of Nick's hand.

"You're very welcome." He tapped the passes. "And thank you."

Torturo shot him a quick backward glance at the door and Nick smiled. He watched the performer ride off and looked more closely at the passes. Good for one admission to general show or adult show. He wondered what that meant.

He went back to his work and tried to ignore the insistent erection that poked at the bottom of his desk. He wasn't gay. He couldn't be gay. He was a Christian and being gay was completely incompatible with that. Brother Bob at church preached such vicious sermons, that Nick was certain that if he ever even looked gay, he'd be executed there on the industrial green carpet, his blood spattering the white walls with their dark wood chair rail, a payment for all the havoc homosexuals were wreaking on society and the family and the government.

Since he was sitting right here working, and not chasing after the man or excusing himself to the restroom to masturbate, he was clearly straight. Maybe he would steal that kiss from Lisa on Friday. He needed it.

He looked up from his desk an hour later when the door banged behind his uncle to see the square had been plastered with posters. Torturo and his bike leaned against a street lamp. Torturo seemed absorbed in lighting his pipe and took a long draw as he watched Nick watching him. When the pipe drew to his satisfaction, he licked his lips. Nick shivered, wanting and terrified. Torturo clearly saw it, for he tipped Nick a wink, *a knowing wink*, Nick's conscience seemed to say, then after a moment, he mounted his bike and road away north, toward Peculiar.

CHAPTER 2

PECULIAR

The carnival had chugged into town on the abandoned Burlington-Northern tracks, the cowcatcher of the gleaming black steam locomotive plowing through waist-high weeds. Which was ridiculous, of course. The heyday of carnival rail travel was long over. No one had seen a show come to town on the railroad in fifty years or more. Still, no one gave it much mind that Thursday morning.

In the quiet little houses of Peculiar, parents chivvied their kids to catch the school bus, before going to work themselves in the city. They returned to a town transformed.

Every telephone and light pole now sported a colorful flier for the Phantasmagoria Carnival. The windows of the post office, Laundromat, and grocery store, as well as the lumberyard fence bore smaller copies of the sideshow paintings. The Phantasmagoria would open Friday evening and run through the Labor Day weekend.

Two boys stood on Broadway, waiting for the crossing guard, greedily and excitedly inspecting the posters, which had bloomed on the hardware store fence while they were reviewing how to multiply fractions.

"Nagina, half-woman half-snake!" read Charlie from the poster that showed a desert and a creature that looked like Medusa from the movie, *Clash of the Titans*. "One of Nature's mistakes or the offspring of our First Mother Eve and the Serpent? Alive!"

"See Torturo, the Pain King, to whom physical agony is nothing!" read Jeremy, pushing his glasses up on his nose. "He eats glass, sleeps on nails, and dances on knives!" He looked at Charlie, his eyes big with excitement. "Cool." The poster showed a handsome man racked on a bed of nails while a shapely female assistant reached toward him with a flaming torch.

"Radical!" Charlie agreed. He read the poster. "The only Ten-in-One Show still riding the rails, featuring born freaks, oddities of nature, and human performers of all sorts! From Elijah Grant, the Carolina Giant, to his wife, Tabitha, the One Cubit Woman." They crossed Broadway and the main street, ignoring the guard's glares. "This is going to be so good."

"Race ya!" Jeremy said. "First one home gets to tell both moms!"

Torturo smiled as he watched them go, then pushed open the door to the Peculiar Tea Room. A slight lady with red curls and a sweet smile greeted him.

"Hello, what can I do for you, sir?" she smiled. "Will it be some tea? Or maybe your fortune? You're from out of town, aren't you?"

Torturo gave her a very friendly smile. "I am, indeed. And tea and my fortune are exactly what I want."

"Make yourself comfortable." She bustled about heating water in a kettle. "Cards, runes, or tea leaves, dear?"

"Cards, I think. Or maybe all three. I have the time and the money."

"Any preference on your tea?"

"Earl Grey, please. I love the classics."

"Lovely choice." She measured loose tea into a bright yellow pot and poured the water over it. After a moment's hesitation, she flipped the sign on the door to read, *With a client, come back in 15 minutes.* She sat down and poured into a pair of matching cups. "So, Mr..."

"Plum. Jacob Plum."

"And you can call me Kiwi. My partner is off today." She sipped her tea. "What are you looking for, Mr. Plum? A basic reading? Future? Past? A Love Forecast?" she teased.

He gave her a hopeful look. "The basic reading, with an eye to love?"

She smiled. "I can't imagine a handsome man like yourself has much trouble in that department." She finished her tea and took out a well-worn pack of tarot cards, shuffling them. She set them in front of him. "Cut them into three piles, please."

Jacob did and watched as she laid out a card, then circled six more

13

around it and put three under it. He was no expert, but he knew that the number of upside down cards could not be good. Kiwi's smile had gone and she was frowning at the spread.

She tapped the inverted High Priestess in the center. "This is your core issue. You're confused, conceited, and insecure. You're headed down the wrong path and into self-destruction." Her fingers moved to the reversed Knight of Wands at the bottom of the circle. "You brought this about by your own appetites. You're a sexy, exciting, and stylish man, Mr. Plum. But you have a bad temper, commit rash actions and are always on the move." She looked up. "You're with the carnival, so that figures."

Torturo looked at her. "Guilty as charged. Go on."

"It does get better." She touched the Ten of Pentacles to the left of the Knight. "This is your expectation. It's a very good wealth card, showing security, home and family." She moved to the reversed Ace of Pentacles above it. "This is the history of your situation. It's not pretty. Luxury, debauchery, overindulgence. It goes with your knight and the self-destructive inverted High Priestess."

"Exactly," he whispered, almost to himself.

"Here," she indicated the Eight of Swords, reversed, at the top of the spread, "are your challenges. You have to free yourself from a difficult situation or move on past some failure or humiliation.

"This is how you will evolve and learn. Oh dear. The Seven of Cups is Temptation personified. You'll pursue illusion, perhaps into intoxication and delirium, and all your effort is chasing phantoms." She shook her head. "You won't be learning, it appears."

She tapped the Eight of Wands on the right. "Your outcome looks all right. With decisive action you'll reach that goal." She nudged the Ten of Pentacles. "Be bold and daring, especially in love."

"I can certainly be that." He flashed her a dazzling smile, making sure all three dimples were on display. She blushed and returned to the reading.

"Your beloved is showing up as the Five of Wands. You're going to have to be very daring because that's a conflict card. Look at the men sparring. An intense struggle, yes, but it brings out the best in the participants." She looked to the middle of the bottom row. "In this circumstance, you will be the King of Wands."

He grinned cheekily. "Wands, eh? I've heard that before about my wand."

She threw him a look that she clearly meant to be stern, but he could see the smile lurking on her face. "Not that wand. The King is a great and daring leader, dashing and magnetic. It's you to a T. Don't be afraid to give others some authority. Your last card is the person who will bring it all together, The Knight of Pentacles. He's slow and steady, very predictable and the voice of honor and duty."

She shook her head. "You're a cad and a rounder who needs to grow up, move out of the past and grow into your kingship. Love is going to be a struggle, but well worth it because your lover will be steady as a rock when you get it together."

He gave her an even broader smile, more sure than ever about the little salesman. "Exactly as I thought. Thank you, Miss Kiwi." He laid down the twenty for the reading and a pair of free passes. "Would you mind putting one of our posters up?"

"Not at all." She taped it to the window. "Thank you. And come back any time." She flipped the door sign back to open and started cleaning up the tea things.

*　　*　　*

The next morning in the grade school gym, as the children waited for the later buses to arrive, their classmates who lived on YY highway had more to tell. The carnival was all set up. The Ferris wheel reached to the sky, the Zipper beside it.

"A Ring of Fire and a scrambler and a merry-go-round and a big round thing!" Nine-year-old Christy informed her classmates breathlessly. "And all kinds of shows and games and stuff."

"And a real freak show!" put in her brother Andy, with all his twelve-year-old authority. He was a sixth-grader so all the kids in the area piped down. "Real ones. We saw a couple of dwarfs setting up."

"Dwarves," corrected Mary, who'd been into Lewis since third grade and Tolkien since fourth. She never looked up from the fat fantasy novel she was reading. Everyone ignored her.

"And a giant. He was way tall. Taller than Mr. Lewis." The kids looked shocked at Andy's words. The principal, Mr. Lewis, stood taller than most of their fathers. "Taller than Mr. Sullins at the junior high, even."

"No way. Nobody real's taller than Mr. Sullins," said Joey. "He's almost as tall as Darth Vader."

"Yes way. He was holding up the pole of a tent while the dwarfs—"

"Dwarves," Mary corrected again. They still ignored her.

"Pounded in the pegs," Andy finished. "And the freak show. It's like the stories mom's told me about when Bushwhacker Days would set up uptown instead of out in the park."

The bell rang and the kids trooped to their classrooms. There would be very little seat-work done in any classroom that day. The three-day Labor Day weekend was coming and spelling tests and math quizzes would be the order of the day instead. It didn't hurt that all the teachers were distracted by the Phantasmagoria as well.

As the sun lowered in the August heat, the calliope filled the air. The sound carried uptown, a distance of about half a mile, luring folks who had decided they might go Saturday or Monday out to the old empty field, now turned into a neon playground, heavy with the scent of sugar and ozone.

Cotton candy machines whirred and funnel cakes fried and the odor of onion rings and corn dogs lay beneath them. Parents, leery of the costs involved, were shocked. The prices posted were straight from the 1960s, fifty cents for the corn dogs, a quarter for the cotton candy. Ride tickets cost twenty-five cents or a wristband for five dollars. Games were twenty-five cents a try. The freak show had separate admission and two different shows.

"No one under eighteen allowed in after ten at night," read Charlie. "Well, crap." The carnival trip had started off on the wrong foot. Jeremy had gotten his butt grounded for not doing dishes. Andy from next door had come along and that was all right.

"'S all right," said Andy, tugging at him, urging him down to look at the duck pickup booth. "We can go before ten."

Charlie held up his digital watch, brand new for his birthday in June. "It's nine-fifteen."

"Well, crap," Andy said.

A handsome man with a thin mustache came out of the giant black Ten-in-One tent, his off-white summer suit immaculate and his panama hat pulled low. He pushed it up and looked at the boys.

"Sorry, kids. The freak show doesn't start until ten tonight. But come back tomorrow and you can catch the matinee." He gave them a smile and then drew a nail that looked as big as a railway spike from a pocket of his jacket.

Andy's and Charlie's eyes got big as he poked it through the septum of his nose. "Torturo!" Andy gasped.

The man laughed. "Alive on the inside! Just like the poster says." He pulled the spike from the septum and then started working it up into his nose. "Don't try this at home. Go over to a friend's house and make sure his mom doesn't mind blood." He got the whole four-inch long spike into his nose as the boys gaped.

Torturo handed them two passes. "That's all they'll let me show you out here. Come back tomorrow, on me, and bring your parents and friends!"

"Thank you, Mr. Torturo," Charlie said, staring at the red pasteboard.

"Thank you, Your Majesty," Andy corrected him. "He's a king, remember?"

Torturo laughed, pulled the spike from his nose and waved as they dashed off, clutching the precious free passes. A pretty red-haired woman put her head out of the tent.

"Tortie, you're a big softy." For a small-time carnival, her accent spoke of tea and crumpets and leisurely afternoon strolls in Hyde Park. Her voice had entranced him the first day he'd heard it and still left him hard every time.

"No, Alice, m'dear, I'm hoping one of them has an older brother." He tweaked her cheek, eliciting a gasp from someone still inside the tent, and ducked back inside to join her. "Besides, two free child admissions will get us at least a couple of paid adult admissions."

"And you call me the slut." Alice giggled as her sister Dinah stepped closer. The leg they shared provided balance as Dinah moved to her usual position, about a hundred thirty-five degree angle from her sister's left hip. Torturo felt surrounded. The conjoined twins each stole a kiss from one of Torturo's cheeks. "We need a couple of piercings, love. Can you set us up? We have a new idea for the adult show."

Torturo cupped Dinah's breast and Alice's buttock. "Anything you like. Come to my trailer."

Alice pecked his cheek. "Maybe we should rehearse for the adult show, too?" She shot a look at her sister. "Dinah's been off with her timing."

Torturo grinned. "We'll talk while you're under the needle."

"Bright and early tomorrow, say nine?" Dinah said.

"Just knock loud."

They went to get ready for the show, the calliope music and the Midway talkers filling the thick-smelling canvas tent and the small-town crowd roiling outside the cloth.

*   *   *

Against his better judgment, Nick went to the show. He wandered the carnival grounds, bored. His old classmates and the current crop of students walked the Midway, arms around their girls, throwing balls at milk bottles, trying to pop balloons with darts. Some succeeded and were hauling around stuffed animals the size of a third-grader.

Nick hoped Lisa would enjoy this tomorrow. He was vetting it tonight. Her parents were stricter than he was and he had had to bargain long and hard earlier this summer to take her to Worlds of Fun, complete with promises to avoid any music shows at the amusement park. So far, the Midway passed inspection.

He hoped he could win her a giant teddy bear. It seemed the right sort of thing to do. Rides that went in a circle—which was most of them—made him throw up, but they'd probably do at least the Ferris wheel.

The clowns, mostly of normal height but a fair number of them little people, creeped him out as they slipped through the crowd hawking balloons and inflated toys. He'd never liked clowns and they seemed to be everywhere. The candy butcher had been a little under-dressed for Nick's taste, with her large breasts pushed up by her low-cut uniform, and he figured he'd have to be alert for her tomorrow and steer Lisa elsewhere when she showed up. The Guess Your Weight guy was cute, but he flirted with anything female, so Nick knew they would have to give that a miss as well.

He walked idly, eating on the foot-long corn dog he'd bought and looking at the shows. The World's Largest Rat. Gross. Not something Lisa would like. The smell from that tent alone made him hurry. The World's Only Living Unicorn would be good. He steered away from the Live Hootchie Cootchie Girls tent as fast as he could. That was completely inappropriate. He stepped past the fortune-teller booths, one of them claiming to be Marie Leveau and another the Cumaen Sybil. Well, that was Satanic. He made a note to cross to the other side of the Midway, where the games were, after the unicorn.

Mistress Valeria, Your Photo Not As You Are But As You Should Be, sounded interesting. They'd definitely have to get pictures done. He watched a trio of girls come out. One of the two shorter ones showed her picture to the other two.

That's totally you, Karin," the tall one said. The other short one nodded. As he passed, Nick caught a glimpse of the photo, which showed Karin in clothes from the Middle Ages, a pack by her feet, playing a flute.

"Emrys Gwalchmai," the little one said. "We always knew it."

"Kind of afraid to get mine done," the tall girl said. "Not sure I could show it to the folks."

The face-painting and the ear and body piercing booths held no attraction for him. He paused in front of the giant freak show tent. The next show started at ten, no one under eighteen admitted.

He'd caught the eight o'clock and watched the Siamese twins sing. He'd seen the world's smallest woman do a classical ballroom dance routine with her husband, the Carolina Giant, or at least his hand. Nick had squirmed as Nagina had crawled through a pit of snakes, her own hair writhing with them and the snake costume she wore around her lower half twisting and squirming like the puppeteers couldn't get her motion right.

But Torturo captured his attention. The Pain King had risen from a bed of nails when the spotlight came up and greeted the crowd with a cheerful patter about how important it was to get plenty of rest. He wore an old-fashioned gym suit, buff shorts and tank top with black edging, like Nick had seen in textbook pictures. His whole spiel sounded like the old health class movies, cheerful and full of common sense. But the act...*oh the act!* As Torturo talked about the importance of dental hygiene, he had swallowed a dozen razor blades and sent a chunk of dental floss after them, only to extract them, threaded on the floss. When he talked about a good breakfast, he had caught a chicken an assistant had released and geeked it.

Nick had stared as Torturo bit the bird's head off, spat it to the side, and drank blood from the neck. He'd tossed the chicken to his assistant with instructions to have it baked for dinner. Proper aerobic exercise was apparently dancing on a ladder of swords and then weight lifting. Nick shuddered at the memory of Torturo hoisting a variety of heavy objects using his pierced nipples.

He wasn't sure he could take Lisa to that. She'd love the rest of the show, the acrobat and the hairy escape artist and the twins, so maybe they could just leave before Torturo's act.

Nick wandered a little more, threw some rings around the necks of bottles and won himself a fake leather biker hat. He felt silly wearing it, but had no idea where else to carry it. He waited back at the tent when the little man in the classic carny costume, right down to straw boater and sleeve garters, climbed to the podium and started his pitch.

"Step right up, ladies and gentlemen, hurry on in. Alive on the inside, the only operating Ten-in-One featuring Nature's Marvels and

Mistakes. We have Alice and Dinah, two sisters with only three legs between them. Eternally joined at the hip, they make their way through life together. We have the Carolina Giant and his wife, the World's Smallest Woman. How do they live? How do they love? All will be revealed for a nominal fee of a double sawbuck. That's right, ladies and gentlemen, a single picture of Andrew Jackson gets you ten, Ten, TEN shows in one tent!"

Not knowing what possessed him to do it, Nick dug in his pocket and produced a red pass. He handed it up to the little man who made it vanish.

"Only the biker boy is bold enough to brave the Ten-in-One! Dark, erotic and mysterious, see Torturo, the Pain King, in the most shocking performance ever given on a public stage."

Nick ducked through the canvas flap, taking his hat off automatically, and found his way to a seat in front of the lighted stage. He set the hat on the bench beside him. His better judgment screamed at him to leave, to run even. "Flee fornication," rang in his mind, but another voice, a soft, compelling one, told him to sit and watch.

And watch he did, as the sweet little Tabitha, who had sold Bibles during the earlier show, came out and used her husband's penis as a stripper pole. Elijah lay back in a recliner, a board on his stomach with his cock through it. An extension half again as long as the shaft had been added and stood straight up from the head.

Tabitha, dressed in a tight white sheath dress, elbow length gloves, and tiny clear plastic shoes that sparkled with glitter, strutted out onto the board. She danced, stripping away her clothes until only the gloves and shoes remained. She climbed her pole like a rope in gym class and then twirled down it, both upside down and right side up. She did a set of vertical splits against it, her slim perfect legs spreading along the blood-dark shaft. She hooked her legs around it and slid down.

When Elijah came, showering the little women, the extension slipped out of his urethra, revealing it for a sound. Tabitha stretched luxuriously, covered in the pale fluid and licked her arms clean of it like a cat.

The crowd applauded and the lights went down. They came up to reveal Marvello the magician and Hannah the Bearded Lady, their matching van dykes and handlebar mustaches groomed to perfection. Marvello still wore full evening dress from the earlier show, but Hannah wore only shoes, top hat and a smile.

They did the guillotine trick from earlier in the day, but instead of her head through the slot, Hannah presented her breasts through the twin openings. She whimpered when Marvello closed a clamping bar down on her nipples to prevent her from withdrawing. He sent the blade crashing to the floor, slicing through the cantaloupes on either side of her, but leaving her unharmed.

Then Marvello set up a series of three swords. Hannah lay across the points. But rather than being suspended only by the neck one as she had been in the afternoon show, he left the one at her waist. To the audience's surprise, he spun her on it. She lay spread-eagle in the air, as if bound by invisible chains, and the sight of the rings in her labia caused a number of gasps from the crowd.

After three revolutions, she sank slowly down the sword, impaled and apparently dead. Before anyone in the crowd could panic, Marvello lifted her off of the sword and kissed her. He kissed her eyes and ears and nostrils. He kissed her lips, breathing in almost as deeply as if he were doing CPR. Then he kissed the tips of her breasts and the gaping wound the sword had made. To the audience's great shock, he spread her legs and kissed her vulva, embracing the lower lips as passionately as the upper.

At that, Hannah stirred and sat up, claiming a kiss from him. They took a bow together and vanished. Nick squirmed in his seat, uncomfortable yet aroused from the kissing of the two bearded mouths.

The lights came up on the conjoined twins. They wore emerald green corsets and stood with their arms around each other. A chain ran from each one's left nipple to her sister's and likewise from the right. A similar chain joined their mons. The one on the audience's right, Dinah, Nick remembered from the afternoon show, ran a slow hand over Alice's fiery curls.

Alice seized her sister by the shoulders and kissed her, with a wet, open tongue clearly visible. Dinah's hands came up and cupped Alice's breasts as they kissed and she moaned around Alice's tongue.

One of Dinah's hands worked its way between them to tug at Alice's end of the lowest chain. Alice yelped and pinched one of Dinah's nipples hard. Dinah retaliated by bending in to suck at Alice's breasts, closing her teeth on one nipple and pulling away, for the benefit of the audience. Her fingers were between Alice's legs and rubbing furiously.

Alice climaxed noisily, begging for more.

A spotlight picked out a figure high above them. Naked, Torturo lowered himself from the highest point of the tent suspended by a hook in his anus, a pair of rings in his penis and two nipple rings. The chain to which these all linked was attached to a rope that went over a pulley. Using the rope, Torturo lowered himself toward the Sapphic twins.

Nick, already uncomfortable watching the women, felt himself getting hard in his pants at the sight of Torturo. He considered fleeing while all eyes were on the Pain King, but found himself unable to move.

The twins moved apart as Torturo lowered himself between them. Dinah nipped his buttocks as he passed and Alice licked a stripe up his penis.

"Hello, girls," he said with a rakish grin. "Need any help?"

"Oh yes, please," said Alice.

"Not at all," grumped Dinah.

Torturo turned to her and handed her a dildo with wicked-looking spikes. She wiggled one for the audience, showing that these were not soft rubber. "I think maybe we can let you have your fun, too?"

"Of course, darling." Dinah smiled. She took the dildo and hooked it to a special strap on her corset. Nick watched, a part of his mind wondering where they had gotten them and whether Lisa might be amenable to one. He put the thought out of his mind at once.

He watched as Torturo stood between the twins, kissing them in turn before focusing his attention on Alice. Along with the rest of the crowd, he gasped as Torturo caught his hand on fire from a nearby candle. When Torturo spread the flames to Alice's breasts and then extinguished them with his mouth, the audience sighed in relief, only to gasp again when he set his cock afire.

In a marvel of timing, he thrust into Alice, snuffing the flame, as Dinah rammed the spiked dildo into him at a single stroke. He shuddered and groaned. Nick shuddered with him and felt himself growing damp and sticky.

Torturo indulged on the twins, his cock flaring anew with each out-stroke, singeing Alice's neatly trimmed triangle of hair. He shoved back on Dinah's toy, clearly loving it and having it hurt him at the same time.

The trio came simultaneously, in a shout that nearly raised the top of the tent. Torturo kissed the twins and slowly withdrew from both of them. He kissed them again, playing with their piercings. They took their bows and left.

"I never have the heart to tell them they aren't enough." He smiled as he hung cinder-blocks from each pierced nipple and one from each

22

of the holes in his foreskin.

Nick could bear no more and fled the tent before the rest of the acts, determined to have a cold shower and pray long and hard. He couldn't take Lisa around people who behaved like that. It was absolutely out of the question.

He showered, scouring himself under the stinging icy water until he was almost blue. Shivering, he bundled into his robe and went to do his Bible study.

Paul went on and on about men with long hair and women with short hair and how the man was the head of the woman as Christ was head of the church. Nick knew Lisa would let it be just that way. Her own hair hadn't been cut since she became a woman at thirteen.

Psalm 129, however, was no help. All the talk of plowmen making long furrows in the psalmist's back brought to mind the twins' nails as they had scratched at Torturo. Being cut free from the cords of the wicked, although he tried to claim the verse, only brought his mind around to Torturo's suspension rig. And gathered into the arms...no, he didn't want to think about that at all.

He knelt to pray, begging God to cleanse his mind of all he'd seen, to not let him become a filthy-minded lecher for whom even scripture had double and lewd meaning. He claimed the psalmist's promise that God would free him from oppression and the cords of the wicked.

Breathing a bit easier, he crawled into bed and lay flat on his back with his hands above the covers. That was when he realized he'd left his hat behind, like Joseph leaving his cloak in the hands of Potiphar's wife. He did his best to think of ledgers and sales records until he slept.

But his dreams were full of the Pain King.

CHAPTER 3

LISA

Nick woke sticky again, memories of erotic dreams discomfiting his morning. He stood under a tepid shower, remembering the way dream-Torturo had set Nick's own, unpierced cock afire and then knelt to take it in his mouth and put it out. He looked down at the traitorous organ, half hard and twitching at the memory. His hand drifted down to circle it, and he hesitated for a moment, unsure whether to strike it or stroke it. He jerked his hand away and turned off the water.

Without thinking any more, he got out of the shower, toweled briskly and dressed for work. The memory of the show and his dream intertwined until he was unsure whether he'd actually seen Torturo take the spiked strap-on or whether Torturo had grown spikes himself as he reamed Nick. He shoved away from the table and poured his coffee down the sink, not wanting it anymore. He dropped his toast, barely two bites missing from it, in the trash and went to work.

The drive went well for the first minute or two, but the image of Torturo on his knees, a wicked smile tipping that thin mustache up, made Nick step too hard on the gas as he left the on-ramp. When he shook himself and slowed back down to an acceptable fifty-five, the idea of the Pain King's pierced tongue on the bottom of his cock nearly put him in the ditch. He was still shaking when he parked the car at the dealership.

He was thankful that he had customers, even if they were only shopping. Talking about the cars and what the customers needed in one was comforting and distracting. It let him clear his mind of the disturbing images of the night before. He didn't have to think of Hannah's nipples, clamped to keep her from pulling away, or of the twins kissing each other or of Torturo, his long body naked under the lights, his uncut cock jutting out proudly as he let the twins kiss him.

But when the customers had gone, without letting him get the sale, he took a cup of coffee and stared morosely at the clock on the wall. It ticked down the last hour until noon and when both hands stood straight up, he grabbed his sport coat and headed out the door.

"See you Monday, Nick," his uncle called. "Take your girl on the carousel for me."

Nick waved, unwilling to admit he had no plans to go back to the carnival. He drove straight to Lisa's house and picked her up. They called up to Raytown for a pizza at the Fun House and got it to go. The Fun House wasn't safe. Not only was it in a bad area, but it served beer and allowed smoking. It still made the best pizza around.

Nick took her to Belton Park for a picnic with the pizza, which was a mistake. The old caboose that had been converted into a play area for the kids made him think of the train and the Phantasmagoria and Torturo. He ate the pizza, trying not to blush.

"Sweetie, I wanted to go to the carnival tonight," Lisa said, her gentle face wreathed in soft smiles. "That is, if you want to, I mean."

Asked so sweetly, Nick found himself readily agreeing. "All right. I've already checked it out. There's some stuff to avoid, like a fortune-teller, but I think you'll have a good time. It's not expensive at all."

He would take her on the rides and try not to ralph, win her a giant teddy bear, and they could even do the matinee freak show. He'd buy her the souvenir sheet music and Bible and copper snake bracelet from India if she wanted them. He might even buy her one of Torturo's autographed cards. Or maybe two, one for her and one for himself.

They went down old 71, since Lisa really never liked the big highway. It was a pretty day, clear and warm, so Nick opened the T-top on the Laser and they enjoyed the sunshine and breeze. Every now and then he'd glance over at Lisa, her brown hair caught back in a low ponytail, a few errant wisps whipped around her face by the wind that tugged at her floral dress, her brown eyes shining when she smiled at him. She loved him.

In that horrible instant, Nick knew he didn't love her, never had and never could. It was what Brother Bob said at church. Men didn't and couldn't feel love, which is why God had to command them to love Him and to love their wives by actions, not by feelings. Nick swallowed hard and resolved that Lisa would never know. He would provide a good home, a good living, and children for her. He would be kind and do all the little caring things the women's magazines in the doctor's office said he should. She deserved it. She would believe he loved her until the day she died. And afterward, when he was in hell for the lying desires that had seized him in the last day, she would have God to wipe away her tears and comfort her grief.

He reached over and took her hand. She startled, then relaxed with a very large smile. He almost never touched her, citing the slippery slope that contact led down, from hand-holding to kissing to deeper kissing until they were defiling themselves with fornication before the wedding.

Nick held her hand all the way to the Phantasmagoria. He parked and hopped out, opening her door and handing her out. He held her hand, something he never did in public, all the way through the gates and onto the Midway. He stole a glance and saw Lisa looking up at him with such adoration on her face that it made his chest hurt.

They strolled along the Midway, looking at the games first. Lisa was not adventurous, but she did pick up a duck, choosing a pink one and got a poster of a New England village, the white steeple rising out of the autumnal valley that a small line of print identified as New Hampshire. At the string-pull, she got a small purple teddy bear. She smiled and pressed the muzzle of it to Nick's cheek with a kissing sound.

The shooting gallery, with its old-fashioned line of ducks moving back and forth, drew them. Nick picked up the cork gun and sighted along it. He paid his money and fired at the ducks, knocking down four with six shots, which got them a Chinese lamp.

Taking the fat, red, laughing Buddha that the booth man offered first was out of the question. There would be no idols in the Harper house. Nick let Lisa pick between a large round paper lantern with a light inside, or the hexagonal style with red tassels, that had a pretty lady on a bridge. She took the hexagon, which Nick thought looked like the ones on the walls at their favorite Chinese restaurant. They took the prizes back to the car, so the lamp wouldn't get damaged.

"Fresh lemonade," Lisa noticed as they walked out. "That sounds good." Nick nodded and bought a couple of cups. It was perfect, sweet and tart and cold. She held his cup while he opened the trunk and stashed their goodies.

They threw the empty cups away and continued exploring. The smells of cooked sugar from the cotton candy and elephant ear booths tempted them. Nick checked his watch and saw they had an hour and a half until the next freak show, at six.

Lisa shivered at the sight of the posters for the *World's Largest Rat!* and *The Beautiful Body Without Any Head! A Miracle of Science!* that they passed. She smiled and blushed at the Hammer Throw, where several of the local football players had taken off their shirts in the heat and were trying valiantly to ring the bell at the top of the backboard. A tall, very good-looking dark-haired boy rang it and his friends cheered. He handed the four-foot tall purple gorilla to his little blonde girlfriend who wasn't much taller than it was.

"Go do it, Nicky," she said. "See where you rate."

Nick left his shirt on and stepped up. He handed over his quarter to the boothman and picked up the hammer. He looked at the ratings on the backboard and scowled. "Girl" read the lowest, "Pansy" above that, "Drag Queen" was followed by "Light in the Loafers." "Gym homo" and "Muscle queer" were near the top. The top, where the bell sat, just read "Super-fag." He didn't want to do this.

He picked up the hammer anyway. Lisa wanted to watch him. So he swung the hammer experimentally and then brought it crashing down on the pad. The weight shot up the backboard and clanged on the bell.

"My Superman." She sighed, with a smile. He looked at the backboard and saw it had ratings of various comic book super heroes, with Clark Kent at the bottom, progressing up through Aquaman, Wonder Woman, Green Lantern, Batman, and topping out with Superman. He must have read it wrong.

She picked out the panda bear, which meant another trip to the car. This time, they focused on the attractions as they came in. They shied from Marie Leveau and the Cumaean Sybil and Mopsus, All-Seeing Son of Blind Tiresius, knowing that going to any one of them could open the family to demonic possession for generations.

Nick nodded at the photo booth. "Want to try this one?" Lisa looked at the pictures, puzzled to see so many familiar faces in unfamiliar clothing and settings. The organist from church stood along a boardwalk in a picture hat, her bustle behind her, with a parasol in her hand. The high school Spanish teacher, usually the most proper of women, wore a dark chiton that bared her breasts and held a lyre. Nick made sure Lisa didn't see the one of their youth minister, sprawled on satin pillows and nibbling a grape, his eyes painted and his face looking ridiculously soft and beautiful.

"She just dresses you up, right? Like when we had that picture made up at Worlds of Fun?" Lisa cherished the picture. It had been Nick's idea to get an old-time engagement picture made. She was wearing a Civil War ball dress and Nick, in Confederate uniform, knelt before her, sliding a ring onto her hand. Everyone thought it was lovely.

Nick nodded, a little uneasy now. He was relatively sure that Lisa harbored no wicked secrets and the camera would only make her lovely and not wanton. They went into the little tent. Mistress Valeria, an Amazonian woman with black hair, a roman nose and olive skin, smiled at them.

"Hello, children. You come for your pictures?" Her accent was vaguely Italian, putting Nick in mind of paintings of sunshine on the vineyard walls, wicker-wrapped Chianti bottles with candles in them and garlic bread.

"Yes, please," Lisa said. "Together?"

"No, no, bella. The camera, she can only capture one at a time. You and then your handsome husband."

Lisa smiled. "Fiancé," she corrected. "So where are the costumes?" She looked around the little tent.

"There are none. The magic is all in the camera."

Lisa flinched at that and turned to go. Nick stopped her. "It's all done with computers and trick photography," he reassured her.

A little calmer, Lisa sat down in the chair. Nick watched as Valeria took her picture, with no more fanfare than a Sears photographer. Nick took his turn in the chair.

Valeria smiled at them. "You will come back after the six o'clock Ten-in-One. The pictures will be ready then. For you, I make a special deal. I charge three dollar each, but for the pair of you, only four for two pictures. Retakes, one dollar." She handed Nick back the dollar from his five.

Lisa wanted to see the Living Unicorn and she cooed over the pretty little white goat with the single horn. It was frisky and friendly and bounced right over to Lisa, wanting to be petted. She bought a handful of pellets from the machine for a dime and fed them to the unicorn, petting it. It nuzzled in her hand for more food. Nick bought a handful and stooped down to join her, but the little beast turned its nose up at his offering and went back to Lisa for more petting.

He dumped the pellets into Lisa's hand and stood back up, almost angry. Of course, the animal couldn't tell if he was a virgin or not. He considered himself pure, even if it was only by stretching the definition to exclude dreams and certain kisses from history majors. It must not have liked his aftershave.

Lisa said as much. "But I like it," she added, taking a deep breath of the citrus and leather smell of his Aramis cologne. She didn't take his hand, but washed up using the wet-wipe packets at the exit. Then she tucked one hand into his elbow and moved a little closer.

At the face-painting booth, they watched a little girl from their church get bright yellow flowers to match her T-shirt painted on her face by one of the dwarf clowns. Nick, feeling very bold, stroked Lisa's cheek.

"Some pretty purple ones to match your dress? Or a butterfly?" he offered. "Right here." Before she could react, he kissed her left cheekbone, his lips barely brushing her soft face. Lisa looked at him, shocked and pleased.

"Oh, Nicky. No thanks. But I would like another kiss."

He smiled and led her away from the painting pavilion. They had time for a few rides before the show. Nick knew it would be best to break up the around and around motions, but bought wristbands for them. In the line for the scrambler, which the carnival called The Whip, the sign showing a whisk and mounds of whipped cream, he turned her gently to face him and kissed her on the lips, his own mouth closed.

Lisa wrapped her arms around his neck and held him in the kiss as long as he would stay. It wasn't long. He pulled away a little, gave her two small quick pecks and then slipped out of her arms.

"Nick," she breathed, all flushed and her eyes big. "You're naughty today."

He smiled his most disarming smile, the one that always sold cars. "Yeah, I am. It's the carnival." Then his face crumbled into worry. "Is it okay? I mean, you're not scared or hurt or offended, are you?"

Lisa smiled back and tucked her arm back into his elbow as the line moved forward. "I'm fine. I'd begun to worry that you didn't like me. How could I keep you happy as your wife if you didn't want to kiss and touch me?"

"I love you, sweetheart," he lied and kissed her cheek again. It was more kisses than he'd given her in the last six months and he loved the way she almost glowed with happiness.

Nick didn't lose his lunch on the scrambler, or the carousel. He astonished Lisa by knowing that it turned backward, clockwise, because it was European. The great carved horses reared and tossed their heads in the company of leaping cats and bounding rabbits and placid camels. He led her up the winding stair to the second tier and got them a seat in an egg-shaped chariot, drawn by the four horses in front of it. She looked surprised when he put his arm around her for the ride.

"A coach and four for my princess," he teased. They rode out the first waltz and showed their wristbands for a second. This time, Lisa took a fine black horse with roses all over his saddle and a scarlet plume that waved in the breeze. Nick picked the more stationary stag beside it. He rode with his eyes closed, the pizza starting to come back on him.

They sat for a few minutes, watching the people. Lisa loved watching people. Nick privately suspected she wished she were able to let go and enjoy so much license as the others. But she was a good girl and knew that the only real freedom was in absolute obedience to God, which meant guarding every idea and action.

From the loudspeakers came the raspy voice of the talker. "Step up, step up, friends. The Ten-in-One is about to start. The Phantasmagoria, the only Ten-in-One Freak Show still riding the rails with made freaks, born freaks and working acts, all for your education and amusement. Come in, come in, see Wolfgang, the Wolf-Boy. Half man, half wolf, he takes after his namesake, Wolfgang Mozart. Ten, ten, ten acts in one!"

They didn't wait to hear more. Nick led Lisa over to the enormous black tent and handed up the free passes to the Ten-in-One's talker. Lisa just stared a little.

"How many Annie Oakelys you got, tiger?" the little man asked, punching them with a star-shaped punch and handing them back. "A souvenir for the little lady."

They got seats inside the tent and Lisa looked at him. "Where'd you get the passes?"

Nick flipped up his shirt collar. "I got…connections, bay-beee," he drawled like a 1950s hood. When she smiled, he said, "I got the passes from Torturo, one of the performers. He came into the dealership and I put up his posters, so he gave me three passes. I used one last night to check out the show."

Lisa nodded. "So what did he mean about Annie?"

"I have no idea."

A small tap on his shoulder sent Nick looking around. Tabitha, the

One Cubit Woman, stood beside their seats. "May I see your tickets?"

Nick showed her the punched red tickets. "What's an Annie Oakley? The guy outside asked how many I had."

The little woman laughed, covering her mouth with her slender hands. "It's slang for a free pass. Annie used to shoot holes in them for the guests. We can't do that anymore."

"Ah, insurance reasons," Nick said sagely.

"No, we just don't have a trick shooter." She smiled and moved on to check the next couple's tickets.

"She's tiny," Lisa said. "And so beautiful."

Nick nodded. "Wait'll you see her husband."

The show began. Lisa watched, shifting uncomfortably as a very good looking black man wearing evening tails and a van dyke beard with handle-bar mustache came out on stage. He smiled over the audience.

"I am Marvello, Master of Illusion," he announced. "I do, however, require an assistant." At that cue, two roustabouts wheeled an elaborate Egyptian mummy case onto the stage. Marvello threw it open to reveal a half-unwrapped dessicated mummy, its flesh black on visible bones and its teeth bared in a rictus. The audience predictably recoiled.

"Hannah, darling? Can you hear me?" he called.

From all around the tent came a sepulchral woman's voice. "I hear you, Marvello."

"I need you." Something flickered in the mummy case. "Across the years I call to you, beckoning you from your long sleep to my aid," he intoned, as the mummy swelled with life, now clearly female and draped in the artful wrappings. "Come to me, my wife of all eternity." With that, he stepped to the mummy case and extended his hand into it, helping Hannah, now dressed in the wrappings, death mask and headpiece, step out of it.

She took a quick bow and ducked backstage to change into an abbreviated form of the evening tails that Marvello wore. She wore heels and net stockings that came to the high, French-cut legs of her body suit. Her van dyke and handle-bar mustache were as immaculate as his.

Lisa looked more and more uncomfortable with each illusion, until a little scream escaped her at the guillotine trick. She clutched Nick as the blade rattled home. At the end, Hannah and Marvello circled the audience selling autographed pitch-cards of themselves for a quarter and a small vanishing box magic trick for seventy-five cents. Nick offered, but Lisa didn't want either thing. Nick got the card of Hannah suspended across the points of three swords.

"Sorry, sweetheart," he whispered and wrapped a comforting arm around her. It didn't help. She screamed again as Nagina, the Punjab Snake Goddess slithered down the main aisle, her cobra's tail flicking against the bleachers, her wings fanning a little as she moved. The little black snakelings in her hair writhed and hissed. Lisa buried her face in Nick's shoulder through the duration of the snake-charming act. Nick watched avidly, trying to figure out how Nagina managed to move in that costume.

Lisa looked up again when the music changed from the Indian pipes to a Big Band sound. Nick stroked her hair as she shuddered at the tip of the snake's tail vanishing behind the curtains.

"I think you'll like this part, Lisa," Nick whispered.

A man almost as tall as the tent pushed a dollhouse as tall as a normal man onto the stage. He pulled a pair of white gloves, one of which had a top hat sewn to it, onto his trashcan-lid-sized hands.

The house opened to show the tiny woman they had met earlier getting dressed. She was buckling the last strap of her dancing shoes. The man knocked on the door of her house and she opened it. The hand, wearing the top hat, stood in the door. She hugged it.

"Oh, Elijah, are we going dancing?" She tucked her arm into his thumb.

"Of course, my dear." He walked his fingers across the platform to a small stage. She climbed it and he put his arm through the curtains. The band played and Elijah sang in a great rumbling bass.

"Heaven. I'm in Heaven. And my heart is beating so that I can hardly speak. And I seem to find the happiness I seek, When we're out together dancing cheek to cheek."

As he sang the old Irving Berlin tune, Tabitha and his hand went through the classic Fred Astaire and Ginger Rogers dance routine. For an encore, they did "Smoke gets in your Eyes."

Lisa applauded wildly. They took their bows and Tabitha smiled at the crowd. "I send my husband to heaven by dancing with him. If you'd like to know how to go to heaven, we have the road map right here. The World's Smallest Bible, only seventy-five cents, comes with its own magnifying glass and for an extra quarter I'll inscribe it to you."

They circulated through the audience, Tabitha standing on one of her husband's massive palms, with a stack of tiny Bibles on the other. Nick held up his dollar. Elijah took it and Tabitha asked, "What name?"

"Lisa," he said. "Lisa Fleming."

The little woman handed down the book and Nick took it. On the presentation page it read, "Presented to Lisa Fleming this thirty-first day of August, Anno Domini Nineteen Hundred and Eighty-Five by Elijah Grant, the Carolina Giant and Tabitha Grant, His One Cubit Wife." He passed it to Lisa and they both thanked the couple.

Lisa jumped a little at the next act. Nick had to admit that Wolfgang was a startling sight, covered with the long brown hair that grew from every follicle and writhing around in a straight jacket. The wolf-boy lifted his head and howled.

"Good evening, folks," he said, his Germanic accent turning it almost to "goot." He thrashed a bit. "I am Wolfgang. You know, it's just that phase of the moon." He gave a chuckle that was something too close to a growl for Nick's comfort. "It makes my colleagues here feel safer to have me...restrained." He chuckled again, the sound of small animal bones snapping beneath a predator's jaws, and shrugged out of the straight jacket.

The crowd gasped as he charged to the edge of the stage, only to divert course at the last instant and go to the baby grand piano that Elijah wheeled out. He sat down and played Mozart's "Eine Kleine Nachtmusik." A collective laugh of relief went up.

"My parents named me Wolfgang, for Wolfgang Amadeus Mozart. But when I came out like this... Mutti got rug burn giving birth and Papa wanted to organize an angry mob. I scampered away from home at three weeks old." The crowd laughed again.

"I have a lot of practice escaping," he said as Hannah came out in her top hat and tails and handcuffed him. She helped him step into a trunk. "They keep trying to lock me up." The end of the sentence came out muffled, because Hannah drew a black silk bag over his head and tied a rope around its neck.

Then Hannah locked Wolfgang in the trunk. She stood atop the trunk and raised a black silk curtain. When the curtain fell two seconds later, it was Wolfgang who caught it.

"But it never works," he finished. He unlocked the trunk and opened the bag to show Hannah, dressed in a red spangled leotard, handcuffed inside. He freed her hands and kissed her cheek, then favored them with Mozart's Piano Sonata 11, "Nocturne," before taking his bow and leaving the stage to sell small folders with his picture in one side and his sheet music in the other. Nick handed over fifty cents and Wolfgang autographed it for Lisa.

He was replaced by a tiny Chinese girl, barely five feet tall, her black hair in a tight knot on her head. A goldfish bowl, full of swimming goldfish, rested atop her hair. She wore a gold bodysuit with gold wrist and ankle bracelets. Very carefully, she lay on the floor of the stage, then rose up to balance on her forearms. Nick watched as she brought petite bare feet up to her head and picked up the goldfish bowl without spilling any or disturbing the fish. With a look of complete concentration, she set the fish on the floor in front of her face and planted her feet flat on the stage in front of her shoulders.

The crowd watched, rapt as she went through contortions almost impossible for anyone with a normal spine. She finished her act by placing her bottom on her head, her legs forward in front of her and balancing on her chin on a rotating, filled wineglass. She made two complete circuits and then gracefully brought her feet forward until she stood on them, glass in hand. She toasted the audience and drank the wine before taking a bow and almost dancing off the stage.

She circulated through the crowd, selling silver spoons with the handle in the shape of a Chinese fish and a small inset of her picture as she lifted the goldfish bowl. When Nick bought one, she pointed to the Chinese characters on the bowl. "The maker signs for me."

"That was worth seeing," Lisa said, staring at the picture in the handle as the stage dimmed again. Nick agreed. He didn't tell her the girl was so flexible that she could lick herself and did during the adult show.

The twins were next. Alice and Dinah wore pretty green dresses and stood demurely on the stage, their shared leg directly in the center, half-facing each other and holding hands. They smiled, introduced themselves and nodded to Wolfgang, whose piano had been moved to the side of the stage.

He played "Evening Prayer" from the opera *Hansel and Gretel*, a duet for soprano and mezzo-soprano. Alice sang Hansel's part and Dinah, Gretel's. Their voices twined together, weaving the old song in and out and soaring to the end. Lisa applauded wildly, loving the performance. The twins gave her an extra sweet smile as they autographed their folder with picture and sheet music.

Jene left Nick confused and Lisa shaking her head. The hermaphrodite wore a one-shouldered scarlet leotard, the strap over the right shoulder to support Jean's breast. Gene's lower body was clearly visible through the clingy material. Jene came out, spinning balls of fire on strings. They did it over and under legs, over their face while bending backward until Nick worried Gene would set his half-mustache and beard on fire.

"Wow," Lisa whispered.

Then, they ate the fire, taking a flaming skewer into their mouth, only to spit the flames back out in a blaze, igniting a candelabrum set near the edge of the stage. For the finale, they swallowed a flaming sword.

The plastic glow balls on a string, to practice twirling before moving on to fire, were autographed in two different hand-writings. Gene Carlisle had the lefty's cramped back-slant, while Jean Carlisle had rounded loops.

They cleared for the final act. Nick tried to rise, wanting to get Lisa out so she would not be exposed to the filth he knew was coming, but his knees refused to work. He could do nothing but watch as the roustabouts set up the apparatus and wheeled out Torturo on his bed of nails. Nick tried not to watch. Failing miserably in that endeavor, he tried to reduce it to something similar to all the other acts they'd seen this evening. But Lisa's soft sigh as he stood up and stripped off the tank top of the old gym suit drew Nick's eyes back in time to see Torturo eat the razor blades. Next to him, Lisa hid her face again, either repulsed or too aroused to watch more.

Nick watched with sick fascination and was horrified when he felt himself getting hard in his slacks. He told himself it was Lisa and the way they'd been all over each other all day. They hadn't been well behaved at all. But deep down he knew that was as much a lie as his "I love you" had been. It was the man on the stage, now thrusting a spike into his nose, that had him aroused.

Lisa looked up in time to see him bite the head off the chicken. Nick caught her as she fainted and held her. He didn't know what else to do. Torturo winked as he guzzled the blood and threw the dead bird to a handler.

His eyes remained on Nick as he attached the clips to his nipple rings and hoisted the cinderblock. The audience gave a collective shudder. He thanked them and offered pitch-cards of himself for sale. One was from the act, the other just a head and torso shot. Nick bought two copies of each.

The Pain King didn't even ask his name as he signed the first set. "Put her head between her knees. That will help," he suggested, as he signed the ones for Lisa. He gave Nick a smile. "You know, you left your hat behind last night. Why don't you come by my train car and pick it up in a few minutes?"

The crowd had thinned out, making room for the next show so there were few bystanders to listen to Nick stutter at the proposition. He somehow knew if they went to Torturo's train car, neither of them would leave a virgin. Lisa stirred in his arms, distracting him from the places his mind was leaping to. He couldn't think about that, about kissing Torturo and Lisa both, of watching the Pain King make love to his fiancée and then—

Lisa looked up to see Torturo smiling down at her and gave a little scream that jarred Nick back to reality. Nick cuddled her.

"You horrible, horrible man. Get a real job, why don't you? One where you don't abuse animals or yourself." She stood up, pulling at Nick, shrill with anger in her fear and horror.

"My dear, this is a very real job. I work a thirteen-hour day, far longer than most men. If you don't believe me, you could try it. I can do the piercings for you right now."

The smile, doubtlessly meant to be charming, made Nick's blood run cold. His cock twitched at the thought of Lisa under the needle. But, in his mind's eye, her faced morphed into his own and the treacherous brute positively jumped. He could only stare as Torturo ducked in and kissed Lisa's slack mouth, pressing deep and open-mouthed like the kisses he'd seen in movies, before he'd stopped going.

Lisa jerked away. "You had no right. I'd never..." She slapped him. "That was Nick's wedding kiss, you wicked, wicked man!"

She burst into tears and fled the Ten-in-One tent. Nick followed, Torturo's laugh ringing in his ears.

The exit took them out through an exhibit of deformed babies in alcohol. Nick, hard on Lisa's heels, caught her in front of the two-headed monstrosity.

"It's all right. Shhhh," he soothed, drawing her into his arms and stroking her hair. "It's all right."

"No, it isn't." She sobbed. "It can't be. He violated me and took what was yours and only yours to enjoy."

"Lisa." Nick finally realized where they were standing and the closed, dead eyes floating behind their glass walls all creeped him out, making him think they could open at any second. He hoped she was too upset to see where they were. They'd spent more than one weekend protesting abortion clinics. Looking at these things for too long might change her mind. He led Lisa out and they sat on a bench. He offered her a pocket handkerchief.

When Lisa had quit crying, Nick asked, "Do you want to go home? I can come back and get our pictures."

She shook her head. A small sheepish smile escaped her. "No, but I'm really hungry. That sounds silly, since we just ate. Please, no chicken?"

"I'll go get something and bring it back," Nick promised. "You sit tight."

*   *   *

Lisa watched him head for the Greek concession. Nick was short and she lost track of him in the crowd. She loved gyros and he knew it. Such a lucky lady she was. But now, she had to pee. She squirmed, trying to make the urge go away. She spotted the port-a-potties not far away and decided she could get back before Nick did.

The escape to the port-a-potty was uneventful, but as she went back to the bench, she slowed for an instant.

"Child," came the low voice from where a coffee-colored hand beckoned her into a tent. "Come talk to old Marie." Lisa startled at the southern and oddly French sound of it. She stepped into the woman's tent and recoiled at once seeing the astrological chart and the pack of tarot cards.

"I have to go." She stared for an instant, then averted her eyes. She wouldn't look at the tools of the devil. "My fiancé will worry." She laid a hand on the tent flap.

"Lisa," said Marie.

The sound of her name stopped her.

Marie's bony fingers shuffled the cards and laid them out. "You need me now. Sit. Stay sat."

Something in her tone told Lisa it would be a very bad idea not to obey. She didn't want to look at the cards. Oh, it was wickedness and demonic. Her gaze went straight to the first when Marie tapped it.

The old woman read out the cards, one by one. "I see wealth and happiness and many children for you," she said.

Lisa relaxed a little. That was the plan. That was God's will for every woman. Maybe the cards weren't evil. The next words drew her up short.

"Shaun will make a perfect husband." Marie smiled, her teeth bright in her dark face.

"I'm engaged to Nick," Lisa protested. She tried not to stare. She had never talked to a black person before. Marie frightened her in many ways, not just her profession and occult powers.

Rather than correct herself, Marie shook her head with a sad look. "You'll never marry no Nick. Not now, not never." She turned over a card showing the Five of Swords. Lisa drew away from the dead man and his bloody wounds. "I look for your Nick, I see only loss, child. No Nick. Look for Shaun."

Unable to bear another word, Lisa ducked out of the tent and found Nick waiting for her on the bench, his own sandwich half-eaten.

"Sorry, nature called," she said. She took the gyro and bit into it, but the cucumber yogurt sauce was sour on her tongue and the meat tasted spoiled under rancid seasoning oils.

She looked over at Nick, who was finishing his, slurping the last sting of onion out of the pita with a smile. "Nick? Did they cut these from the same roast?"

He nodded. "Yeah. Good, isn't it?" He noticed she'd only taken a single bite. "Is yours okay?"

"It tastes really funny, like spoiled or something. Out in this weather, food goes bad so quickly." She offered it to him.

Nick took a bite of it. "Tastes fine to me, sweetheart. I think you're still shaky from fainting."

She tried it again, the second bite worse than the first. Gamely, she ate, sipping often at the lemonade to cut the taste. Nick left her again for a minute to get their pictures from Mistress Valeria. Hating herself for the waste, she tucked the unfinished half into a trash can.

"Mine didn't turn out," he said. "Yours is really cute."

She opened the pasteboard folder to see herself in a coat-dress and pearls, her hair done in a fifties sort of upsweep. She smiled as she laid a table for five, a small brown-haired boy opening the kitchen door in the background.

"I look like my mother. But that is nice. Just like we're going to be, right?" She shoved Marie Leveau's words *you'll never marry no Nick*, out of her mind. She glanced at her watch. "It's almost nine."

"Time to get you home, Mrs. Harper," he teased.

She was more than ready to be led to the car. She buckled up and held the souvenirs on her lap. She wanted another peek at the picture. She'd photographed really well. Her mother was the beauty of the family. Usually, she herself just looked a little mousy. When she opened the folder, she just saw a photo of the locomotive of the Phantasmagoria.

"I hope you didn't pay her for this," she said as Nick got in.

"She let me have it for a quarter as a souvenir of the show. And apologized for not having the camera aimed correctly."

Nick drove her home silently. She watched him, just as silently. She liked to watch him. It made her feel all soft and squishy inside and kind of tingly. The kisses he'd been giving her all day were definitely making her feel that way. In her driveway, he looked at her. She leaned in closer, hoping for a kiss.

"I'm sorry about all that. I didn't mean to upset you." Nick stared out the windshield, not looking at her. She wished he would.

"It's all right." She looked at her hands, ashamed of herself for giving in to her carnal desires. Nick not looking at her made her feel dirty and spoiled. The freak had ruined her. "I just... I'd never been kissed like that. I was saving that kiss for you at our wedding."

Nick smiled and lifted her face to look at him. "It's not too late to keep saving it." He pressed her lips lightly. "I'm giving it back to you. Keep it safe." He kissed her again, his mouth still closed. "And when you do give it to me, it will be better than wine, sweeter than raisins or apples."

She got out, her lips tingling, and went inside, knowing Nick wouldn't leave her driveway until she was safely indoors. In private, she wondered which man was making her tingle, Nick or the handsome freak.

CHAPTER 4

MIDWAY

That particular Saturday, Torturo lounged in the entrance of his booth, waiting for customers. Very few people wanted to have ear piercings done so early in the day. The really sexy pierces tended to wait and slip in under cover of darkness. He sipped from a tall glass garnished with a lemon slice. Most people, seeing the glass and the nearby gallon jug would have assumed it was sun tea. They would be partially right. He alone knew it was laced with a pint of whiskey. He would kill the whole gallon of tea before the weekend was over.

He watched the crowds as they moved among the games, rides, and attractions. It had been so long since he was one of them. When he had moved among the crowds on the Midway, the women had worn calico or gingham dresses and straw hats, the men bib-overalls. All the clothing had been well-worn and often mended, unlike the blue jeans worn by both sexes, so new and stiff with dye and sizing that the wearers could barely stagger.

He watched a family, the daughters clearly related by their pretty mother, walk along. The older girl, maybe seventeen and very tall, wearing jeans, a black T-shirt and a couple of necklaces, hung back, as if not wishing to be seen.

He watched the father, a small man with the look of someone who is despised and can't quite figure out why, as he walked holding the younger girl's hand. When the man opened his mouth, his nasal whine carried clear across the Midway and Torturo understood the look of loathing on the older girl's face.

She said something, too low to be heard. The man cut her off with a snarled word and a slashing gesture. The pretty woman moved a little down the way and pretended she couldn't hear it. Fear, perhaps that the man would notice she was there, showed clearly on her face. Torturo saw the man's eyes shift to her and then over the curves of her daughter, who was clearly none of his getting.

The girl rolled her eyes and looked around as her family walked on. She spotted Torturo in his booth and her eyebrows went up. He winked at her. She smiled and hurried to catch up. He saw the man slow, dropping behind. As he watched, the man took a sidelong glance to get the girl's position. When she was almost in range, he stopped and slammed his elbow back to catch her in the gut, in a movement that would look accidental to anyone not watching the whole drama.

The girl had seen him slowing and matched him at the last instant, stopping out of range of his elbow. When he whirled on her in a fury, she smirked and said something so clearly nasty that it made the little man's ears go red. He stalked off to catch up to his wife and younger daughter.

She caught Torturo looking and winked back. Then she touched the tip of her tongue to the cupid's bow of her upper lip and moved on to greet a short, buxom dark haired girl in a gold tunic and black pants wearing a gold mesh choker that matched her own. Her pleasure at seeing the little one was obvious and Torturo did not miss that her eyes went straight to the girl's low neckline and her lovely creamy breasts on fine display.

Torturo smiled. He always liked seeing adventurous women. And ones that could stand up were even better. She was not going to stay under that roof long, he was willing to bet.

::*Not her*,:: came a still voice in the back of his mind. ::*She's mine.*::

Torturo scowled. He knew what that meant, especially on Labor Day weekend. The Phantasmagoria did not run on steam and cash alone, but on blood and spirits. The Show wanted her. He took another long drink of whiskey. "You think it makes it easier when you pick ones I'm interested in, don't you?" he grumbled at the Show. There was, unsurprisingly, no answer.

He idly watched the parents and the younger girl for a while. They went into the petting zoo. The older girl went off to ride the Tilt-A-

Whirl with her friend? Girlfriend? It didn't matter.

His attention fell on a tall, stocky blonde girl, accompanied by a shorter dark young man. He watched the girl go in to see Mopsus the Seer, while the boy watched the rides. When the boy noticed him, he winked. The boy flinched and busily began studying the promotional pictures Mistress Valeria had out. Invert, but hiding, Torturo decided. His blonde girlfriend was in for a nasty surprise.

The boys from the day before came back with a third in tow and introduced him. They showed him they still had the passes and only looked a little disappointed when he didn't offer them a third. They stared, awed at the piercing booth.

"Can you pierce anything?" Charlie asked, gently touching the three eyebrow spikes Torturo had above each eye.

"Anything I can pinch." Torturo reached out and pinched Charlie's cheek.

"Punk rock!" Charlie laughed.

"Even on girls?" Jeremy whispered, his tone that of reverent awe. Torturo knew exactly which bits of girls the boy was thinking of. He was young enough that sex was still a mystery, but one he was starting to want to solve.

"Even on girls." Torturo opened his own shirt and pulled up his undershirt to show them his pierced nipples. "Looks pretty much like that. Usually not in threes though." His own had spikes that went under the nipple in an X and the ring itself. Andy almost reached out and touched it, but stopped himself.

The boys giggled. "Thank you, your majesty," they said and dashed off for a ride on the octopus. Such a pity they weren't a few years older, he thought.

He went back to people-watching. He'd been twenty-three in 1932 when the Phantasmagoria had come to Hitchcock, Oklahoma. It had been the biggest thing to hit Blaine County in years. Folks walked and rode in from three counties away.

And he had seen the twins. Alice and Dinah had come out in their old-fashioned dresses and sung the "Evening Prayer." They were the single most beautiful thing he had ever seen. They had smiled right at him. A messenger had come to him with a note to see them in their coach.

Torturo—who had not been Torturo then, but only Jacob Plum—went, ashamed of his patched shirt and mended trousers. He had spent his last lone penny on one of their cards, so he could carry the memory of them with him, always.

They had kissed him and washed him and made all his dreams come true. He had fallen asleep aboard the train and awakened far from Hitchcock.

He watched three older boys whoop through the crowd, ducking around lines and making plenty of racket. The short one with curly hair pointed at the giant rat display. His straight-haired stocky companion pointed to the Ring of Fire. The taller boy, a dark saturnine youth, guided them both into the mirror maze.

Torturo shook his head. The maze would be safe enough at this hour. He didn't trust it after dark. He remembered watching one night and counting entrances and exits. Not everyone who entered came out. He had never ventured in himself and had no desire to do so. No one else seemed to care.

A voice, slightly accented with French, came over the loudspeaker. "This is Clovis de Lorraine, Voice of the Phantasmagoria. There will be a masked ball tonight after the midnight performance of the Ten-in-One. Admission is free. The Phantasmagoria will provide all that is necessary. A mask and costume will be required to enter the dancing pavilion. Dancing will end an hour before dawn to allow clean-up time for the tent meeting and hymn sing. No masks may be worn to that event. Thank you and enjoy your visit."

Torturo looked up at the speaker. Clovis must want several from this town and very badly. Well, he would only supply one. The girl. He knew she'd be at the ball. Clovis would have never declared it if she was the type to skip it.

The thrill seekers rode the rides. He watched the tall captain of the baseball team, or so his shirt proclaimed to anyone reading, win his rather short and homely girlfriend a large teddy bear. She smiled up at him like he was God incarnate. Torturo hid a smile. Someone would get lucky tonight.

He glanced at his watch. Almost time for the two o'clock. A shadow fell over the booth. The tall girl with the wicked stepfather stood there, her short, lovely companion beside her.

"I am not getting my ears done, Cyn," the little one protested, her blue eyes startling against her black hair. Torturo wondered if she had as much fire as her friend.

The tall girl looked down at him where he sat. "My friend is a little reluctant," she said, jerking her head at her companion. Torturo saw her ears were pierced and little chain mail triangles dangled from them.

"We're just looking."

"Feel free." He smiled and watched them look at all his stock. As the little one worked toward the far side of the tent, he noticed the tall one was edging toward him. She stopped in front of his chair and swallowed hard, getting up her nerve.

"Mostly, I dragged her along because my folks worry about me. I came in to ask if you did," she turned a little red and cleared her throat, "nipple piercings," she finished in a lower voice.

"Sin…" Torturo deliberately inflected her name, turning it into pure wickedness in his mouth. He smiled as she turned a little pinker. "Lovely name. And suited to the question."

"Cynthia." She wrinkled her nose. "And do you?"

He made a show of studying her breasts. She didn't flinch when he touched the side of one. In fact, she pressed into his hands. "Twenty-five dollars for two rings." He touched the soft curve of the other side and squeezed them gently. Her breathing got faster. "A special price, since they're so lovely."

She blushed but did not move out of his hands. "Uh…all right. And…" She stuttered a little, clearly unsure how to handle the compliment. "Thank you," she managed.

Torturo released her with great reluctance. He was ready to yank her in, kiss her and shoo her little friend out of the tent. But it was too early. "Tonight, then?"

"Uh-huh." She nodded. "I heard the thing about the masked ball." She got even quieter and spoke very fast. "Will you dance with me? Please just one?"

Torturo picked up a needle and made a show of being preoccupied. "I don't know." He watched her face fall. "I can certainly manage one dance. But I had hoped to be your date."

Sin stared at him as if he'd grown a second head then and there. Nothing came out of her mouth but series of "uhs." She nodded, but then looked at him suspiciously, the gaze of a girl who had been set up too many times. He knew his proposal sounded odd coming so soon on the heels of meeting her, but she had seen him watching her earlier.

He gave her the most charming smile in his repertoire, showing all three dimples. "That's a yes? I did like the way you handled the old man."

Her eyes narrowed more as he smiled. "How do I know you won't be here, laughing at me for being a dumb kid?"

Torturo turned off the charm and looked at her as earnestly as he knew how. He took one of her hands in his. "Darling, I wouldn't ask if I didn't want to. And I do."

Sin looked relieved at that. "All right. Shall I meet you here? I'm a good dancer. I took ballroom dancing instead of gym class for the last two years." She shot a quick look at her friend who was ostentatiously studying the necklaces. "Later. I'll sneak in to the adult show. I can pass for eighteen," she whispered.

He gave her hand a gentle squeeze, pressing a free pass into it, and let go with a show of reluctance.

Cyn's companion joined them, shaking her head, tossing her waist-length braid. "You know you'll chicken out. Like you did on the rappel cliff."

"Who's a chicken? I went down that cliff," Cyn protested as they left. He noticed her eyes trailing over her friend's ass.

"Buck buck buck," her friend clucked.

"Let's get one of those deep fried pickles," Cyn suggested.

Torturo stifled a groan at the image of her mouth wrapping around the pickle. He imagined it on his cock. He would bet the flirty little dyke liked boys, too. He would love getting her alone, seeing those perfect breasts bared to his needle. He knew it would take very little to persuade her into giving her piercing artist a special tip. She might not be for him, but he could still enjoy her. He rubbed his already-hard cock through his pants.

He closed the booth. He had just time to take care of the problem before the next show.

He went through the day, enjoying himself immensely. This was a typical small town. Grudges and secrets, abuse and love all carried through it. He watched older blue-haired ladies cut a pretty woman dead while fawning on her husband. He saw little teen princesses, at least one so drunk she could barely walk by three in the afternoon and their athlete boyfriends. One man, physically handicapped with oversized legs and using a cane to get through the crowd, looked at the children in his path in a way that made even Torturo shudder.

Most would have shuddered from fear. He did it from ancient memory. He let that thought sink like an unquiet zombie. If he thought of his father, he would never make it through the next show. He flagged one of the clowns and told them to keep an eye on things, pointing out the chester on the Midway.

One of the teen princesses brought her boyfriend over and made him get his left ear pierced. Torturo obliged, setting the blue stone in the dead center so fast the boy barely had time to yelp.

At the six o'clock show, he was unsurprised to see Nick on the front row, a pretty little brunette on his arm. He watched the young man and his girl through the opening acts, the still voice in the back of his head whispering that Nick was indeed the one meant for him. It told him to get Nick aboard on Monday and the Phantasmagoria would make sure he stayed, forever.

He could see Nick didn't love the girl, despite his gentleness with her and his care of her. She adored him and couldn't tell that he felt nothing at all. Yes, he would be doing them both a true service. Nick would be cruising the gay bars within a year if they married and the girl would know.

Torturo took a breath and stepped onto the stage for his routine. He couldn't take his eyes off of Nick, those bright blue eyes capturing his imagination until he knew he was hard in his gym-suit. He glanced down and saw Nick had the same problem and was dealing with it with much less grace.

When the girl fainted, Torturo saw his opening. He finished the act quickly, keeping his eyes locked on Nick as he hoisted the cinderblocks. Even those didn't hurt today, they just made him harder. Only a few people bought his photo cards, but Nick bought five. Two dressed ones for his girl and all three, including the nude—which he didn't request an autograph on—for himself.

"Put her head between her knees," he suggested as he signed the cards for Lisa. Nick obeyed at once and Torturo hid a smile. This one was completely trainable and programmed to respond to authority. Perfect. "You left your hat last night. Why don't you come to the train car in a few minutes and get it?" He almost made it an order, but enjoyed the flustered stuttering from Nick.

Lisa came around and Torturo handed her the cards with a flourish. She gave a little yelp when he smiled at her. "My apologies, miss. It's not often we get ladies of your delicate constitution these days."

She shied away and made the rude suggestion he get a real job. He was watching Nick when he offered to do the piercings so she could try doing his job. Nick looked like he was about to come in his pants at the thought of Lisa with piercings. By the protective way Nick moved his hand in front of his hard-on, Torturo knew he was remembering last night's show and wondering about piercings of his own.

He seized the moment and kissed the girl's open mouth. She stood stupidly for a minute and then yanked away. She never did kiss back.

Nick had apparently been a complete gentleman, or invert, whichever. Then she hit him and fled, crying.

Nick had followed, but Torturo saw the last glance back at him. Under the anger was a deep wanting. He laughed. He filled the tent with it and sent it rolling down the Midway after them like one of Zeus's thunderbolts.

Alice and Dinah peered out. "Is it time for the next show, Tortie, darling?" Alice asked.

He kissed her, getting a far better response than from Nick's little mouse-girl. "Not yet, my dears. But I think we've found a new member of the Phantasmagoria."

Dinah nuzzled his neck. "That little rabbit can't do much for you." She sniffed, dismissive of Lisa's ordinary prettiness.

"Not the girl. Her boyfriend." He shivered as Alice's hand closed around his shaft through the beige cotton of his shorts.

"Come someplace private, darling, and we'll take care of you." Alice twisted one of the rings in his foreskin.

"That would be lovely." He let the twins lead him to their train carriage and followed them in. Soon, he promised himself, he would have a double bunk of his own.

*   *   *

The next show, he was rather surprised to see the family he'd been watching earlier on the Midway. He noted that Cyn put her sister and her mother between herself and her stepfather. The stepfather knew it all. He had the grace to be polite for the singing and the acrobatics and the dancing. But he had to blab to everyone about how Wolfgang did his escape and how Marvello's illusions were all mirrors and wires. He actually gave a short dissertation on how Jene's fire-eating worked, one that included the words "cold fire." Torturo hated hecklers and he hated spoilers more.

Jene hated them, too. "Sir," they said. "I need your ever-so-knowledgeable assistance for this next bit."

He had no idea they were mocking him, Torturo realized as the man climbed the stage and looked smug.

"So, our clever friend, what is your name and occupation?"

"Lee Dennison," he answered. "I'm an engineer."

"Of course." Jene smiled. Torturo rolled his eyes. Engineers were the worst. Not exactly scientists, they had enough smatterings in all the studies to think they knew everything. "Chemical engineer?" they hazarded.

"Mechanical engineer," he answered.

"Then if you would, please, Mr. Lee Dennison, Mechanical Engineer, use any match or lighter you have on you to ignite this torch please?"

He pulled a half-used book of matches from his shirt pocket and struck one with the practiced ease of a pack-and-a-half a day smoker. He lit the torch. "You're using a cool-burning oil in that," he said loudly.

Jene just picked up the torch, sucked the fire into their mouth and then sprayed it back at him, igniting the hair on his arms. "I am?" They smothered the fire in a woolen blanket, leaving behind only first degree burns.

"I can sue you people for this," he snarled. He sat down and his wife pulled a tube of clear gel from her purse. He sulked as he rubbed it on his arms.

"Good luck trying." Jene sniffed and finished their act.

Torturo had already decided to make that show particularly gory. Instead of the usual needle through the arm stunt, he ran it through his tongue, bleeding a lot. Cyn's little sister passed out. Two faintings in one day, which was high for the last few years.

He made sure to geek the chicken very messily. When the spoiler said it was fake chicken, Torturo replied, "Ask Mr. Wymer down the road. We bought it from him."

The wife looked very smug. She finally spoke up. "Please do tell my father he's raising fake chickens, honey." The last word left Torturo feeling chilled from the frost in it.

The spoiler shut up until they left. As they passed out the pickled punks' tunnel, Torturo heard him say the things were rubber. His wife contradicted him and mentioned she'd seen one of those born. Maybe there was a bit of spark in the lady yet.

The last evening show went off without a hitch. He did a second ear piercing on a shy, very smart-looking blond boy. Sin dropped back by his tent before the adult show. She sat on a folding chair in the back, examining the jewelry, saying she wanted to be sure of her piercing choice.

A trio of dark-haired boys hung around until he considered asking if they wanted anything done. At last, they shoved the taller white boy forward. The Mexican-looking boy and the shorter white boy—the one he had noticed earlier with the blonde girl—egged their friend on.

"Come on, Tom. You said you would."

"Yeah, but you guys have to, too," Tom insisted.

The other white boy nodded. "I'm next. Julian, you can go last."

Tom's friends busied themselves looking at the jewelry. Tom selected a small red stone and Torturo set it before he could change his mind. The second boy took his place in the chair holding a clear crystal earring.

"Nice choice, John," Tom said. He caught sight of Sin, who had slid off the chair and was practically crouched under a table to be out of their line of sight. "Sneaking around, bitch?" he demanded.

Sin ignored him and continued looking. Tom walked over as Torturo was finishing with John. The Pain King watched as the boy kicked Sin in the thigh. Tom spoke low and fast, demanding her attention.

"I'm talking to you, four-eyes. I bet you're thinking of taking that faggot freak to bed." He jerked a head at Torturo who pretended to be absorbed in piercing Julian's ear with a green stone. "Knew you were a disgusting slut."

Torturo stepped into the boy's line of sight. "Hardly a faggot if I'm enjoying the charms of this delightful young lady. Something I'm sure none of you ever have or will." He looked at the three young men, frowning. "Do you often harass other customers in a shop or insult men with sharp needles in their hands?"

Tom sneered, all teen bravado in the face of a larger opponent. "She's almost a boy anyway. Dyke wants to be and everyone knows it."

Torturo moved closer to him and ran a hand down his face. "No need to be so jealous. There's plenty more if you're wanting it." Before Tom could react, Torturo kissed him, just to give the boy something to think about. He stifled a smile when Tom opened up to him at once and he heard a soft whimper.

He did smile when he pulled back. He winked at Julian and raised an offering eyebrow to John. "Anyone is welcome to play." The three boys turned and showed their heels, fleeing into the safety of the darkness. Sin looked up at him, her honey-colored eyes adoring.

"That…" She flushed. "That was the sexiest thing I've ever seen." She took his hand and let him help her to her feet, clearly hopeful he would kiss her, too. "Thank you. They're a pack of jackals and I'm the weak antelope at the edge of the class herd."

He shook his head. "Not so very weak at all. Far braver than any of them. You see what you desire and acquire it. They simply look and want, constrained."

Since she looked so expectant, he decided not to disappoint her. He drew her close with one arm around her waist and tipped her face up with his free hand. She wrapped her arms around his neck and pressed her breasts against him. He gave her the lightest of brushes, just enough to get a feel for her lips. She looked disappointed when he eased away.

"That's it? You French that creep and all I get is that little peck?" She seemed to be working up to a full mad. He pulled her in tightly and laid one finger across her lips.

"Sin, to kiss you properly would spoil all the delightful anticipation. And the way I plan to kiss you is certainly not appropriate for the middle of the Midway, which you seem to have forgotten." He smiled and stroked her lips with that finger. "I promise, you'll have all he did and more, in due time."

"I'll be at the adult show," she promised.

He nodded and sent her out of the booth with a swat. He closed the piercing tent and went to get ready.

*　　*　　*

He was not at all surprised to see Nick sitting near the front for the adult show that evening. He also noted Sin living up to her name on the second row in tight jeans and a tighter T-shirt, with a different short, buxom brunette. Must be her type, he decided, and smiled as he watched her. The earlier kiss and his anticipation of her made him hard before the show started. The friend whispered nervously to her and she looked a little scared herself. Just as he had figured, she was underage. It didn't matter to him. He watched her and her top-heavy friend for a few minutes. He liked them young. Not as young as the man he'd seen earlier, true, but not old enough to have been spoiled by leering, pawing teen boys. Not old enough to associate sex with something messy and shameful that boys did and girls put up with.

The audience was mostly male, as it always was. Young men, without dates and without any place better to be on a Saturday night, filled the benches waiting for some fantasy fodder. Torturo saw the three boys whose ears he had pierced sitting in the middle.

The show went on. He heard a lot of heavy breathing through the other acts and a few gasps as he lowered himself in for the twins. A low soft moan that he recognized as an orgasm came from the crowd when he lit himself afire and entered Alice. A whispered, "That had to hurt," accompanied Dinah's spikes.

After the twins had left, the house lights came up to half. He turned as he always did and addressed the crowd. "That's better. If we're having an erotic experience together, I would like to see you. I adore my twins, but they really are never quite enough. I need a volunteer." He beckoned the little brunette to the stage.

She blushed and gave Sin a look. Sin urged her to go. She started but the call of, "Go for it, Boom-boom!" from the trio of boys slowed her. Torturo beckoned her up. She was almost beet-red when she got there and was very carefully looking at his face and not his naked body.

"What's your name, my dear?" He smiled as if he hadn't heard the rudeness.

She shot a glare at the boys. "Suzie." She breathed a little easier. "Suzie Bloodworth."

Torturo smiled and beckoned the twins. "If you'll go with Alice and Dinah, they'll get you dressed. You can watch from backstage."

The twins each took one of her hands and led her behind the black curtain. She shot a reproachful glance at her friend as she went.

Torturo picked up an enormous apple. "Dinah was lovely. But I do like something a little larger." He licked the apple, careful not to puncture it with the three spikes in his tongue. He bent over the table, his back to the audience and spread his legs. Slowly, he worked the apple into his ass.

He beckoned a short young blond man, with the compact and powerful physique of a wrestler up on the stage. "What's your name, sir?"

"Max Reinhardt."

"How much do you bench, Max?"

Max smiled. "Two-fifty."

"Pick up that weight, if you would please, Max."

Max lifted it and the audience could see him working at it, his fair Nordic face turning red. "Oof. That's about fifty pounds."

Torturo nodded. "Thank you. You can sit down. A hand for my helper, here, folks." The audience applauded politely as Max went back to his seat.

Torturo's cock was still flaccid. He attached heavy chains to his foreskin piercings and hooked the chains to the weight Max had just set down. He was effectively trapped in place. "Is she ready?"

"Almost," Dinah called.

"All right, folks. The only way that this weight is getting off the floor is if I get aroused. As Max said, it's about fifty pounds. And here's my help."

Suzie, now wearing a royal blue corset that pushed her ample bosom up and out on display, stepped out uncertainly. Torturo smiled and the crowd saw his cock twitch.

"A bit more help, Suzie, my dear." He bent in for a kiss, making it slow and deep, like in the movies. She was blushing bright red and a rosy flush had crept over her face and the tops of her breasts.

Torturo's mouth followed the blush and he buried his face between her enormous soft breasts. Suzie just stood still, blushing furiously and breathing very fast. There was a loud snap, one he knew most of the audience should recognize as a mousetrap going off.

Torturo came up out of her bosom with a mousetrap on his tongue. His cock was completely rigid and the fifty pound weight hung in mid-air, four inches from the floor. He lifted the bar from his tongue.

"Ow." He grinned. "Thank you, my dear. A very large round of applause for Suzie who was a very sweet girl and a lovely helper." He lowered his voice. "Please, keep the corset as a memento."

The applause rolled and Suzie sat down, still wearing the corset. Tabitha came out a moment later carrying her blouse. Sin smiled at her and Torturo continued the act. He tried to vary it from night to night, so that one adult show was a little different from the next.

Tonight, for the finale, he set up a small campfire in a barbecue brazier and stabbed a barbecue fork through his still-hard cock, making sure to futz around a bit and cover himself at least once, long enough the audience could think he'd substituted a sausage. He sat on a camp chair, over the brazier, roasting his penis in the fire and singing "Oh Susanna."

Suzie kept blushing. The smell of cooking meat filled the tent.

At length, he stood up. "Ah, nothing like a weenie roast." He rode out the wave of laughter. He brandished the barbecue fork, yanking his discolored cock back and forth. He offered it to the front row, most of whom recoiled as he moved down the line. He wasn't surprised when Sin moved up and tried a lick.

She drew back, fanning her mouth. "That's hot!"

"Freshly roasted." He gave her a wink. Finally he stopped in front of Nick. "Need a bite?"

"Yeah," someone from the back said, "have a bite."

Soon the whole crowd took it up. "Bite. Bite. Bite."

Nick hesitated and then leaned forward. Torturo could see the progression of his thoughts, that it had to be a trick, had to be fake. Knowing how small towns worked, he suspected Nick was weighing how fast the news would get around. Clearly, he decided that no one could talk because it would mean admitting they had gone to the adult show. He planted his teeth behind the head and bit. Torturo groaned as he broke the crisped skin and then continued through the cooked meat of his cock.

Torturo drew back, the head missing and blood spurting from the end. He took his bow and hastened off the stage, to where the twins waited with the gauze. In all the years he'd been doing that stunt, no one had ever taken him up on the bite.

Alice and Dinah bandaged him and he headed for the piercing booth. He still had whiskey there and it was closer than the train. He'd regenerate, he hoped. He had never actually had a body part severed before. He needed the whiskey as he'd never needed it before.

*   *   *

The crowd dispersed and Nick sat looking sick. He spat the bite he'd taken into his hand. It wasn't a sausage. It wasn't a fake. It was a real piece of human penis and he'd had it in his mouth. His mouth tasted of blood and he wanted to throw up more than he had after the second carousel ride.

He waited until everyone was gone and went to the piercing tent. He had no idea what he was going to do. So he set the bite on the table and fled before anyone could see him.

*   *   *

Torturo saw the young man slip out of his piercing tent and went in to pour himself a drink. Sin arrived a few minutes later and pretended to be looking at jewelry.

On his worktable, like a misshapen grayish shooter marble, looking absolutely bizarre without a shaft behind it, sat his cock-head. Nick had returned it. Torturo wondered if he still thought it was a prop, or if he was just too confused to do anything else.

"Hi," Sin breathed, flushed and excited. He wished he could match her feelings at the moment.

"Hello, dear. So are you here for the piercing?" He picked up the

53

whiskey bottle and took a large drink.

She nodded. "And…more?" she suggested. She moved in close and said, "I want my first time to be really special, something I can't get here. I don't want the local boys who don't know anything." She took a large breath and blurted, "I want the fire like you gave the twins. I've fantasized about it for years."

He smiled at the girl. She'd said the words he'd wanted to hear. "Come to my carriage in ten minutes. We'll dress for the masquerade. I'll do the piercing afterward, so you don't hurt all night. And I'll make it very memorable." He pecked her cheek and headed across the Midway. He walked fast, despite the fading ache where he'd been bitten, turning the cock head over in his pocket. Torturo climbed into his train car and stripped. He could hear the Phantasmagoria in his head. He knew what would help.

He pressed the severed head of his cock back to the healed-over end of the shaft with one hand. He pressed the palm of the other hand and his forearm against the paneling of the train. He leaned his head against it and breathed quietly. The skin fused and the flesh grew back. He felt the tingle of coldness followed by returning sensation in the head.

After five minutes, there was no evidence that the car salesman had bitten off the end of his cock.

He arranged the cuffs above the berth and set up the lighter fluid and a candle. Sin was going to get her memorable first time after all.

CHAPTER 5

MASQUERADE

Cyn steeled herself and knocked on the door of the train car. Second thoughts crowded her until she wanted to run. Of course, he didn't care about her. He wanted her body or a joke at her expense. Maybe both.

She'd been on edge all day since her family had come home. Mom and Lee had been at each other, as usual. The damn dog had taken a gigantic dump on her bedroom carpet, again as usual. She'd gotten that scrubbed up, wishing she'd taken Nicole up on the offer to spend the weekend. Dinner was the usual overcooked hamburgers, a salad, and a fight. She ate, not wanting it atop all the fair food. She did the dishes, then went back to her room. After a brief argument with her better judgment, Cyn tucked a contraceptive sponge into her jean pocket, then slipped downstairs and out the back door after leaving a note on the table so Mom wouldn't worry.

"Spending the night with Suzie. See you at church tomorrow." She stayed with Suzie reasonably often, so it wouldn't set off alarm bells. Since she was meeting Suzie at the carnival, it was technically true. She got her three-speed out of the shed and pedaled off into the summer evening.

The Phantasmagoria by twilight felt different than it had by day. It had been creepy by day. Now it felt downright sinister. Cyn laughed at herself. Just virgin jitters. She didn't plan on going home a virgin. In the back of her mind, a small voice asked if she really planned to go home at all.

Maybe, it suggested, *you could get a job with the carnival. They could use a tall, pretty girl either in the hoochie show or selling candy.* Cyn dismissed the thought. She had her life planned. She'd already sent her college applications. She was going to breeze through her senior year, graduate with honors, spend most of the summer with her dad and get the hell out of Peculiar. Then it was just a matter of how far and fast she wanted to go. Traveling carnivals, no matter how appealing, didn't figure into her future.

She coasted down YY by the duplexes. She and her mom had lived on Shari Lane for a while, before Lee. The Phantasmagoria gleamed topaz and ruby ahead. She parked her bike, locking it to the rack near the gate, ignoring her better judgment which told her to keep on riding, spend the night at her grandparents' house and call Mom when she got there.

For a brief instant, the lights all went out. The soft breeze stirred the flaps of canvas and whistled among the metal skeletons of the stopped rides. No people moved in the dead stillness. She looked down the Midway and saw only empty booths and rides. She shivered, remembering the way Fairyland had been so dead on her last visit right before the amusement park had closed. She shut her eyes at the sight of a skeleton propped against the side of a booth, still dressed in a ragged striped shirt and crumbling straw boater.

When she opened them, she saw the lights had come back up and she wondered how she could have missed the throng. The skeleton was the cute duck pickup guy, who flirted shamelessly with Suzie. Atop the Ferris wheel, Debbie and Michelle screamed in their high, squeaky cheerleader voices to start it back up. People she knew roamed everywhere, shooting at targets, picking up ducks, spinning around on the rides, and lined up for attractions. At least now she had an alibi.

She hurried over and joined Suzie at the booth, putting the thought of the man's bright blue eyes burning from empty sockets in a bare skull out of her mind. "Hiya," she said. "Look, Suzie, I'm out illegal-like. I left a note saying I was staying at your place. Can you cover for me?"

They headed to the snow cone stand. Suzie pumped her with questions and Cyn gave evasive answers.

"It's a guy, isn't it? One you don't want the folks to know about." Suzie smiled and gave her a wink. "Your secret is safe with me. Just come on over after you see him. We never lock the side door. You aren't doing anything goofy like eloping, are you?"

Cyn laughed and squeezed Suzie around the waist. "Darling girl, why would I elope with a mere man, when you know you hold sole and only possession of my heart?" Suzie giggled and Cyn went on. "Hark, what dark in yonder window grows? It is the east and Suze the approaching night."

"All right, all right already. Sheesh. Someone's gonna snitch if you keep acting like that."

Cyn nodded and let go of her. "The last thing I need is for Mom to find out I like girls, too." She gave Suzie a wicked grin. "I have a free pass. You want to crash the adult show? I'll go halvsies if you come along for immoral support."

Suzie giggled. "I have the car. Sure."

"I have to go by the piercing booth beforehand, though. Meet me at the tent when it's time." Cyn hurried off to see Torturo.

The adult show was more than they had hoped. Better than late night Cinemax. Better than the liberated porn tapes they'd found in Cyn's dad's drawers. Suzie was still pink after her volunteer stint as they walked to the parking area. Cyn tried not to be jealous. Suzie may have gotten her boobs licked, but Cyn planned to end the night in Torturo's bed.

"Don't come in too late. Don't wake anybody," Suzie said as they walked toward the gate afterward.

"You aren't staying for the masquerade? Costumes are provided." Cyn pointed toward the other giant tent on the grounds, its white roof aglow with light.

Suzie shook her head. "I've had enough excitement for one night. See you in the morning."

"Thanks." Cyn gave her a smile. "You're a pal." She made sure Suzie got safely to her car and then hurried back.

The summer night lay over the Midway. Only a few late thrill seekers rode the rides. The booths glowed but their light felt sickly in the country darkness. The clowns were doing no business with their balloons and candy. She caught a glimpse of a furry face at an upper window of the funhouse and it went out like a candle.

"Hyperactive imagination," she said to herself and hurried a little to where Torturo's little stand sat in the shadow of the huge black Ten-in-One. She glanced at the mirror maze as she went, catching her reflection in every mirror but two. She sidestepped a clown carrying a bundle of balloons, a box of cheap toys slung around his neck, and glanced back to see how those two mirrors were angled. The clown did not cast a reflection. She rubbed her eyes and looked again. All the mirrors showed her and the clown and the Midway.

Nobody knew Cyn was terrified of the dark and had been since the night she'd first seen *The Wolfman* on TV when she was four. Vampires were sexy, but werewolves disturbed her deeply. She'd done her best not to freak out about Wolfgang. The trunk escape had helped. Long a Houdini fan, she'd thrilled at the chance to see it done live, even knowing how it worked. Now the imagination that had landed her the editorship of the school literary magazine worked against her. She wondered where the hairy escape artist was. She told herself she couldn't possibly have heard a howl over the music and machinery. It was just a tired carnival, no different from a dozen others she'd been to. She scoffed at her own nerves. Who knew losing her virginity would be such an adventure?

She stepped carefully around the ropes and tent pegs and slipped into the piercing tent. Torturo looked very pale. He set the empty tumbler on the table and managed a smile for her.

"Come to my railcar in ten minutes, darling. The Show should have our costumes there." He headed out. She glanced at her watch.

It was a long wait in the tent. The noise of the carnival slowly abated. Only an eerie sounding waltz filled the air, drifting in from the masquerade. Cyn shivered in the warm night. The lights of the Midway went out, one by one, ending with the Ferris wheel. By the light of the full moon, the carnival looked even creepier. She turned her back on the Midway, trying not to feel as if she had a target painted between her shoulder blades. This time, she knew she heard a howl and remembered there were coyotes in the area. She tried not to think of the fact that only some canvas stood between her and a snarling, potentially rabid coyote.

Finally, it was time. She walked to the train, expecting at every step to have someone tell her to go away or worse. She checked each car as she approached, starting at the engine. A small silver plaque on the second car read "Torturo the Pain King."

Her courage screwed to the sticking point, Cyn knocked on the door of the train car. She wanted this. He wanted this. There wasn't going to be any trouble. Second thoughts crowded her until she wanted to run. Of course, he didn't care about her. He wanted her body or a joke at her expense. Maybe both.

His smile looked more genuine and the gray look on his face had been replaced with a healthier shade as he opened the door. He wore a pair of silk pajamas and a dressing gown, looking like an old movie star rather than a carnival performer.

"Do come in, Cyn. Your dress is hanging on the screen. I haven't had a chance to change yet."

She climbed up into the train, relieved to be inside. The car was one room, with a berth and a table and a little bathroom. A changing screen blocked off one corner. Her dress, a huge thing resembling a wedding cake straight out of the eighteenth century hung on it. A tall powdered wig, all ribbons and stacked curls topped with four ostrich plumes, sat on a wig head. A black domino mask on a stick, the eyes outlined with white sequins and a pair of dancing black slippers with ribbon ties completed the outfit.

"I love it." She sighed, the dress alone sending her straight into bliss. "I always wanted one." She looked around at the red velvet and brass fixtures. "Wow. Very Victorian."

She wasn't ready when he pulled her close for a kiss. She knew about kissing, but there was none of the overeager fumbling or timidity of boys her age. She opened for his tongue, finding it not slick and clumsy but sweet and sure in her mouth. She stroked it with her own, remembering to breathe, unable to believe she was really kissing this handsome man. The peck earlier had left her all shivery and weak-kneed, although she'd been careful not to let him see that. Now, she had no qualms about melting in his arms as he satisfied everything she had always known a kiss could be.

"Ah, not a complete innocent." He smiled. "Is there a boyfriend or fiancé I should worry about?"

"He's a hundred miles away," she said. "Literally. None of the local boys will touch me with a ten foot pole. Or even an eleven foot one."

"The more fools they," Torturo said, and kissed her again with even more passion.

She felt his cock, hard and free inside the pajama pants, rubbing against her hip and belly. Her breath came faster and she felt a knot starting about where it was pressed to her. She never wanted the kisses to stop. If he kissed her neck, she would be lost.

When his lips did indeed work down onto her neck, she moaned, pressing up into his mouth. He held her just a little tighter and nibbled. She gasped and threw her head back. "More!" she demanded.

With a thrust of his hips, he matched her groan. "God, woman." He bit harder and she yelped, her nipples poking through both bra and T-shirt. She pressed even closer and one hand left his neck, slipping between their bodies to wrap around his cock through the silk pajamas.

"You're huge." She felt her eyes getting big at the thought and her breath quickened.

His eyes shifted between brown and green and gold, depending on how the light hit them. Now, they looked purely predatory. "All yours, lovely Cyn. Whatever you want," he promised, his voice honey and fire, making her tingle as much as his kisses.

But her gaze fell on the dress. She'd always wanted to go to a formal masked ball, wearing something very fancy. It was only one o'clock. There was plenty of time for everything. She squeezed his cock, loving the hard, hot feeling of it in her hand. "Let's dance. Hold that thought until we get back here."

"It will definitely hold," he said and took one more kiss, his hands sliding back up to her breasts. She jerked as he rubbed his thumbs over her nipples, tiny sparks flying through her belly to sparkle between her legs. He let her go and headed for the bathroom.

"Uh, better let me go before I get into that," she said, pointing at the dress.

"Of course." He gestured her toward the door with a little bow.

She finished and came back out. He stepped in. She stripped fast and wormed her way into the dress. Torturo was going to have to fasten it for her. She sat down and put on the slippers, tying the ribbons around her ankles and up onto her calves. Using the mirror, Cyn settled the wig on her head, realizing she was now almost seven feet tall.

Torturo came out of his bathroom in knee britches and stockings, a satin coat and embroidered waistcoat with a lot of lace around his throat and wrists. His wig had a ponytail held by a black velvet ribbon and several side curls. He'd powdered his face and hair, rouged his lips and a beauty mark sat near one eye, carefully not obscuring any natural dimples.

"I should do makeup," she said, staring at him. "You're gorgeous. I mean, more gorgeous." She shook her head to clear it and stood up. "Help me here, please?"

"Of course, darling. You look lovely." He did the hooks on her back with a deft hand. "There's makeup in the bathroom and a better mirror." He grazed a hand over the top of her breasts, which were pushed up and exposed nearly to her nipples. He lowered his face and kissed the tops of them, a promise for later that she felt clear through her body.

She hurried through her makeup, going for the completely artificial look as he had. She set a heart-shaped beauty-patch on her right cheek. When she came out, she spread the ostrich feather fan and batted her eyes coyly over it at him.

"Now, we're ready. My lady?" He handed her the mask as she folded the fan. She took his proffered arm and let him lead her along the darkened, empty Midway to the dancing tent.

It glowed white in the night. Cyn stepped carefully, the soft slippers not made for walking on uneven ground. She held tightly to Torturo's arm, convinced he could defend her against anything, including Wolfgang.

She recognized the music as a waltz and smiled up at her handsome escort. "I hope you like to dance."

Torturo smiled and nodded, then kissed her, there in public with one hand on her half-bare breasts. If her mother heard, she'd be in for the guilt-trip of her life. If it got too bad, she'd go live with her dad. Torturo was totally worth it.

They glided onto the dance floor, surrounded by people in various costumes. A fox swished past, on the arm of a samurai, her bushy tail slipping out from under the kimono. Cowboys and Roman slave girls, Cleopatra and Robin Hood all waltzed by, but Cyn only had eyes for her escort. He'd kissed a boy in front of her and now he was wearing makeup and she found both of those facts hotter than she knew she should. She liked men in makeup, from the few MTV videos she'd seen at her dad's place.

Torturo spun her through a polka and for once her feet didn't tangle on the step-step-step. She looked up at him, laughing and breathless.

"Oh! Can we rest a little?" She panted, flushed from heat and motion.

"Of course." Torturo found a seat and pulled her down on his lap. She gave a soft laugh and he kissed her quiet. "Do you want to be naughty? No one knows who you are."

"Yes," she whispered.

He kissed the tops of her breasts. She shivered under his hot mouth and blushed red when the motion made her breasts, with some small help from his hands, pop out of her dress. He stared a moment.

"You rouged your nipples?" he asked, running his thumbs over them to make them hard.

She nodded. "I'd read about it. It's okay, isn't it?"

Torturo kissed her in a way that left no doubt it was more than okay. She knew she'd never catch her breath if he kept doing that. Her whole skin felt tingly, like she was going to break out in goose bumps.

Cyn tucked her boobs away and patted her wig to make sure it was still on right. Torturo let her up and stood. They watched the dancers, some of whom looked almost transparent under the party lights. She thought she saw a couple of classmates, but when she looked again, they were lost in the whirl of dancers.

She let Torturo lead her through a reel and another waltz. The creepy feeling from earlier was back. She needed to get back to the train and down to business before she chickened out.

In the break between songs, she stood on tiptoe to reach Torturo's ear. "I'm ready. Take me back, please?"

He smiled and led her from the bright tent where the orchestra had started a tune she didn't recognize. It sounded almost off key and out of time, but Cyn had never been good with either. She didn't care. Torturo was going to make love to her.

* * *

They returned from the masquerade, Sin buoyant and half-dancing back to the train. Torturo had enjoyed himself. He'd never learned to dance, but the Show fed him the knowledge. Sin was, as promised, a good dancer, even if she did lead. He finally gave up trying and let her since she seemed to know what she was doing.

He opened the door for her and swept her in, kissing her as he kicked it shut. She disentangled for a moment and set down her fan and mask, then swept the wig off and went back to kissing him. The motion made her bosom pop out of the top of her dress, as it had while he held her on his lap during a break. He looked again at her rouged nipples. He'd been delighted then, kissing them gently before tucking them back in.

Now he didn't tuck them back but bent to lick one hard nipple as he unhooked the back of her dress. Awkward, but an action he was quite familiar with. She let the dress fall to the floor and stood wearing only a pair of white cotton panties and the dancing slippers.

Torturo looked at her for a moment, wanting to remember her as she was forever. Truly lovely and without knowledge of her own beauty, she stood, beckoning him as if he needed an invitation. He accepted at once.

She responded to his kisses with heat that hadn't been there even that evening. He held her for a moment, wishing he could keep her, but Clovis had marked her as his own. He bore her back to the bed with fierce kisses and then softened to soothe her. She kissed back, as eager for his tongue as he was for the taste of her.

He kissed her neck, lingering in the spots that made her squirm the hardest. Her nipples had lost most of their rouge but stood tall and dark anyway. As he sucked one and then the other, listening to her gasps of pleasure, he slipped her panties off. The slippers molded to her feet and presented no impediment. He nibbled at one tender tip and she spasmed under him in orgasm.

Amazed at her responsiveness, he parted her thighs with one long finger. She whimpered as he stroked a slow circle of her vulva, first with the finger and then with his tongue. She tasted exactly as he had known she would, all sweetness but with an underpinning of knowledge. Too much knowledge.

She made no protest as he entered her with one finger and then two, his mouth never leaving her. He found her tiny clitoris, small for such a hot woman, and flicked it until she screamed, flooding and pulsating around his fingers.

::*Give her to me*,:: Clovis whispered in his head, sounding hungry. ::*Give her.*::

::*Mine first!*:: Torturo thought angrily, knowing the Phantasmagoria would hear.

"Yours," she whispered.

He looked up, startled. "What?"

"You practically screamed it at me, darling. Of course I'm yours." A brief frown crossed her face. "I wish I could be yours for more than a night."

"Hush," he whispered, rising to kiss her. He was not surprised she took his mouth even more eagerly than before. He chuckled as she licked him clean, her tongue seeking every trace of her flavor.

He returned to her neck and slipped the fingers back into her. When he nipped this time, she came again. He bit harder, careful not to break the skin, and her hips bucked against his palm. Another bite, hard enough to leave a mark, sparked another orgasm.

"If you were mine, I'd make a necklace of teeth marks around your pretty throat, darling. You come so sweetly when I do."

"Necklace," she said, "or collar?"

He caught his breath with desire. Clearly pretty girls were a different breed than he remembered. "Collar...oh you...I think you have the right idea." He drew his fingers out of her slowly and sucked on one as he lit the candle and prepared a light coat of lighter fluid for his cock. "You wanted the fire, too. What a wicked lady I found tonight."

She just nodded, her brown eyes big as she watched. He lit his cock from the candle, the yellow flames leaping as he plunged down into her. He smelled a bit of scorching hair and the heat of the flames went out as he filled her in one strong thrust.

She caught her breath and laughed, a wild joyful sound. "Yes!" She kissed his mouth. "Yes, yes, yes!" She kissed his whole face and then quieted. "Thank you. That was what I'd expected. Not as hot though."

He gave a couple of pumps and she quit talking, her mouth back on his, sucking his tongue like it was one of the ice pops the booth next to his sold. He moved slowly, enjoying himself. She caught the rhythm and met him, tightening down on the outstroke.

"Clever little virgin."

"Not anymore," she said. "Is that working? The book said it would feel good for you."

"It's beyond good, sweet Sin. It's great."

"Harder please." She thrust up against him and nipped his throat, one hand leaving his back to play with his triple pierced nipple. She tugged at the ring.

"More of that," he demanded, moving harder in response. She tugged each ring in turn, pausing to play with the skin of the nipples. Once she managed to get her mouth down and nip him. He pounded her until she screamed again. "Noisy," he teased and bent his head to bite another link in the necklace, then another and another.

She came with each bite, until overwhelmed by her response, he spent himself as well. He rolled off to lie beside her. She lay on her back, staring at the ceiling, a bruised ring of bite marks from under her left ear to her right collarbone, looking as blissful as he'd ever seen a woman.

After a moment, she rolled to face him and kissed him very sweetly. "Thank you," she whispered.

*   *   *

Torturo stood, looking at the corpse on the bed. Sin had said yes to everything, even his hands around her throat during the last lovemaking. As he had to, he squeezed. She'd come harder each time he'd tightened his grip. He'd seen the light go out of her eyes just as he came.

She lay in his bunk now, pale everywhere, the velvet ribbons of the slippers startling against her skin. He wanted something to remember her by. The door of the car blew open and a whirlwind carried in papers and photographs on a thin mist. The mists were memories people had of her, being drawn out of them by the Show.

He reached over and touched her necklace, a broken coin engraved with her boyfriend's name. The earrings were impersonal and the nipples rings—and he reveled in the memory of how aroused the needle had left her— were too new. No, something that was purely her. He slid the silver and green class ring off her finger. The stone flashed rainbow fire and he looked over the few details it provided. Raymore-Peculiar High School Class of 1986. Cynthia M. Wishom. She'd been in drama.

Torturo opened a drawer and took out a chest filled with similar objects. The whirlwind had grown stronger and more objects, thick medical records and photographs, were covering her. After a second's hesitation, he took one of the nipple rings out of her and looped it through the class ring. He shut the token in the chest and watched her burial.

She was cocooned in the mist, all the papers covered by it. The last few wisps trailed into the train car. As he watched, she seemed to sink into the berth, vanishing as if she'd never existed. Around him the Phantasmagoria shivered with new life.

"Good-bye, darling Sin. Thank you," he whispered, running one hand over the bunk where she'd lain. When he turned to get ready for bed, the gown and wig were gone.

Torturo napped on the red velvet couch, his dreams full of Sin's wild laughter and tight heat.

CHAPTER 6

SUNDAY

Nick walked home in the darkness, his stomach roiling. He paused after crossing YY to vomit in the drainage culvert. He'd thought it was just a sausage, right up until his teeth had sunk into raw flesh. But no, he'd had a real penis in his mouth. That upset him as much as the taste of blood and the knowledge he had maimed a man.

He was queer. His mind rejected that idea, unable to reconcile it with his beliefs. He had been tricked, thinking it was a fake. None of that changed the fact he had committed sodomy. There was no hope for heaven for him now. God did not save queers.

He crossed the tracks and slipped across the back yards and into the kitchen door of his duplex. He stood under the shower for a long time and spent until one in the morning praying.

He went to bed, setting his alarm for church.

The next morning, all he could stomach was toast and coffee. He prepared for church by doing his morning reading. But neither the Psalms praising God by listing the mighty kings He had killed, nor Paul's discussion of spiritual gifts and being a part of the Body of Christ was working. He knew what part of the Body he'd ended up and it wasn't a mentionable one. It was actually rather blasphemous to think that way.

Sunday school wasn't bad. They were doing a study on Revelation. That was always interesting. The smell of the church, book must and wood, perfume and the ghost of old coffee, calmed him. The service went slowly, the singing and praying soothing to him. He sat with one arm along the back of the pew, ostensibly around Lisa's shoulders, and shared his hymnal with her.

Brother Bob got on his usual hobbyhorse, determined to ride gays into the ground if he could. He spoke forcefully about the perversions, about the way they destroyed life for real people, about the way they flaunted themselves and ensnared children.

And would you act like that? asked a small new voice inside him. *If you let him have you, do what men do with other men?* Nick became aware he was listening to that voice describe the pleasures he could have—which had nothing to do with perversions, destroying real people, or seducing children— and not paying attention to the sermon when he saw the rest of the congregation stood up for the invitation.

Tempted to go forward and throw himself at the base of the altar weeping over his sins, he mumbled through the song and waited out the recessional. It wouldn't do him any good.

"You'll be joining us for dinner, won't you, son?" Mr. Fleming asked.

Nick nodded without really thinking. He caught himself driving out of town on YY, turned around at the old drive-in restaurant, and headed out east of town on J Highway.

He moved through the day like a sleepwalker. All day, the carnival pulled at him, but he refused. Three times, he realized he was walking to the car to go back, when he'd only meant to go to the bathroom or leave the front room. He wasn't going back. He wouldn't ever see the man again. He ate the large dinner Mrs. Fleming made, not really tasting it.

His head wasn't in the game of croquet and Len, Lisa's little brother, sent his blue ball spinning into the lilac bushes before Nick could realize he was even in peril. After the prickly task of retrieving it from amid the thistle underneath the twiggy bush, he sat on the porch swing with Lisa. She curled into his side. He put an arm around her, then ignored her, thinking only of Torturo and the taste of the cooked meat in his mouth.

"Your head's been a million miles away all day, honey," she said, jerking his attention back to broad daylight and Sunday afternoon.

Nick nodded. An idea struck him for how to get rid of the disturbing pull completely. "Lisa, what do you think of getting married tomorrow? We can just go down to the courthouse and have a judge do it."

She shook her head. "Tomorrow's a holiday, Nick. Besides, Mom has her heart set on a big church wedding. But you're sweet to try to surprise me." She pecked his cheek.

He looked at her, having trouble breathing. His lies crowded in on him, choking his breath away, making him want to spill his guts and at the same time never speak again.

"Lisa, I—" He couldn't continue. He couldn't destroy her sweet innocence with truth. "We'll do it Mom's way then," he finished lamely. He kissed her cheek, dry and passionless, a change from the sweet kisses he'd given her the day before. He ignored her puzzled, hurt look. "I'd better go home and change for church."

Lisa nodded and brushed at the bit of gravy he'd gotten on his shirt at dinner. "Soak that or it'll never come out, honey." She sighed, letting her hand rest on his shirtfront. "If tomorrow weren't a holiday, I'd be taking care of it."

"I will. Lisa, I wouldn't make you do laundry before we're married." He hugged her, the feel of her slim soft body in his arms sparking no reaction. He went home and changed clothes.

Evening church was a blur. His head was back in the Phantasmagoria until he had no idea what the sermon was about. Instead, he saw over and over the round tines of the barbecue fork going into Torturo's cock. He wrenched his thoughts away, but even the hymns sounded dirty. He felt incredibly unclean.

He repeated Phillipians 4:8 to himself, under his breath. "Finally, brethren, whatsoever things are true, whatsoever things are honest, whatsoever things are just, whatsoever things are pure, whatsoever things are lovely, whatsoever things are of good report; if there be any virtue and if there be any praise, think on these things."

Lisa looked at him funny for whispering to himself. He walked her out to her dad's car and then went home himself. He sat cross-legged in the middle of his front room floor repeating the verse, trying to drown out the faint music of the carousel that drifted in.

It didn't help. He went to bed early, putting in his earplugs.

On Monday, he managed not to think too much as the crazed Labor Day shoppers, lured by 0.9% interest for twelve months and a five hundred dollar rebate, asked him question after question about the cars on the lot.

At lunchtime, he glanced up and saw Torturo and his bicycle leaning against the light post across the street. He pretended to be busy figuring out his new computer. When he looked up again, Torturo gave him a sexy wink, a wicked grin and then mounted his bike and rode off.

Nick slipped out to the Wagon Wheel for lunch, needing comfort food. He heard a familiar rolling laugh from the cash register as his shrimp arrived. Torturo stood there, flirting with the girl behind the register. When he looked up again, it was only Mr. Sevy, who did crop dusting.

He went to his uncle and said something wasn't agreeing with him from yesterday and asked for the rest of the afternoon off, agreeing to work a full day on Saturday. It wasn't totally a lie. He felt not at all well.

Nick drove home, slowly, carefully—71 was not the best paved highway in the state and he didn't need to be bounced about. An unusual number of emergency vehicles seemed to be going the other way. He pulled off as an ambulance passed him, probably heading up to Research at Belton. That meant the patient was too injured to go to Cass Memorial, which was seven miles closer.

He said a small prayer as it turned off its siren, indicating the patient had died. He drove on. Despite his caution, he missed his turn and ended up in the parking area for the Phantasmagoria.

Feeling oddly disconnected and outside of himself, he let his feet carry him along the Midway. The suggestive little voice in his head said he really needed to catch the last Ten-in-One Show. He paid his three dollars and sat down in the middle of the tent, hoping the last-day crowd would cover him. No one seemed to notice him.

Torturo and the twins saw him, though, and all three of them flirted outrageously with him. He sat for a while after the show ended, until the roustabouts started removing the benches. The jarred babies had already been packed up.

He wandered out on the Midway and saw the rides were shut down and the booths were being dismantled. Roustabouts and clowns with no costumes, but still in makeup, lowered booth sides and parts of rides, packed away guns and rubber ducks, stuffed animals and baseballs. Nick watched for a few minutes as they dismantled the Ferris wheel, all the men moving together like a machine to take it down. Torturo's piercing booth still stood, but most of the stuff was already packed in the shipping containers and the tables were folded. It was ready to be struck and loaded. Torturo lounged in the work chair, drinking what looked like iced tea.

"Hello, Nicholas," he said when Nick peered in. "Back for another taste? We missed you yesterday."

Nick sputtered, but his feet carried him in anyway. Surely he didn't mean to be standing quite so close, or leaning in near enough to smell Torturo's unique scent of aftershave, sweat, whiskey, and something just him.

"I want—" he started.

"Of course you do. Everyone wants." Torturo stood up and closed the distance, standing so near Nick could feel the warmth radiating off his body over the warmth of the early September day. "But what do you want, Nicholas?" he whispered, his breath teasing Nick's ear.

Nick shivered under the warm breath, the suggestive words. A voice he didn't recognize as his squeaked, "You." He shuddered when Torturo dropped the door flap, closing them into the hot canvas tent. Torturo's mouth came down on his. Nick shook and pulled away.

Torturo laughed. "For wanting me, you have a funny way of showing it." He turned Nick's face back to him with long gentle fingers. "Nicholas, I'm going to kiss you again. Then we're going back to my train car. We'll be more private and it's not nearly as close." He fanned the air, which had already grown stuffy and too hot, with one hand

Nick nodded. When Torturo kissed him again, he met it. He opened his mouth at the first brush of the slick tongue on his lips and let Torturo taste all of him. He'd only been kissed like this once, by the drunken girl in college. She'd tasted of spoiled olives and ash from the cigarettes and beer, and her tongue had felt slimy in his mouth. Torturo's was just wet enough to be pleasant and he tasted faintly of tea and whiskey, but more like himself.

He breathed into Nick's mouth, stroking along the roof of it, and Nick sucked at him a little, feeling the trio of barbells pierced through his tongue. When Torturo let him up, his mouth had gone dry and his eyes were wide.

"Now, to my carriage. We'll be more comfortable there for anything else you might want." They passed the roustabouts who were already starting to pull the stakes that guyed his tent down.

Nick stared around him as they entered the car. Dark rich wood, polished to a high gloss, scarlet flocked wallpaper, brass fittings, crushed red velvet furniture, and a very neatly made bunk with a vintage patchwork quilt all made the car look more like a museum exhibit than a working train.

"Head's through there." Torturo gestured to a green door with brass scrollwork and a brass handle.

"I'm fine, thanks," Nick managed. He sat down on the red velvet bench built into one wall and watched Torturo take a bottle from an ornately carved cabinet.

"I need a drink." Torturo poured two. "And so do you. We only have a little time before the train leaves, Nick. So use the liquid courage to tell me what you want and I'll give it to you."

Nick looked at his hands for a long second. He didn't take the drink. "I'm damned. Damned just for wanting this. So if I'm going to hell for being homosexual, I want to at least taste it once." He swallowed. "I've hidden it. I've fought it. But Brother Bob is right. I'm already damned." He looked up at Torturo. "So complete it for me. If I'm an abomination for having the feelings, let me be damned for the act as well. I have to know. Just once."

Torturo took a long drink, draining his glass. Nick suspected he'd heard all this before. "It's going to be more than once," he said, and Nick shook at the certainty in his voice.

Nick shook his head. "No. You'll rape me and then I'll go home to my apartment and live out the rest of my life, married, kids, church three times a week, and knowing I'm damned."

Torturo banged his glass down on the table and scowled. "I only take those to my bed who are willing. I am many things, but a rapist is not one. Either come to me willing, Nicholas, or leave now."

"I am willing," Nick said, his voice very small. "But it's not love and it's not real sex, so what does that leave?"

Torturo leaned across and kissed him, slow and gentle, taking his time. Nick nearly shivered from the way the kiss made ache. "It is sex, Nicholas. That's all it is. Do you want me to fuck you?"

Nick shivered at the sound of the crude word, one he hadn't heard spoken or even thought in five years. He nodded.

Torturo laughed, a thin, bitter thing, nothing at all like the deep, rich sound he normally employed. "And how do you think I'll manage that feat, given that you bit the head off my cock two nights ago and hadn't the simple decency to apologize or offer to kiss it better?"

Nick gulped and felt the blood drain out of his face. In his desire, he'd forgotten about that. "I'm really sorry about that. I thought it was a prop, you know, a fake. After all, you really couldn't stick a fork in your...yourself and then roast it. Could you?"

Torturo just nodded. "Everything is real here, Nicholas. Marvello may be the Master of Illusion, but I'm the Pain King. That means I do it all."

Nick stood up. "I'm sorry. Sorry I wasted your time."

"Sit down."

Nick found himself wanting to obey that quiet command. He shook his head and went for the door. "I'm being stupid. I've offended you, imposed on you, insulted you, and injured you. I am sorry. It would be better if I went. Tomorrow, you'll be gone."

Torturo stood up and unhooked his trousers. Nick steeled himself to see a mangled mess. Torturo drew out a large, thick uncut cock with a ring pierced through either side of the foreskin. He slid the skin back and showed Nick he was intact once more. Nick just stared.

Torturo laid one hand along the side of Nick's head. "You've already tasted it. Try it without the teeth," he coaxed.

Nick bent forward and kissed the head of Torturo's cock, shivering with excitement and fear. He didn't understand how the man could be intact. The simple act made his own cock jerk awake. He'd never felt like this when touching or kissing girls. He slipped his tongue out and ran it under the loose skin. He felt Torturo cup the back of his head and he relaxed. The big hand felt right.

"Take it in your mouth, Nicholas," Torturo murmured. "Suck it, lick it, kiss it all better."

Nick opened his mouth and took it, as he had the night of the show. But he didn't close his teeth and the skin was soft and not cooked crisp. It wasn't horrible. Torturo tasted of clean salty skin and something else, filling his mouth with a taste that was uniquely male. Nick sucked gently and licked at it.

Torturo pressed him to take it deeper, the hand on the back of his head insistent. His soft voice seduced Nick as he said, "Roll your tongue around it, then press it to the roof of your mouth."

Nick followed the directions, unsure if he was doing well at all. Torturo gave a soft little gasp and Nick pressed it to the roof of his mouth again, swallowing as he did.

Torturo stroked his hair. "A quick study and so very good, Nicholas. With practice, you'll be a splendid cocksucker. Now, use your teeth. But only do this on me. Others don't care for that treatment."

Nick nibbled a little, closing his teeth at the base of the shaft and then drawing off, letting his teeth rake over the length of it before nipping the head and then biting down on one of the rings and tugging. He bit hard at the soft foreskin, which had drawn back. He nibbled at the taut V where it joined the head.

Torturo's moans increased with his teeth and Nick soon found he bit harder than he'd intended, because it drew such a strong response. He closed his teeth sharply about halfway down Torturo's cock and sucked more intensely.

Warm bitter saltiness flooded along the back of his tongue as the cock in his mouth jerked. Nick swallowed reflexively, almost at the same time he realized Torturo had just orgasmed in his mouth. He pulled away, a look of revulsion on his face.

Torturo pulled Nick to his feet and kissed him, hard and deep, seeming to seek his own taste in Nick's mouth. Nick pressed close and put his arms around Torturo's neck. He felt his own erection straining at his underwear and rubbed it against Torturo's thigh, unable to control himself.

All his control and discipline, all his purity and high thoughts fled from him. He wanted to finish, and spend the nasty white stuff out of himself with a shout of pleasure. He knew Torturo would let him, would aid him even.

"Time for me to suck you," Torturo said, pushing him toward the bunk. Nick backed into it and sat down hard.

Torturo went to his knees before Nick and unzipped his dress slacks, then shoved his tight white briefs aside. "Beautiful," he whispered as Nick's cock stood at attention before him. He licked along the length, teasing. Nick caught his breath and whimpered.

When Torturo took the head into his mouth, Nick shot at the first flick of his tongue.

"I'm sorry," he said. "I didn't mean to—"

"Hush." Torturo kissed him again. He'd gotten hard again, Nick saw. He reached out to touch the rings, but drew back at Torturo's next words. "I'm going to fuck you, Nicholas." He reached over and opened a night table and pulled out a large tube of gel.

"Yes," Nick said and shoved his pants off. He went to his hands and knees on the quilt and saw Torturo smile.

"You've dreamed about this. I know you have." Torturo eased him to kneel up and undid his shirt. Nick licked at Torturo's nipples, toying with the piercings.

"Yes. Do anything to me."

Torturo pushed him back to his hands and knees. Nick felt right in that position, ready to be abused. At the first touch of Torturo's tongue on his ass, he groaned. The Pain King rimmed him slowly, pierced tongue wet and clever on Nick's tight sphincter.

"Oh God," Nick moaned, the blasphemy wrenched from him.

"Like it?" He could hear the leer in Torturo's voice.

"So dirty, so hot," he managed, unable to say more. When Torturo went back to it, he lost all his speech and could only whimper. Torturo replaced his tongue with one long thick finger and Nick moaned. "Please...please, you're making it feel too good."

Torturo chuckled and slipped a second finger in. "It is too good. Why do you think you crave it? Why do you think God hates it? He hates all things pleasurable, because they distract us."

"Should hurt," Nick managed, shoving back and taking the fingers clear down to Torturo's palm.

"Do you want it to?"

"It should. Ram me, hurt me, make it bad." Nick kept rocking on Torturo's fingers and whimpered when he pulled them away. He watched over his shoulder as Torturo smeared the lubricant gel on himself. Nick saw the lack of condom, but didn't care. If Torturo infected him, he'd have every reason not to marry Lisa. And he deserved no better than to die of AIDS anyway.

"My pleasure." Despite the promise, Torturo seemed to ease into him, not ramming or pounding. It didn't hurt beyond a little stinging and Nick stifled a small sob in the pillow at how much he enjoyed this deeply perverse act.

"Now, Nicholas, how many times can I get you off again?"

Nick shook his head. "Please no." Torturo just laughed like the devil himself, deep and loud, and moved within him, driving him into incoherence. Nick came again, shooting all over the quilt. He felt Torturo thrust into him a few more times and then stop, pulsating.

"Yes...just like that," he whispered. "Infect me. I deserve it. Filthy adulterer."

Torturo bit his neck, hard, above his shirt collar. It would show and no one would believe Lisa had bruised him. He turned to protest, but Torturo kissed him. Nick lost himself in it and finally came up for air.

"This is crazy," he muttered

"Is it?" Torturo quirked an eyebrow at him.

"Insane. I get more turned on kissing you than I do my fiancée."

Torturo smiled. "Because you want me more than your fiancée."

Nick shook his head and sat up. "Preposterous. I can't possibly want you more."

Torturo pulled him back down. Before Nick could think, he lay flat on his back under the bigger man's body. "You know it, you just don't want to admit it. I wanted you, too. From the second you looked up at me from all that paperwork, I wanted you." Torturo took another kiss. "I considered asking where your restroom was, having you show it to me and showing you some of these pleasures in there that first day."

Nick shook his head and tried to squirm away as the train lurched. "I have to go. You'll be leaving soon." He reached for his pants, only to get waylaid by another kiss. He felt himself stiffening a third time. Torturo smiled and kissed his way down Nick's body to suck him again. When Nick came, very quickly for a man who had just climaxed twice, he didn't feel Torturo swallow.

Torturo kissed him again, this time passing Nick's own semen between their mouths. Nick pulled away and covered his mouth. He found the strength to roll Torturo off of him and get his clothes on.

"I have to go." He covered his mouth again "I just…oh God."

"Come with me." Torturo stretched his long body out on the bunk and let the mellow lamplight gleam on his piercings.

Nick looked at him liked he was crazy. "I have to work tomorrow. It's my bowling night, too."

"I won't be back," Torturo warned. "We never play the same town twice."

Nick took a couple breaths as he tied his shoes. "Why do you think I picked you to damn me so thoroughly? At least this way, never seeing you again, I can move on, marry my girl and live right the rest of my life. And maybe God will forgive me. Maybe." He didn't believe it.

Torturo chuckled. "I thought I did better than 'damning' you."

"You were incredible," Nick confessed. "That's exactly why I'm damned."

"Then you might as well join the rest of us, if that's the case."

The train lurched again and Nick headed for the door. "I have to go."

Torturo sighed. "Farewell, then, Nicholas."

Nick flung the door of the train car open, intending to have to jump for it. "Shit!" he yelped, startled into vulgarity by the sheer enormity of what he saw. "There's nothing out there!" He clutched the sides of the door frame as icy blackness tugged at him.

Torturo bounded across the car in a flash, pulling him back in. "Shut it! Quickly." He dragged Nick back to the bunk.

"What's going on? What the hell?" Nick shook his head in denial, unable to believe what he'd seen. The door closed of its own accord.

"We've moved on. And we're going to sleep." Torturo pushed and prodded them into a comfortable position to share the narrow bunk.

"I can't stay," Nick protested. "I have to go home. I have to work tomorrow."

Torturo shook his head sadly. "Too late. I am sorry, Nicholas. We talked too long."

"So now what?" Nick yawned hugely.

"Sleep," Torturo whispered his eyes closing as he drew up the light cover. "Sleep, my Nicholas."

CHAPTER 7

ALL ABOARD

Torturo awoke to see Nick already up, sitting on the side of the bed, holding his head in his hands. He groaned and stretched. Nick jumped at the sound.

"I hoped it was all a bad dream," Nick said.

Torturo stroked his back and kissed his neck. "No. It was a good dream."

"Good for you, maybe." Nick relaxed under his hands. "You didn't throw up in a culvert after a mouthful of blood and cooked organ."

"Except for that part, I remember it being pretty good for you, too." Torturo leaned over and kissed Nick, brushing his lips gently over his new lover's cheek and lips.

Nick stayed still, not responding. "That part was…" He ran out of words and instead, kissed Torturo hot and urgent, with wet tongue and open mouth. He looked confused when he pulled back. "But now, I'm what, five hundred miles from my house? How am I going to get home?"

Torturo shrugged and moved in again, wanting more of Nick's kisses. The last one had left him hard and he pressed against Nick's back. Nick stared at the floor.

"I don't know where we are. Or when," Torturo said.

Nick looked up. "What do you mean, when?"

"I mean, I don't know how much time has passed since we slept.

You'll get used to it." He wasn't sure he could explain the hibernation just yet. It didn't matter. He stole a kiss now that he could reach Nick's mouth and wrapped himself around Nick's body, rubbing his cock against Nick's back.

Nick just stood up and looked at him as if he were crazy. Torturo hated that look. He'd seen it on many, many faces over the years.

"I need a shower and clean clothes and I want..." Nick sank back to the bunk. "I don't even know what I want."

Torturo licked the back of his neck. "You seemed to want me fucking you."

Nick shuddered, whether from the tongue or the words, Torturo didn't know. "So crude."

He laughed and started dressing, "Yes. And hot. And messy." He kissed Nick's cheek as he bent to retrieve his socks.

"I'm really damned now, aren't I? I took a ride on the hell-bound train."

"Welcome aboard." Torturo grinned. "You're in good company. After all, you get me."

Nick looked at him and slowly smiled. "If it's all the same, I'd rather have breakfast. I'm starving." His stomach rumbled a counterpoint to back him up.

That, too, was a typical reaction. Torturo laughed as his own stomach growled and he finished dressing.

"All right." Torturo opened the door of the train car on a cool autumn morning. Nick shivered in his short-sleeved dress shirt. Torturo offered one of his sweaters and suit coats, which were far too big on Nick's small body. Nick rolled up the sleeves of the sweater. Torturo smiled at him, enjoying how cute he looked. Cute was not an adjective that he normally applied to men, but Nick's slight form in the oversized clothes, boyish face and look of anticipation all seemed to merit it. "Follow me."

*   *   *

Nick followed Torturo to a tent with a flag flying high above it.

"Mess tent. Soup's on when the flag's up," Torturo said. Nick's stomach growled more urgently at the smell of bacon and eggs and coffee.

Everyone seemed to already be in there, eating as if they were all starving. The giant had a gallon pot of oatmeal and ate it with a spoon the size of a water dipper. Hannah's bowl was the size of a soup tureen and she was halfway through it, a few stray oats in her mustache. The twins smeared jam on toast, Alice having blueberry and Dinah having grape. A whole loaf's worth of nibbled crusts sat beside their plate. Tiny Tabitha had tackled a full-sized bowl of oatmeal and two strips of bacon, which were longer than her arms.

Nagina laughed at something Mingxia had said, her wings fluttering with her mirth. Mingxia sipped from a cup bigger than her head. Nagina returned to her oatmeal.

Torturo picked up a coffee mug almost as large as his whole face and filled it with some of the best coffee Nick had ever smelled. He picked up a tray and Nick followed suit, getting his own soup-bowl sized coffee mug.

Torturo charmed the cook, getting ten strips of bacon, a dozen eggs scrambled with cheese and cooked very soft, and five slices of toast. Nick had a more modest plate with a soup tureen of oatmeal and five strips of bacon.

Nick devoured the food and went for seconds, ignoring Torturo's grin when he sat back down with more oatmeal and some eggs.

"So, anyone have the paper yet?" Torturo asked, after getting a refill of his coffee. He'd demolished his eggs and bacon and had stolen a piece of toast from the twins.

Alice passed the paper and two more slices of toast over. He read the date aloud. Nick shook his head, certain he could not be hearing right. "October 24th, 1985. Argillite, Kentucky. Halloween Faire to host Phantasmagoria Carnival."

He read the article aloud, to odd bursts of laughter Nick didn't understand. He ate the last bite of the eggs and bacon as Nick rejoined him with his third tray. They finished eating in silence as the others drifted out.

After the Giant and his wife and the twins had left, Nick looked at Torturo. "What am I? Just a tag-a-long?"

"They wouldn't have fed you if you were," Jene said from down the table. Jean wiped their mouth and then slapped Gene's hand as he reached for another piece of toast. "You've had eight," she scolded her left side. "It's good marmalade," he returned. She conceded and they had another slice.

"They're right," Torturo said. He got up and retrieved the coffee pot. "You'll work. A place will open up for you. What can you do?"

Nick shrugged and swallowed the end of his own toast. "I can sell stuff. Kinda what I do."

"Can you sell the Show?" Torturo poured Nick more coffee. "Extra warm up? Mountain mornings are chilly." He held his whiskey flask over the cup, but Nick shook his head. He added a small dollop to his own coffee and tucked the flask away.

"Easily," Nick said.

Torturo went vague-looking for a minute, as if listening to something that only he could hear. Then, he smiled at Nick. "Your clothes will be waiting in my train car. You'll be sharing with me."

They bussed their dishes and headed back to Torturo's car. The Backyard was already fenced off and small tables and chairs were set out for the performers. Nick watched the Ferris wheel go up, its cheery white paint and red and yellow lights replaced by black with purple and orange lights. The creepy sight made him shudder.

To distract himself from thinking too much, he asked, "So what am I now that I've been hauled along?"

"You already asked that, Nick."

"I mean privately." They went into the car, glad to be out of the north wind that blew down off the mountains. Nick looked embarrassed at having asked the question.

"Mine... if you want it."

"But your what?" Nick persisted. "Your," he hesitated and forced the words, "sex toy? Your house boy?"

"My beloved." Torturo drew him close to punctuate it with a kiss. Nick looked confused and Torturo stopped, simply holding him. "It's not so strange, really, is it?" he asked, a puzzled look on his face.

"That's something you say to a woman, because she expects it," Nick said flatly.

Torturo snorted. "Well, that's not very romantic."

Nick shrugged. "Romance is something you do to keep her happy." He knew all about romance. He'd studied magazines and books on how to make his woman happy and have a successful relationship.

Torturo shook his head and lit his first cigarette of the day. "So young to be so jaded, Nicholas."

Nick sat down on the velvet bench. "I'm not jaded. I'm realistic. I don't believe in romance. I don't believe in 'in love.'" He made little quotes in the air with his fingers.

Torturo shrugged. "Then believe in want and friendship. It's close enough."

"I believe in want," Nick admitted. He knew all about want, too.

"Itches wanting to be scratched that should have been ignored."

Torturo filled his hip flask and then took a mouthful straight from the bottle. He trailed one hand along Nick's face. "It's a shame you don't like me more. I'm a very good friend to have."

"I don't know you well enough. Besides...friends? You can't be friends with something you dump a body fluid into." Nick's face twisted. He didn't want to think about last night, or September or whenever it had been. He didn't want to remember how he had felt as if he were exploding, turning into the whole universe and how Torturo had felt curled around him holding him and kissing him. In those moments he experienced nothing but warmth and safety, a sense of being home. Now, in the cold morning light, he knew the feelings for the deceptions they were.

"You would have really hated your wife, wouldn't you? Consider yourself very fortunate I swept you away before you could get married. I couldn't imagine a marriage to someone I didn't even consider a friend, but rather a thing and something like a toilet into the bargain."

Nick looked horrified at hearing his beliefs put so bluntly. "I wouldn't hate her," he protested. "She wouldn't be a friend. She'd be my wife and that's an entirely different thing." He couldn't articulate the difference. The most understanding he could muster was that a friend meant a person different from himself, while his wife would be a part of him. But he suspected Torturo would have something to say about that, too, so he shut up.

Torturo leaned in and kissed him and before he could stop himself, Nick found his arms going around the big man's neck. He pressed closer, a small whimper of need escaping him.

Torturo pulled away and shook his head as he looked at the clock. "Come on. We have work to do. After we take care of the animals, there are posters to put up and free passes to give out. Marvello and I do most of the outside work since we're the most ordinary looking."

*   *   *

He led Nick to the animal tent. The creatures crowded around him. He first patted the horse and then, to Nick's great surprise, the unicorn.

"How in the world can you touch it? I mean—"

"You mean with my drinking and smoking and very active sex life?" Torturo grinned as the unicorn poked him a little searching for a treat. He fed it a carrot. "It's not about who you fuck, Nicholas. It's about truth. She only deals with those who are truly themselves. Those who are trying to be what they aren't, she has no use for."

He fed all the animals. Nick watched the two-headed pig bury both mouths in the trough. Torturo returned to the unicorn to brush her out and polish her hooves and horn.

"It's pretty. It loved Lisa."

"Your girl was exactly what she seemed. I'll bet she didn't let you within five feet." He looked at the unicorn and smoothed her mane. "Did you, Precious?"

"I don't understand. I'm honest." Nick pulled away as the pig, finished with its food, investigated his shoelaces. "Don't like animals much anyway."

Torturo snorted and went to curry the gray mare who waited her turn. "Well, Petunia likes you at least. I grew up on a farm. I love animals. That's what I was hired on with the Show to do originally, you know. There were a lot more animals then."

"Yeah?" Nick sat down on a hay bale and drew his feet out of Petunia's reach. "Like what?"

"Horses mostly. They made the set up and take down easier. We had half a dozen and a couple wagons. The horses also worked as a pony ride."

Nick cocked his head. "Did you ride? I like watching trick riders."

"Not for the Show, but I do ride the one we have left. She's getting old, though, and we won't replace her." He checked the mare's hooves, hiding his regret. His lady was almost twenty, very long lived for a horse.

Nick shrugged. "I'm pretty much a small town boy. My folks had a garden, but never animals. Mom was allergic."

"Home's not a home without at least one dog, I say." He finished with the mare and moved on to check out the six-legged dog. Frisky bounced over to be petted, in fine fettle this morning, his much shorter extra legs scrabbling at the air. From the corner of his eye, Torturo saw Nick draw back a little.

"I hate dogs. Yappy little biting things, like the one across the street. Stupid beast cornered me and bit my ankles until I fought him off with a briefcase."

Torturo looked at him, disgusted. "The Mighty Nicholas Harper, terrier slayer."

"I just got it between the dog and my ankles and made a run for the door," Nick protested.

Torturo laughed at that. It fit Nick. "You've never met a German shepherd, then?"

Nick shuddered. "Oh yeah. Guy down the way had one. They're giant poop machines with big nasty teeth."

Torturo finished watering the petting zoo. "And the best friend you'll ever meet sometimes." He petted the cyclops kitten and checked its ears, then made sure the four-legged hen had a clean nesting box.

Nick wrinkled his nose. "They stink, too."

Torturo shrugged. "So do we. So do I, right now." He gave Nick a suggestive grin. "Care to join me in the shower?"

Nick hopped off the hay bale and Torturo wrapped an arm around his shoulders. "I need it. So, how'd it get to be Thursday at the end of October anyway? It was Labor Day. Where did the whole two months go?"

Torturo, very sweaty and smelling of animal feed and hay, said simply, "We slept through them. We hibernate between stops." He considered, looking for a way to tell Nick something good and added, "And we don't seem to age while we do."

Nick took this in silently as they went into the car. At the door, he stopped. "I can't do this. I'm leaving." He looked up and Torturo gave him a puppy-dog look of big eyes and exaggerated sadness. Nick shook his head. "I can't lose months of my life at a time. I'm going home. I'm going to grovel to Lisa and marry her."

"You won't be happy," Torturo said. "And neither will she. I can make you happy."

"All you make me feel is filthy," Nick sneered.

"So, are we on for the bath?" Torturo asked. He knew only fear made Nick talk so. Everyone got scared and angry at first. He remembered yelling at both the twins and slapping Alice in a blind rage when he'd found out what was going on. Alice had only forgiven him when Dinah reminded her of her own bad behavior with a butcher knife when they'd come aboard. Nick shot him a look of pure contempt and walked out of the Backyard. "Guess that's a no."

Nick barged in on his nice warm bath about twenty minutes later, shaking with rage. He dropped to his knees beside the tub. "I can't go home. Every tent flap I walked into, it dumped me in this backstage area. Every time I walked out the main gate, I found myself walking right back down the Midway."

Torturo nodded. "You need to follow what you want."

"All I want is to go home," Nick said.

"To all that loneliness? To a wife you don't call friend and don't love?" Torturo still couldn't believe that. He'd known couples that had married out of convenience, because they were fond of each other, but they were at least friends and co-workers. He couldn't fathom Nick's idea that a woman was more akin to a tissue.

"To my home and my job and my girl. To my *life!*" Tears of rage rolled down Nick's face, seemingly unnoticed. His balled fists clenched by his side and he nearly quivered.

Torturo reached out, wiped one of the tears and stroked his shoulder and Nick relaxed under his hands. He pulled Nick toward the oversized tub and started easing off his clothing. Nick helped him, surely unconsciously. He tugged and Nick joined him in the bath. They shifted around until Nick's back nestled in the warm water against Torturo's chest and Torturo wrapped his arms around his lover.

"Darling, I know it's hard. But you're one of us now. And it's not so bad, really. You just have to follow the rules." He kissed Nick's neck and rubbed him with a soapy washcloth. "I'll bet you're great with rules."

Nick seemed to melt against him; the fury had passed and left him spent and limp. Torturo kissed him under the ear.

"We go where the Show allows us. We never leave the grounds after nightfall. We hibernate between stops." He paused, thinking. "We all change. Some more radically than others. Be prepared for it."

"I guess I'm trapped," Nick laid his head back on Torturo's shoulder. "Might as well enjoy it."

"Or you've been set free," Torturo suggested. The water had gone cold and, although reluctant to disturb Nick, he needed to get on with the day. They got out, dried off and he went to the other room to see what the Show wanted him to wear. In moments, he pulled on a charcoal gray wool suit with pale gray stripes and a dove gray ascot. He pinned an orange rosebud to his lapel.

Nick stared, seeming unaware that he only wore a towel, watching him dress. Torturo could feel the hunger in Nick's face and see the effect he had on Nick's body.

"Free would be free from my desires and physical urges." The words came out of Nick's mouth, but the rhythm and cadence were all wrong. Torturo knew he'd been taught that belief, had absorbed it, but had not made it his own. His own body gave lie to the very idea.

Torturo knotted his tie in the mirror. "Why would you want that?" He caught Nick's blue eyes in the glass and held them with his own.

"This is life. Live it while it's yours."

"But, it's the only way to be good," Nick protested. Torturo wondered if he knew how feeble and false the words sounded, especially after the resignation in the tub.

Torturo turned around and saw Nick catch his breath. He looked good and he knew it. "And what's so great about being good?"

"It's the only way to prove you actually love God. Enjoying anything is the surest way to ensure a painful and hot eternity. This life is a testing ground, a snare and a distraction."

Torturo shook his head. "You poor, poor man." He reached for his hat. Even if Nick couldn't leave the grounds, he had work to do. He saw the confusion and dawning realization on Nick's face.

"You don't believe." Nick shrank back even more than he had from the dog.

He bent and kissed Nick's forehead. "Trust me, love. I've had it beaten into me already. God is a cruel father."

Nick looked shocked at that. "No. No." Torturo could see Nick couldn't get his head around it. He tried rationalizing. "God is very just and perfect and unable to abide anything that isn't. That can look like cruelty to limited mortal thought, but we aren't to rely on our understanding."

"You're not perfect, Nicholas. You never were."

Nick looked at the floor. "No, I'm not. No one is. I, at least, make the effort. I don't wallow in sin like you do."

Torturo's laugh sounded nasty this time. "Every thought, every sight under control? Hardly. The man I saw in that car dealership wasn't pure. He was consumed with lust, with desire for me." He leaned in and licked Nick's ear. "Did you stroke off under your desk in that big empty dealership, dreaming of me rogering you over the top of it? I did. I pedaled back here, thinking with each bump what you'd feel like under me."

Nick shook his head. "I splashed cold water on my face and read the Bible I keep—kept—in my desk. Numbers is always good for cooling down."

Torturo nipped his earlobe and felt Nick shiver. "You're a liar, my darling." He ran one hand down to Nick's towel-covered crotch and found him hard and ready. "I don't keep such a book here, Nicholas. But, I think we can make do."

"I know." Nick's voice had gone very soft and he breathed more rapidly as Torturo kissed him. He gasped and clung as Torturo stroked him. "Such a hypocrite," he whispered. "But I can't fight anymore."

"Why fight? Live." Torturo kissed him again as Nick shot into the depths of the towel. He held his lover for a minute and then said, "Let's see what the Show has for you to wear. I expect you'll be able to get out if I'm accompanying you."

Nick never let go of Torturo's waist as they opened the wardrobe to find a black wool suit in his size, with a flashy orange vest and a black bowler hat awaiting him on the shelf. He fumbled with the pumpkin-printed bow tie until Torturo came up behind him and did it. Nick shivered when Torturo's arms went around him and hissed softly when Torturo pulled the tie tight. He scowled at the ghosts and pumpkins dancing on the band of his hat.

"Let's go." Torturo set the hat on his head and led him off the grounds and into the little Kentucky town. After the first stop, he insisted Nick do the talking. He handed out posters and approved their placement, but Nick sold the Show. He had to admit, the little man was a good salesman. The Show had made a fine choice.

When they got back to the grounds, the roustabouts had almost everything ready for Friday's grand opening. Torturo looked it over approvingly. He loved Halloween carnivals. The booths had all shifted from their summer merriment to something more sinister and creepy. The rides had all changed color to suit the occasion. Black and orange dominated the Midway, with splotches of blood red, livid lilac, and poison green like wounds and bruises.

Nick looked horrified. "Satan's birthday," he mumbled under his breath and Torturo caught it.

"Is that what they're saying these days? Do you even hear how ridiculous you sound, Nicholas?" He laughed. The roustabouts looked up and joined the laughter. Torturo led him past the octopus, reconfigured into a black widow spider, and the whip which now sported vicious-looking spikes and chains, like a torture instrument, although well away from the passengers. Leering skulls grinned down from the Midway streetlights in place of bulbs. Two of the dwarf clowns shot streams of green slime from water guns into the mouths of screaming plaster clowns, blowing up jack-o-lantern balloons as they tested a game booth.

Torturo chuckled as the duck booth operator howled along with Warren Zevon, singing "Werewolves of London" in a very off-key baritone while scrubbing the duck pond and ducks.

"Better not let Wolfgang hear you there, Tony," he called. The man waved a red rubber duck with horns in Torturo's direction.

Nick just glared at them for making fun of him. He turned and stalked to the cook tent for lunch.

Torturo followed him, laughing as he sauntered along. A new carving on the door of the Fun House, re-done to be a Haunted House, drew his eye. A pretty girl, naked but covering herself with her arms, crouched atop the door lintel, a pair of enormous batwings sprouting from her shoulders. He smiled, pleased Clovis had placed Sin instead of simply absorbing her entirely. Most years, only one of the human refuelings got added to the décor.

"Hello, boys," Hannah greeted them. Her appetite seemed undiminished from the morning. A whole roasted chicken, now nearly skeletal, sat before her. Torturo got the same. "I see we have a new talker." She nodded at Nick.

"The Show seems to think so. You should have heard him doing the pitch to the local businessmen, honey," Torturo said as Nick got his own lunch. He had the roast beef. Torturo grinned. "Still can't eat chicken after my act, huh? Lots can't." He wrested off a drumstick and stripped it of meat in three bites.

"I'm pleased you did so well, Nicky." Hannah smiled. "Now when you build the tip, I'm one of the teaser acts."

Torturo saw she was losing him with the jargon. "When you start gathering the crowd for the Show, you can bring her out and talk about her."

Hannah launched into the spiel, her words fast and rhythmic, "Hannah, Hannah from Lame Deer, Montana. Prettiest lady you ever did see, but gotta watch out for that goatee. Just look at her folks, isn't she gorgeous? Not every man can handle a lady like this, but our Marvello can. It takes a master of illusion to cope with the strong appetites of a strong lady. The beard is real. The mustache is real." She paused for a breath. "And that's where you invite a couple of men up to tug my whiskers, dear." She twirled one end of her handlebar mustache. "I would dearly love to shave," she said. "I think I will after the last show."

"Go ahead," Torturo said. "It'll grow back in hibernation."

"Besides, Marv likes to kiss me when I'm all smooth." She smiled up at her husband, who had ambled up sleepily. "We have a new talker, sugar."

Torturo's fingers went white around the knife and he carved a chunk off the breast with extra force.

"Good morning, sweet." He bent to kiss Hannah's cheek. "I overslept again. Hello, Jacob. Is this our new boy?"

"Nick Harper," Nick said and his hand went across the table in a gesture so automatic Torturo could tell he didn't realize he'd done it. He scowled, remembering the day Hannah had offered her hand to the new man, in just that same way. Things had gone downhill from there.

"Marvello, Master of Illusion. The troupers call me Marv. Nice to have you aboard." He folded Nick's hand into his own and shook.

Torturo finished his chicken and got up. "I'll be in the car," he told Nick. Nick just nodded. The twins showed up and started cooing over how handsome Nick looked in his work clothes. Torturo knew it would be some time before Nick came home.

At least he wouldn't have to listen to the pious whining for a while. Nick had some of the ugliest notions of human relations that Torturo had encountered in a very long time. Maybe being around people who didn't reinforce how awful other people were would help.

He took out his flask and had a drink. It was early in the day to be hitting it, but Nick drove him to distraction. He stared at the ceiling of the car. "Are you sure about him?" he asked of the thin air. No answer came, but he hadn't really expected one. The Show had answered him once already today, telling him Nick was to be the talker. The Phantasmagoria itself seldom spoke these days. When he was new, he'd heard it all the time.

He thought of Hannah and Marv. He had another drink. He'd disliked Marv since the day the angry young man in beret and sunglasses had swaggered along the Midway. When Marvello, who had been Marvin Jackson in those days, came aboard, the whole dynamic of the Show changed. Elijah was a strong man, but he wasn't a pack leader like Torturo. Marv was. They still circled each other like wolves fighting for dominance, even after twenty years of weekends.

Hannah had held out her hand to Marv, just as Nick had, on their first meeting. She and Torturo had been in an off phase of their on-and-off relationship. The Labor Day he'd caught her kissing Marv in the Backyard had been the day he knew he couldn't like the magician. He'd called her a cheating whore. She'd laughed and demanded to know how it was cheating when they'd been apart since Easter. That time, refueling the train had been pure pleasure.

He'd had a few more drinks by the time Nick came back about an hour later and hung his hat on the hook by the door as automatically as he'd extended his hand to Marv. He sat on the edge of the bed, looking better than he had since they'd woken up. Torturo raised the flask in salute.

"Looks like I'm stuck," Nick said, but he didn't sound as doomed as he had this morning. In fact, he sounded almost cheerful. "But it's not a bad gig to hear them talk."

"Might as well enjoy ourselves," Torturo said, sitting up and stealing a fast kiss. Nick didn't pull away, which was good, but he didn't return it as he had the night before, which wasn't so good. He tried again, making it deeper and sweeter and, this time, Nick responded before pulling away. "Scared, darling?" Torturo asked, stroking Nick's face. He tugged Nick's bow tie open.

"No," Nick lied. He wasn't in the practice of it and did it very badly. "I just…"

"Want to talk instead?" Nick nodded, excited by the out. "Talk then. After all, we can't be friends if we're virtual strangers."

"You think we can be friends if we're—" Nick broke off and gestured to the bed.

"Fucking?" Torturo supplied. The reticence had been cute at first, but it bored him.

Nick shrugged, blushing.

"I really think we should do more of that. But yes, I believe we should be friends if we're sharing living space and meals and a bed." He stroked Nick's face again, the soft cheeks sweet under his fingers. He wanted to seize it and kiss Nick all over it, tasting his cheeks and mouth, forehead and eyelids before feasting on his throat and lower. "You sell cars. You go to church. What else?"

"I bowled on Tuesdays and led my nephew's Cub Scout troop."

Torturo smiled, playing in Nick's hair. "I don't blame you for being bored and looking for some excitement."

"Who was bored? I had a nice life. I'm bored now. There's nothing to do." Nick pressed into Torturo's hands, surely unconsciously.

Torturo gave him the kicked puppy look. No one else had ever complained of boredom while he touched them. "So you're bored of me? I'm not bored of you." He leaned over and kissed Nick's neck, taking the long slow taste he'd wanted. "Not at all. There will be plenty to do when we open tomorrow."

"We can't…" Nick took a deep breath and tried out the unfamiliar word, "screw all night and morning."

Torturo shrugged. "Then don't. Do what you wish, Nicholas. I am going to rest a bit. You're welcome to join me." He lay back on the bunk and opened one arm, still cradling the flask in the other.

"I want to go home, just leave the grounds, walk into town, and buy a bus ticket. I don't care that I've been missing for two months."

Torturo rolled his eyes. Homesickness was always a problem, but Nick seemed to have it in spades. "You'll get over it eventually. There is no life back in your little town for you. Everyone knows you bit my dick. You wouldn't get your life back anyway."

Nick glared. "Everyone thought I bit a sausage. I can make a new life. Up in the City, if I have to." Torturo waited, listening. Nick shook his head. His next words were to himself instead of Torturo. "And what would I do?" He propped his elbows on his knees and cradled his head in his hands. "Live a queer lifestyle and die before I'm thirty-five." He waved away the flask when Torturo offered it.

Torturo set it on the table as he got up and went to soak in the tub again. From the tail of his eye, he saw Nick slide off the bunk to his knees and bury his face against the mattress with his arms folded under it. He emerged about an hour later, naked. Nick hadn't moved and Torturo suspected he was praying. Nick would be broken of that soon enough.

"You're no saint, Nicholas. You're just a serpent, a false believer. And you know how to deal with snakes, don't you? From above and behind."

Torturo seized the back of Nick's neck with both hands. Nick caught his breath, terrified.

"If I ever catch you at a display like this again, I'll send you on to your God a little quicker than you planned." Torturo tightened his grip, twisting Nick's neck as if to break it.

"Go ahead," Nick snarled. "Go on and send me to hell. It won't be any different. I'll find myself right back here while a demon with your face sodomizes me over and over."

Furious, Torturo tightened his grip on Nick's neck again, prepared to break it. He couldn't live with this. Nick was never going to be his lover, only a whining nuisance. He twisted, hearing Nick whimper at the pain. Then, Torturo caught a glimpse of them in the mirror. Half of Nick's face was gone, sheared away leaving only wet, starkly white bone poking through raw meat and blood-clotted brown hair. Shards of glass perforated the other half, including a large piece in one blue eye. His own face was dark with asphyxiation and a livid rope burn encircled his throat. He blinked and shook his head and only saw the two of them, still dressed for work. The Phantasmagoria showed things like that sometimes. Those times had grown more frequent in recent stops.

He pulled Nick to his feet and turned him around and kissed him. "You're just homesick," he whispered. "It happens to everyone." Torturo stroked his face and hair, catching one forgotten tear with his thumb. "I could have left the Show, too, but I joined it to eat. And I had no other options on that front. I had animals to work with, plenty of food, plenty of booze, and the twins. I love it here."

Nick just sighed, clearly not paying attention to the soothing. "God doesn't hear me anymore."

Torturo pulled away, long tired of this song already. "God doesn't care. He hasn't in a while. There's just a lot of hopeful people trying to be special enough to care about. But it's hopeless."

Nick shook his head. "Not hopeless. He always heard me before. Sodomites and adulterers and fornicators can't have heaven."

"Men are the gods now. And there is one certain thing to remember when dealing with mankind, it cares only for itself." Torturo let his voice go soft and gentle. "As you have reminded me so well today, my darling. You care not a whit for me because you didn't ask a single question of who I am, not even my name. You spoke only of your life and your God and your boredom."

Nick snarled at him again, furious himself. Torturo wondered for a brief moment if Nick was angry that he wasn't dead. "I don't want to know. I don't want to stay. As far as I'm concerned, you're a demon who led me so far astray I'll never find my way back. You've ruined me in every possible way, so why in the name of little green apples would I ask anything about you, Jacob? Jacob, the trickster, the liar, the supplanter. You fit your name." Nick got up and walked out.

Torturo sighed and let him go. Nick couldn't leave the grounds. He'd find some tent somewhere and maybe a sympathetic listener and pour out his troubles. Torturo just hoped it wouldn't be Jene. From all he had seen, Nick still acted skittish about the hermaphrodite, but if Jene offered a friendly ear, that might change. Jene was always friendly where slandering him was concerned, he knew.

He lay quietly for a few minutes before he got up and dressed. Then he ambled out into the Backyard to enjoy the end of the late October sunshine. The twins sat on their special bench, Alice with her arm around her twin, stroking her hair, and Dinah worrying at a fingernail. They looked up and forced a smile.

"I'm not in the mood, pigeons. Nicholas just stormed out."

"We know," Dinah said. "We saw him go past. He will adjust. We all do." She dabbed her eyes.

Torturo sat opposite them and took out his handkerchief. "That dream again?" The twins shared a recurring nightmare.

Dinah nodded. "It were dreadful." Her sweet accent turned decidedly less posh, speaking more of the cheaper streets of London. "We stood on the corner, all unlaced and on offer, holding each other against the cold fog. We kept trying to tease some man into having us both for a pound."

Alice took up the narrative. "He was handsome, he was, all in his black cloak and topper, very flash toff. He offered us two sovereigns, one for each, and took us into the alley."

"He always kills Alice first," Dinah said. "With a bright silver scalpel."

Alice patted his hand. "Oh, Tortie, you weren't there when we woke up. Would you sleep with us tonight, love?"

He leaned forward and wrapped the girls in his arms. "Of course, darlings."

"We shouldn't ask, not with your new lover," Dinah said.

"He'll be happier if I don't bother him." Torturo kissed one cheek of each girl.

"He'll come around, Tortie, darling," Alice promised. "We all do. You would not believe what Dinah and I did when we saw the Show. We snuck aboard the train and hid in separate cars."

Torturo stared at the joined twins. They had never, over the many years together, spoken much of their life before the Phantasmagoria. Nobody did. Part of the price of living almost forever was having no past. "What? How did you manage that?"

"We are petite and we were very naughty," Dinah supplied. "We escaped our suitors and the guards and found the doors open."

It dawned on Torturo. "You weren't together then. Like that night I had the fist fight…the last time I hurt."

Alice nodded. "We awoke, in a car of our own, joined." Her pretty face went very cold and blank at that. Torturo wondered if it had hurt.

Dinah's face grew sad at the memory. "We screamed ourselves raw, tore our hair, and Alice tried to cut us apart with a kitchen knife." She scowled at her twin.

Torturo leaned over and took their hands. "Oh, darlings. You must have been terrified."

"We were sixteen and absolutely horrified. But Eliza came to us and she calmed us. You never saw Eliza. She was very beautiful, but had no arms."

Torturo thought a moment. "I think I've seen one of the old posters, but they don't do women justice."

Alice continued. "She came to us, held us and told us all we needed to know. She combed our hair for us and helped us into the new clothes that we had to wear. She was very clever with her toes."

"We hated her," Dinah put in.

"But only for a while. We thought it was her fault, you see." Torturo nodded, starting to understand. "Your Nicky may hate you a while, darling," Alice went on.

"I don't know if I can take it."

Alice leaned over and kissed him. Dinah followed suit. "We love you. And you can't possibly love him yet."

"No, not yet," Torturo admitted. "But I had hoped."

"We know. He will come to it," Alice assured him.

"He wants you so badly, how could he not?" Dinah, always the more perceptive in emotional matters, kissed him again.

"Until that day, I will be his despicable demon, then." That had been the worst of Nick's diatribe. He gave the girls his best sad puppy face.

"Oh he didn't," Alice snapped.

"Didn't what?"

"Actually say that," Dinah said.

"Oh yes. It seems I am Satan incarnate." That idea caused an amused smile to spread over Torturo's face, ruining the hang-dog look.

Alice chuckled and pinched his cheek. "A wicked, handsome devil." Torturo smiled more.

"Our wicked handsome devil," Dinah corrected. "Tortie, he will get over it."

"If not, I'll beat it out of him."

"And prove to him you're evil?" Alice cocked an eyebrow at him and Dinah matched her in mirror image.

"I am."

"No, you aren't," Dinah said.

"You're our darling who came aboard for love of us so long ago." Alice smiled as he hugged them both. She and Dinah held him tightly, feeling the flush on his face that spoke of distress he could not let out to anyone but them. They each kissed the cheek closest to them and let the Pain King work through a new and unfamiliar sort of agony.

CHAPTER 8

THE TALKER

Nick hiked all over the Midway, familiarizing himself with the layout. He found that still wearing his work clothes caused the roustabouts and clowns to talk to him and answer his questions. He paused at the mirror maze and straightened his hat. He fumbled with the bow tie, trying to remember how Torturo had done it.

Stitches, one of the senior clowns, found him there. He fixed Nick's tie and took Nick under his wing to introduce him around. "Torturo really should do this," he said, his painted face a mass of Halloween style scars with thick, ugly sutures.

"We, uh, kinda had a fight," admitted Nick. "I think it was my fault."

Stitches smiled. "Jacob can be very difficult sometimes. Jene despises him. It was a bad breakup. The twins adore him, most of the time. Nagina and Mingxia avoid him. Most of us know to stay on his good side as much as we can." He pointed at the little stage in front of the Ten-in-One, now painted with orange stripes and a line of dancing skeletons on the rim of the ticket booth and tombstones around his podium. "Give it a try, kiddo."

Nick did his best to ignore the demonic decorations. He was already damned, worrying about Halloween had to be the least of his concerns. He found a comfortable way to stand and did a couple practice runs of his talk. Stitches gave him a smile. They sat on the edge of the stage and watched folks get ready for the next day.

"You know, Nick, no matter what you've said, you can always apologize," Stitches suggested. "Jacob, well, he's not a forgiving sort, but he might make an exception. Especially for you," the clown added with a secretive smile.

Nick gave a wry smile, but stared moodily at the black Ferris wheel. "I said he was a demon."

Stitches laughed. "You're about right." Nick stared at the ground as Stitches continued. "You know, Marvello used to be a talker. He might have more pointers for you."

"I'll ask him, thanks. So, uh, tell me about Jene."

Stitches chuckled. "Jean and Gene Carlisle were the cutest little Beat couple. They turned up one day in about, oh must have been fifty-two. And they were not happy to be one person, for all their talk of merging souls and spirituality. Jene is literally both of them, fused into one body."

"Even—" Nick broke off and blushed. He tried to imagine how they would look naked.

"Even sexually. Nick, you really will have to speak more freely. This," Stitches made a broad gesture, "is the Phantasmagoria. There are no limits here."

"How long have you been here?" Nick finally asked, after he quit blushing.

"Since nineteen twenty-five, a few years before Jacob. We age about one year for every ten, so, I look about thirty now. Or would if I could see my real face." At Nick's puzzled look, he ran one finger down the line of sutures in his cheek. "They aren't makeup, kid."

Suddenly unable to stand the grotesque scarred face any longer, Nick gasped, "Excuse me, please. Starving," and fled to the cook tent.

Marvello and Hannah were sitting, sipping coffee and looking through a magicians' trade magazine. They closed it when he sat down with them.

"Can you help me please?" he asked, stuffing a bite of coffee cake in his mouth. The ravenous hibernation hunger had been only temporarily quelled by breakfast and lunch. He sectioned an orange as he chewed.

"We will if we can, son." Marvello smiled. "What do you need, Nick?"

"Stitches said you might be able to help me with the talking?" Nick drank deeply from his cup of coffee. Hannah refilled it for him. "And maybe with Jacob, too."

Marvello rolled his eyes. "The first definitely, the second not at all. The first thing you need to know about Jacob Plum, Nick, is that he's an abusive drunk. If you stay with him, you will end up as Jene did, begging a safe spot in our car for a hibernation."

"He says he loves me. I don't believe it. Men don't really love. We just want and say we love to get other people to do what we want."

"You're wrong," Marvello and Hannah said at the same time.

"Jinx, darling." Hannah smiled and went for another watering-can size pot of coffee.

They were deep in conversation about teasers and the best way to build a tip when the cook ran up the supper flag. Marvello explained the timer method, that Nick was to play up the price of seven dollars, only to announce a special price of three dollars for the next three minutes. But, of course, everyone got in for three and the rigged timer never ran out, despite its loud ticking.

Hannah delivered three dinners so Marvello and Nick could keep talking. The better Nick did, the better the Show would do.

Nick ate, barely tasting the meat and noodle casserole, listening and absorbing like a sponge. Then he saw Torturo come in. The Pain King scowled to see Nick talking to Hannah and Marvello. He got his own food and sat alone.

Nick shook Marvello's hand and Hannah's and took his half-eaten tray over to where Torturo sat, frowning at his food, sipping his coffee instead of eating.

Before Jacob could say anything, Nick took a deep breath, put his tray on the table and said, "I'm sorry."

Torturo didn't even look up from his coffee. He just poured more whiskey from a hip flask into it. "For what?"

"For everything I said. And for being a jerk to you when you're only trying to help."

"Really." Torturo's drawl wasn't a question and Nick, remembering what Marvello had said and, long attuned to the ways of abusers, hesitated before plunging on.

"Really," Nick hastened to reassure him. "I have a bad case of homesickness and I'll get over it. I'll be better when we start working. And, thank you."

Torturo said nothing to that. He took a bite of the roll and demanded, "What did the magician want?"

Nick shrugged. "Just teaching me the basics of talking. I want to do a good job for you guys." He attacked his lima beans.

Torturo appeared to come to a decision. He reached over and stopped Nick's hand halfway to his mouth. "Go back to the car and wait for me."

Nick gestured at his half-finished food with his free hand. "I'm eating."

Torturo's grip tightened until Nick squirmed and tried to pull away. He felt a small bone in his wrist grate against another. "Take it with you." Torturo's tone brooked no argument.

Nick wrenched his hand away and rubbed it, very leery of him now. "All right. See you soon? I need to talk to you a little."

"I won't be long." He poured more whiskey into his coffee and shoved the still-full tray away.

Nick gave him a smile, grabbed a cupcake and headed back to the train car. He did notice that Torturo didn't smile back. That left him even more uneasy. The curt commands rankled at him. He remembered what Marv had said. There were ways to avoid getting hit and after watching his cousin Karen, he knew most of them.

The secret to handling Torturo would be to be sweet. He had been fine until their fight, when Nick had crossed him and called him names.

Torturo came in a few minutes later. Nick had changed into his jeans and a sweatshirt and sat on the edge of the bed. He stood up and went to Torturo.

"Hi." He tipped his face up for a kiss. Torturo met it, melting and sweet, his hands coming down hard on Nick's shoulders and shoving him into the wall of the car. Nick squirmed, pinned there, half aroused, half afraid. It turned to all fear when Torturo shook him, bumping his head against the hard wood.

"What?" He twisted, trying to free himself from Torturo's hands.

"You're mine, not his." Torturo's eyes burned as he shook Nick again and then pinned him to the wall with his long body. He cupped Nick's face between his massive hands and bent for another kiss. When Nick jerked away, escaping his grasp, Torturo scowled.

Nick's face went hard. "I'm my own and we need to get a few things straight, mister."

Torturo caught him with one long arm and pulled him back for another kiss, this one as sweet and melting as any other he'd given. Nick wrenched away, wanting more of the kiss but not liking the price that came with it.

"No way." He put the table between them. "No way. You don't get to treat me like that and then kiss me."

Torturo chuckled. "That little shake was to make sure you remembered the kiss. You'll know when I hurt you, Nicholas."

"Yeah, I'll remember it. I'm requesting my own car, like everyone else has. I watched one of my cousins get abused enough that I don't plan to take it." He stopped for a moment, listening to the sudden voice in his head.

The soft, subtle voice that had encouraged him to go in for the adult show, the one that had teased him all the time in Peculiar, came back. It whispered to him of how good things would be between him and Torturo. It told him of the Show and how he would own it one day.

"You won't get a car." Torturo ducked around the table and pinned Nick to the opposite wall. "Where do you think you're going to go? It won't let you leave and it won't let you have your own digs, because it brought you along for me." He kissed Nick's neck. "You'll take whatever I give you."

Nick only half-heard the threats. After a couple more minutes of distraction, listening to the voice, he came fully back and crumbled in Torturo's grip. The only thing left rigid about him was his cock. He dropped his eyes, a sinking in the pit of his stomach.

"Just don't bruise my face or hands," he said in the same voice he used when pleading with God. It said he was small and weak and inoffensive and that the other was so much bigger and more powerful. "Those have to be seen." Torturo kissed the spot where he'd bumped Nick's head. Nick only shuddered under his lips.

"Don't play with the magician anymore," he ordered.

"I was only learning to do my job," Nick said in the same small, soft voice.

"You already know. And what you don't, the Show will feed you." Torturo kissed him, heat and desire evident in the touch of his mouth.

Nick just looked defeated and started stripping out of his clothes. He let Torturo shove him back onto the bunk.

"Good boy," Torturo said, stealing another kiss of his neck.

"I'm not," Nick said. "If I was good, you wouldn't need to hurt me." He covered his mouth again, but Torturo peeled his hands away for a kiss. "Make me good," Nick whispered.

"Of course. I love you, Nicholas." Torturo sat up and drew him very close, kissing him long and slow.

Nick just stared at the floor when Torturo let him go. His mind whirled from the mixture of pleasure and fear and pain. This was bad. It was so bad. He would end up exactly like his cousin, six feet under from "falling down the stairs." No one in the town had done a thing because, as everyone whispered behind their hands, smart-mouthed women brought it on themselves. But maybe if he did his best and stayed calm, he could avoid dying for a while.

"I'll do my best for you and the others and I'll be very good," he said, still not looking up. "I'll do anything you say. Just don't hurt me."

Torturo smiled and stroked his hair. "I like to see you hurt. It makes you pliable and willing."

Nick said nothing, but looked at him with big, scared eyes. In a move of pure placation, he went down on Torturo, unzipping and stripping the big man so fast he almost scraped his fingers on the zipper. Despite his terror, Nick remembered what he had learned and sucked beautifully. Torturo stroked his hair, making very pleased sounds. He even gave a warning just before he came, but Nick kept working.

It was all part of the job. He understood at last. He had been given over to his sin. His punishment for his wickedness would be a glutting upon the desires until they burned at him like wormwood. He would get all he ever truly wanted. When Torturo came, Nick licked him clean, fastened him back up and moved away, only to have Torturo draw him back in for more kisses and touching.

"Dad was right. I am gutless," Nick whispered.

Torturo shifted them around and lay back on the bunk. "There is no pleasing any father, ever, Nick."

Nick didn't look up, but with an effort of will, reached over and played with the triple piercing in Torturo's nipple. "Is there any pleasing you?"

"Just love me, darling," he said and kissed Nick's hair. "I want a nap now. And you are welcome to stay."

Nick heard the command and made himself comfortable in Torturo's arms. "I'm not sleepy. I should be. We've been up for hours." He figured this was a safe topic.

Torturo stroked him. "We don't sleep like normal people anymore. We just hibernate and take a few naps. We have to cram our lives into the space between one in the morning and noon. That's our time."

Nick kissed his neck to make up for asking a question. "What do we do during it?"

"Work on new bits for the acts, test the rides. Eat at the mess tent. And we can leave the grounds after dawn but before noon." Torturo kissed his ear. "We have to travel by bicycle. Would you like to see a movie?"

Nick shook his head and then thought the better of it. Saying no was always a bad idea. "Only if you want me to. I haven't seen any movies in a long time."

"Ah yes, part of your purity campaign." Torturo reached down and stroked his cock. "Nicholas, anyone who has to work so very hard at virtue has none to start with. Just give in."

Nick kissed him again. "I did." He tried not to sound as if he'd betrayed himself and his life. He didn't want Torturo to know he suspected he was already in hell and being punished for his sin.

"Yes, and you're going to again." Torturo kissed his neck, his big hands soft on Nick's back. "You do love it so."

Nick knew he was right, on every count.

*　　*　　*

The next morning, a very subdued Nick ate under Torturo's watchful eye in the mess tent. After they left, Jene and Marvello exchanged nods. The drunk had already beaten the boy into submission, that was clear enough. But if Nick froze on the Midway today, they knew what would happen. The Show would turn Nick into a clown or a dwarf and put him to work elsewhere. And there would be no living with Torturo for a while until the Phantasmagoria acquired him a new lover.

*　　*　　*

Torturo stood near the flap of the Ten-in-One listening. He'd already gone out and shoved a spike up his nose to tease the crowd into the Show. Nicholas sounded good. He'd get better with time, but he was already good.

"Lovely Hannah from Texarkana, folks! Give her a hand. You can see more of her inside, a whole lot more if you take my meaning, gents."

Torturo could almost picture the lascivious eyebrow wiggle Nicholas would give them at that point.

Hannah stepped in beside him, wearing a very colorful, yet modestly cut, dress and flats. "Nice choice, Jacob," she said, brushing her lips over his ear. He smiled at the feel of her mustache. "Don't break him, dear."

"I won't."

Hannah didn't move away. "Tortie, love, can you do some more piercings?"

He turned to face her and stroked her beautiful breasts. He'd never been allowed to set a needle to them and he wanted to dearly. "Sure I can. What would you like?"

She smiled. "A triangle."

He let his hands drift lower, feeling her hips and the curve of her ass. "I approve."

"And Marv wants you to add a few rings as well. He's talking infibulation."

Torturo raised an eyebrow. "He's getting daring."

"He wants to padlock me. He figures the rubes will totally freak out."

He matched her wicked grin. "They will. It will be wonderful."

She peered through the curtains and saw Nick having Mingxia do a small contortion for the crowd. Torturo peeked with her. "Tortie," she laid her hand over his, "he'll come around."

He didn't stop looking at Nicholas, noticing how he did well with every aspect of his new life, sometimes even better when he wasn't there. "I hope you're right."

"I was not pleased to wake up in the arms of a handsome man," she tweaked his cheek, "only to find I had grown a beard overnight, remember?"

"Yes, I remember. You cried for days and nothing I could do consoled you. But you realized, eventually, that there was no shame in it."

"Exactly. Sometimes I still shave, because I'm vain enough to want to see my own pretty face."

He smoothed an errant whisker into the point of her beard. "But you're no less pretty with it."

She twirled the corner of her mustache. "And no less vain. Those of us who were significantly changed had radical shocks. You with less visible changes still had shocks."

"I had it easy, I know." He watched the teaser, not wanting to go into this discussion. He and Hannah had been a fine romance. Only Marvello had made their parting bitter. It had taken years for them to come to a comfortable sort of avoidance living and working in the small show.

But part of life in the Phantasmagoria was not talking about life before the changes. He twiddled one of his eyebrow piercings, deep in memory of the horror he'd felt the night a roustabout had broken two of his ribs and four of his teeth, but he'd felt nothing at all. The next morning he'd awakened to find all his teeth back in place and a piercing kit on his nightstand. When he ran a needle through his earlobe, he could feel it, but nothing had hurt. He had set his first earring then and gone to see the twins. Fortunately his pleasure sensations were all still working.

"You came with the Show willingly. That changes everything."

He sighed. "I've waited too long for him, Hannah."

She kissed his neck. "I know, Jacob. I do know. And the rest of us have been poor substitutes, for all that we all love you. We want you to have him. We'll make sure you do." She gave him a wicked smile when he finally looked at her. "Now, about my needles…"

"Yes. Is tonight too soon?"

She gave a wry smile. "Actually, yes. I planned to do it right before hibernation."

He nodded. "For a perfect healing, of course."

"Exactly. And if we do it before, he will want to play with it."

Torturo rolled his eyes. Marvello had only one ear pierced and did not understand how much other rings hurt. "Naughty man."

Hannah pecked his cheek. "Part of what I love about him. Don't brood too much. Your boy will come around."

"Thank you, Hannah." He kept watching his boy as Hannah slipped off to change.

He regretted his treatment of Nicholas last night, but he'd never say anything. He didn't like his boy afraid. He wanted Nicholas hot and willing like the first night. He watched the timer routine and hurried backstage to change before anyone saw him.

The shows went very well that day, each crowd bigger than the last as Nicholas grew into his role. By the eight o'clock teaser, he was calling for volunteers to pull the screwdriver out of Torturo's nose and more to test Hannah's whiskers.

After the midnight show, when Torturo eased his way backstage, Nicholas was waiting for him. Nicholas seized him by the shoulders and yanked him down to kiss him hard. He heard the twins laughing and someone applauded.

"I can't believe it! Did you see the crowd?" His Nicholas kissed him again, hard and wild and sweet.

Torturo smiled down, thrilled by the change of heart. He knew the work would help his boy. "You did perfectly."

Nicholas shoved him a little toward the train. "I love this job. Come celebrate with me." He gripped Torturo's hand and yanked him toward the Backyard. After three steps, it seemed to dawn on him what he was doing. He slowed and stopped. "I'm sorry, I'm being pushy. What would you like?"

Torturo lifted his face and kissed him. "Anything you want. Celebrate, darling. You put in a hard day's work and did it brilliantly. You've found your calling." He tugged his boy along the path they had been traveling. "Take me back to the train and do what you planned to." He tipped Nicholas to face him. "Tell me what you wanted."

Nicholas, still very bold, kissed him. "Your mouth. Your hands. Your tongue. All of it, like you did the first night."

Torturo bent and kissed him. "Of course, darling. I love it when you ask me to do delicious things to you."

They got inside the train car and Nicholas tossed his hat off, grinning as it landed on the hook. He untied the bow tie with the skeletons on it and shed his graveyard scene vest. He tugged at Torturo's shorts and tank top when Torturo slowed him

"Nicholas, it was a lovely evening." He kissed his lover.

"It was." Nicholas's eyes shone like blue stars as he said, "What I really want is too much to ask."

"Never too much, darling. Ask and it shall be given." Torturo got his pants undone and reached in to stroke Nicholas's cock.

"A needle." Torturo barely heard the whisper. "I want a ring."

Torturo paused halfway to his knees. He straightened slowly, his mouth working for words that wouldn't come. He had wanted to pierce Nicholas, but never expected to so soon. "Really?" he finally managed. "Where?"

"Anywhere you want to put it." Nicholas took a deep breath and rushed on before he could chicken out. "I want to feel it and think, 'Jacob loves me. He thinks I look sexy like this,' as I go through my day." Nick looked at the chains at the head of the bed, noticing them for the first time. "Would you like me immobilized?"

Torturo went for his piercing kit, his hands almost shaking with excitement. "Only if you think you can't hold still."

Nicholas finished stripping and lay out on the bed. He laid his wrists in the cuffs, never intending to close them. They snapped shut of their own accord.

"Oh dear." He looked up and yanked at the chains. They were very securely fastened. "I should have made sure you had a key."

Torturo grinned. "I do, don't worry." He reached out and pinched Nicholas's right nipple, tweaking it awake.

"Ouch." Nicholas looked surprised. "You're doing... I thought you'd start with my ears." He breathed very fast and his cock jerked, leaving a small damp trail on his stomach.

"Anywhere I want to put it," Torturo reminded him.

Nicholas breathed out. "Yessss." He smiled. "Both?"

"Only one for now." Torturo swabbed him down with Betadyne and then made symmetrical dots on either side of his lover's right nipple before he clamped it in the forceps.

*   *   *

Nick breathed slowly and watched as Torturo took his time, perforating the skin at the first dot. The needle broke his skin. Torturo bent down and Nick gave the kiss he wanted. Nick whimpered as Torturo rolled the needle in his fingers, the metal just barely inside the meat of his nipple.

He watched as Torturo eased the metal through his flesh, very slowly, drawing it out. His head spun and his stomach flopped a bit. He could never watch needles before. His cock leaked and he couldn't stop making little moans of pleasure and pain.

Finally, the point of the needle tented the skin at the opposite dot. Torturo pressed just a little harder until it popped through. Nick sighed. Torturo slipped the gold ring through his nipple.

"Hurts," Nick whined.

"I know. But your little man loves it." Torturo licked his cock.

Nick held off his orgasm only with difficulty as Torturo sucked him in deep. He couldn't resist the sensation of the triply pierced tongue and came at the second lick.

"Inside me?" Nick looked hopeful. He squirmed in the chains, loving the feeling of being trapped and restrained. "I want to feel you in there."

"Soon," Torturo promised. He kept sucking at Nick's softening cock.

"Please? Jacob...please?" Nick was not averse to begging if it would get him what he wanted. "I need you."

Torturo kissed him hard, gratitude for Nick's words clear on his face. "Yes." He grabbed the lubricant and spread Nick's knees.

Nick kissed anything he could reach. He stifled a gasp when Torturo's chest spikes caught on his new piercing and pulled at it.

"Lovely sound," Torturo whispered, sliding in, very cautiously. He reached up to turn the ring in its hole.

"Please don't," Nick begged when Torturo tugged at the ring.

Torturo laughed and shoved into him hard and fast for three strokes, then lowered his mouth to lick the piercing and hook one of his tongue barbells into it. He backed off when Nick, only half-hard to start with, went completely soft.

"Please, it really hurts," Nick said.

Torturo took his hand away from the ring with visible effort and wrapped it around Nick's cock. Nick thrust into his hand, trying to take his cock in deeper, too. He rocked between Torturo's hand and cock, getting hard again.

"Oh yes. You love it. I knew you would."

Nick gave a small nod. "More," he demanded.

Torturo smiled and pounded him, adding a bit of a wringing twist to the grip on Nick's cock. Nick moaned under the treatment. He came hard and fast, spending all over Torturo's hand.

"Slut," Torturo said affectionately. "I knew you'd come around."

"Thank you," Nick whispered, going limp in the chains.

Torturo kissed his neck. "I'm not done with you, darling."

Nick smiled, only partly making himself. "Finish. Let me feel it."

Torturo thrust more deeply and came after a few strokes. Nick tried to put his arms around Torturo's neck but the chains drew him up short. He had to settle for wrapping his legs around his lover's waist. Torturo smiled down at him.

"So hot." Nick rattled his wrist chains. "Please let me out. I need to touch you."

"Hold a moment. I have to find the key." He groped around and then pulled it out from under the pillow. "See? I'm a magician, too."

Nick gave a soft laugh as Torturo unchained him. Once freed, he wrapped his arms around his lover and kissed him. As his hands slid over the skin of Torturo's neck and arms and back, Nick, caught in sensation, kissed him again, even more yearning this time.

"Sweet, brave boy." Torturo could not resist touching his newly pierced nipple. Nick didn't flinch.

"My Jacob," Nick said, a little drowsy. His throat hurt from work and two orgasms in a short period had left him sleepy. He pillowed his head on Torturo's chest and rested. Warm, strong arms folded him close and the nap overtook them.

They woke before dawn to a loud quarreling outside in the yard. Torturo grabbed his bathrobe and Nick struggled back into his pants. They threw open the window of the car just in time to see Wolfgang duck out of his car, followed by a flower pot that shattered on the ground like a mortar.

"And stay out, you beast!" Jean's voice followed him.

"I'll talk her around, kiddo," Gene's came in reply.

Torturo laughed. More correctly, he sent his long, deep laugh rolling about the Backyard until every window had been flung open and all of the freaks leaned out to witness Wolfgang's marital woes.

"Jean, she is PMSing," Wolfgang said ruefully. "Anyone got some floor space I can share? Guaranteed free of the fleas." He scratched behind one ear.

"You're always welcome here, dear," said Hannah.

"Come see us, Wolfy," Alice chirped.

"We have space," Elijah rumbled.

"It's better I go with you, Elijah." The wolf-boy headed to the giant's car. "Jean will be sorry by lunch, I know this. Gene, he already is."

"Wow," Nick said as they pulled back in. "And I thought we'd had a fight."

Torturo yanked him in close, pulling his face up for a kiss. "Darling Nicholas, your little whining is nothing compared to the hell Jene can put a man through. Two personalities in one body and they don't always agree. They're both bisexual, but she's the jealous type and makes him feel guilty."

"You want me again?" Nick said, feeling Torturo's renewed erection rubbing against his leg.

"I always want someone." Torturo reached down and stroked his cock, easing the foreskin back over the head and tugging the rings.

"If I were in charge, I'd padlock those rings together and then chain them to the ones in your," Nick hesitated and said it, "balls." He covered his mouth with his hands again clearly shocked at his own audacity and desires.

Torturo's eyes widened, pleased with Nick's progress. He knew Nick didn't mean it, that he was just trying to keep up sexually, but he had to ask. "And do you think it will take long for you to find a padlock, you wicked thing? Don't tease me so."

Nick went to his knees to suck Torturo, eager again. He took the thick shaft most of the way down, not gagging as he did.

"Oh, darling." Torturo stroked his hair. "I may have to pierce your tongue, too." He added, very softly, "I make a wonderful bottom, when you want me."

Nick glanced up and gave a happy little moan, then continued sucking.

CHAPTER 9

MONTHS OF SUNDAYS

Halloween ended. Nick went willingly into Torturo's bed for the hibernation, not knowing when they would awaken again. They awoke to a harvest carnival, all cornucopias and intact pumpkins, corn shocks, and cheerful scarecrows instead of the Halloween sort that had looked as if they would prefer to eat the passerby in addition to the crows. The lights were red and orange and yellow and the whole Show felt much more cheerful.

Even Stitches looked better. The sutures had changed and he now looked more like the Scarecrow from Oz than a cobbled-up monstrosity. Nick hunted him down on the Midway Thursday before the Show opened.

"I heard you really got a good crowd in over Halloween," Stitches said. "And Jacob forgave you, too, apparently."

"I like the work," Nick admitted. "Anything I should play up this weekend?"

Stitches shook his head. "Nope. Just do a great job and everyone will be happy."

Nick nodded. They watched the concessionaires set up the candy floss machine. "I could go for some cotton candy," Nick said. Thinking wistfully of cashew chicken and kung pao beef, he added, "I could go for Chinese, too."

Stitches nodded at Mingxia walking over from the dark ride, which had changed from a haunted house to a "The First Thanksgiving" theme. "I wouldn't let Jacob hear you say that when Ming's around."

Nick realized the acrobat was in earshot and blushed.

"Good morning, Nick." She smiled. "You did a very good job last time. I'm pleased you will be staying." She twisted her waist-length hair up into a bun and secured it. "The dark ride is ready. One of the pilgrims was nodding off of the beat," she told Stitches.

"Morning, Mingxia." Nick tried to sound casual. "You ready for tomorrow?"

She flipped over and walked on her hands a few yards. "Always." She popped up on her fingers and let them crab-scuttle down the Midway, carrying her body high in the air.

"I'm sleeping with a guy who has two pounds of metal in his body and she still freaks me out," Nick said. "Let your fingers do the walking," he added with a shudder.

Stitches smiled at him. "I told Jacob you'd come around."

"Didn't seem much point in fighting it. I'm his." Nick unbuttoned his shirt and showed Stitches the ring. "Nice, huh?"

"Very cleanly done. Did he perforate both?"

"Nope. But I bet that will change." Nick buttoned his shirt and sat, dangling his feet off the edge of the stage.

"Probably." Stitches hopped off the stage. "Back to work for me. Have a great day, kiddo."

Nick watched the Show finish setting up. The roustabouts tested the rides to see if they were running properly. He wondered if the guys running the swing wanted a tester. He knew the Tilt-A-Whirl would be a bad idea. He heard footsteps behind him and turned to see Torturo standing there with two large paper cones of yellow cotton candy.

"Happy Thanksgiving, Nicholas." Torturo handed him one and plopped down beside him, taking a bite of his own that left sticky strands of sugar in his mustache.

Nick peeled off a tuft of the floss and popped it in his mouth. "How'd you know?"

"I read your mind." Torturo grinned. At Nick's automatic look of horror, he hastened to reassure him. "Stitches passed the word along."

"Thank you." Nick licked a poof of floss to watch it disintegrate. "It's exactly what I wanted." He tore off another chunk and squashed it into a tough little ball.

Torturo laughed. "You play with your food like a little boy."

Nick gave him a smile. "If I can't play with my food when sitting out here on a gorgeous fall morning with my lover, when can I?" He licked the ball of sugar very suggestively.

"Oh, Nicholas." Torturo sighed happily. "You've come so far so quickly. I was afraid you would do something foolish like plant your delectable bottom in front of the locomotive and wait to be run over as penance for your wickedness."

Nick had the cotton candy down to the paper cone. He ran the top of the cone into his mouth, licking at the last bits of candy. He wasn't about to show Torturo that he'd already had that thought a few times. "Damned and burnt and I might as well enjoy what's gotten me that way." He shrugged. "Life's a lot easier without hope." He tipped his head over to Torturo's shoulder, his voice soft.

Torturo ate the end of his own floss, one arm around Nick. "You're right. It's a nice morning and I shouldn't be spoiling it with philosophy."

"We're all sticky," Nick said.

"Uh-huh." Torturo trailed sugary fingers over Nick's cheek and followed it with his tongue. "And I'm going to get us even stickier in a few minutes."

"You never stop, do you?" Nick sounded amused rather than annoyed. To make up for the impertinence, he nipped Torturo's neck.

"Five times a day if I can manage it, darling." He bent around, popped the last bite of candy in his mouth and kissed Nick, passing him the melting floss.

Nick met the kiss and did his best to make it hotter and deeper than Torturo had planned. The last bit of sweetness melted in his mouth and he shoved his tongue into Torturo's, pressing deep and wet, his sticky fingers in Torturo's hair.

"You want it as much as I do," Torturo said, looking amazed.

Nick grinned. "Why not?" He slid off the stage and pulled at Torturo's hands. Since he knew submissiveness worked, he decided to try for pure brazenness. "Come on, big guy. You said you wanted the bottom." Torturo just stared at him and Nick pulled harder. "Come on. Don't look so surprised. I just figured out there was no sense fighting anymore."

"No, there isn't. You enjoy it well enough."

Nick grinned and tugged. "I know. Now get off that stage before I yank you off." He gave a great jerk and Torturo slid off the stage and landed on his feet, laughing.

"Whatever you want to do with me."

Nick practically dragged him back to the train, not letting the grim resolve in his mind show on his face. If he could not escape his doom, he would embrace it with both arms. Anything Torturo could do, he could take and would enjoy. It wasn't a hard decision to come to. Once they reached the Backyard, he caught Torturo in a lip-lock and steered them toward the car, heedless of the yard furniture and other freaks.

"Sweet boy." Torturo gasped as Nick opened the door and pushed him in.

"Your boy," Nick said. He got them to the bunk and peeled off his own clothes. Nick fumbled with Torturo's buttons as he asked, "So how does this work?"

"With me? Just stick it in." Torturo eased out of his fine wool pants. When Nick nudged him, he rolled onto his belly.

"I meant this part." Nick swallowed hard and licked a stripe up the crack of Torturo's ass.

"That's exactly how."

"What feels good?" Nick nipped one flat, strong buttock.

Torturo gasped. "Biting is wonderful." When Nick licked him again, but avoided the opening, he said, "You tease."

Nick hesitated briefly and then licked at the tight pucker. He poked it with his tongue, then kissed and sucked at it, his skin crawling and his mind rebelling. His cock pressed rock-hard against the bed. Torturo rewarded him with noises of approval.

"Just like that, love." Torturo gave a soft cry when Nick managed to nip him. Nick felt his lover's balls draw up tight. He added a couple of fingers and Torturo took them easily. "You can't hurt me."

Nick took it as a challenge. "Oh no?" He bit Torturo's ass, hard, leaving teeth prints in the skin. Torturo just moaned under him. "I'm going to have you up one side and down the other." He tried the words for effect.

"Do it." The soft sigh was nothing like Torturo's usual confident sound.

Nick nudged him onto his back and knelt over his shoulders. "Suck," he said, holding his cock to Torturo's mouth. The look of adoration and bliss Torturo sent him nearly brought him off. "Just enough to get me wet." Once wet, he pressed the Pain King's knees to his chest and pushed in, entering another person for the first time with no finesse or gentleness. He knew Torturo wanted it this way. Even so, he bent down for a kiss. "My Jacob."

Torturo leaned up for another one and caught Nick's lip lightly between his teeth. Nick, testing him, pulled away very slowly, letting him bite down to hold it. He nipped but did not bite hard. Nick, on the other hand, bit his lips and slammed hard into his ass. When he opened, Nick bit his tongue hard enough to draw blood. Torturo only rode him hard, begging for more.

"You like it so rough," Nick shook his head and closed his teeth on his lover's collarbone.

"What was your first clue?" Torturo found his words slurred a bit with the injured tongue.

Nick laughed. "You taking Dinah's toy." He slammed deep once more at the thought of it and came, surprised to see Torturo come at the same time. He shuddered a couple times and then shook his head. "Whoa." Nick leaned down for a deep, sweet kiss, sweet as only Torturo had ever made them.

"Enjoyed that, did you? Your first time on top?"

Nick nodded on both counts. He took another deep breath, trying to put strength back into arms that wanted to do nothing but dump him atop his lover. He balanced and swatted Torturo hard on the unbitten ass-cheek. "You're a good lay." He got up to wash.

"Love you, too, darling." Torturo smirked, but clearly he was thrilled with Nick's behavior, even though Nick was working very hard at it.

Nick locked himself in the bathroom and soaked until his fingers shriveled. He turned over his behavior in his mind, analyzing and replaying every moment of it, trying to be horrified at himself. He tried to make it stop arousing him, with little success. He was hard before he got out of the tub. There was no hope, only the pleasure of his lover.

He scrubbed his hair, wrapped in a towel and shaved, deliberately not thinking about how easy it would be to use Torturo's straight razor to open a vein. Suicides went straight to hell. Even now, there was still a chance he might not. But his traitorous body wanted nothing more than to go right back to bed and fuck Torturo again.

He dropped the razor in the sink with a clatter and stared at his half-shaved face. Yes, he had thought the word, with anticipation and not distaste. He could almost taste Jacob under him, the smoke and hint of brandy and coffee. He felt the skin of Jacob's ass pressed against his thighs and groin and cheeks. And he wanted more.

He came out, shaky, and started dressing. Torturo got up to dress and Nick swatted him as he passed. Torturo rewarded him with another kiss, and Nick clung around Torturo's neck and thrust against him, half-hard.

"You can't possibly want it again. Nicholas, you're turning into me."

Nick laughed and drew back, finishing his tie but not going soft. "I had a lot of interesting dreams during hibernation."

"What about?" Torturo turned his attention to knotting his own tie now, a conservative green one that brought out the gold flecks in his hazel eyes.

"You." Nick turned and gave him a light kiss on the cheek. "And all the wickedly delightful things we can do."

"That's why you've been more willing then." Torturo put on his suit jacket. "And you'll tell me all about them?"

"Better," Nick promised. "I'll show you."

"Tonight?" Torturo looked eager.

"All this weekend long. I just gave you one. What's the plan for today?"

"The usual Thursday work of posters and pressing the flesh." Torturo emphasized this last by grinding against Nick, demonstrating his flesh was still interested, even more so after Nick's little tease.

"Put that away." Nick punctuated the order with a kiss. "Only I get to press that. When we get back, I'll press it all you want. In we go to talk up the Show." He put on his hat to go out, the bowler's band now decorated with leaves and cornucopias.

"You're so much better than I ever was, darling." Torturo picked up the roll of posters. "And with what might I be pressed?"

Nick looked at their reflection in the mirror. "My, we're a handsome pair." He turned to Torturo and shoved his own hard cock back hard against Torturo's groin. "Hands or mouth or anything you please, my dear Jacob." He clung closer, taking a long sweet kiss. "And everything we both want." Torturo's smile left him eager to go and come back.

Nick opened the door and saw a second bicycle standing next to Torturo's. He swung a leg over the bike, stuck his share of the posters in the basket, and followed Torturo into town. He wobbled a little, not having ridden for a few years.

Once in town, he soon found his stride. A quick, disarming grin, a firm handshake, and a fast patter had always been his best tools and he used them now on every major business owner, from the bank president and postmaster to the man who ran the Laundromat and the thrift store lady.

Soon, every window in Sidney, Montana, sported a Phantasmagoria poster. By eleven, Nick's stomach rumbled audibly and he retched from hunger in a ditch in the park as they pushed their bicycles through it. Torturo laughed when he said he needed a snack, calling him a master of understatement as well as a born ballyhoo artist. They went in to a little cafe.

Nick ordered the hot beef and gravy sandwich and the salad bar on the side. It would hold him until he could get to the mess tent and eat a couple of chickens and half a pig. Torturo ordered the four piece chicken dinner with all the sides and a salad. Between them, they half cleaned out the salad bar.

"Never was much for cukes, but these are good," Nick said around a mouthful of salad.

Torturo, more used to the hibernation hunger, finished his roll and took his time at the chicken. "Hunger's always the best sauce, Nicholas. I went hungry many nights before I joined the Show and everything always tasted good afterward."

Nick shook his head. "What did you do before the Show, Jacob?"

"I was a farmer." The admission clearly came hard.

Nick looked him over, taking in his fine suit, his expensive Turkish cigarette burning beside him, his general attitude of a man of the world. "I can't imagine it."

"Then let me paint you a picture of Jacob Plum, age twenty-two in nineteen and thirty-one. We were just starting to feel what folks would call the Depression in Hitchcock, Oklahoma. Out in the sticks, we were all poor. If I saw twenty dollars in cash money, it was a good year. Mama had been sick for a long time. She was weak and tired and the farm was coming down around my ears. I'd made a go of it for six years, since Daddy left, keeping the taxes paid, getting the crops in and harvested, but this year we'd had a drought and little of nothing had come up and less had borne. That morning, Mama didn't wake up. After I buried her, I took our last dozen eggs, sold them, and went to the Phantasmagoria, because something told me I should. It wasn't right or fitting, but I knew I had to. Maybe I could get in on a game or a cockfight and get the money for the taxes. Or, if nothing went right there, I could stand in front of the train when they left and the county would finally get the farm."

Torturo paused for a breath. Nick shook his head. He'd heard about hard times, but this was harder than he'd ever imagined. "Wow."

Torturo nodded. "The sheriff had been out that morning with the notice. I had twenty-four hours to get my affairs in order and clear the premises. I buried Mama in the burying ground, next to my three little brothers that didn't live, packed myself a bundle and didn't look back. I paid my nickel for the Ten-in-One. There they stood, the most beautiful women I'd ever seen. Voices like angels, hair that looked fit to burn me if I got too close. And three legs between the pair. They summoned me to their car, made me a man and took me along with the Show." He finished the end of his roll. "Everything I am today, I owe to the twins and the Phantasmagoria."

Nick watched him eat the chicken with a slow, measured grace, his large hands using the cutlery instead of picking up the heavily-battered pieces. Nick ate his own sandwich, the rich beef flavor of the gravy satisfying him for a while.

Torturo paid and left a nice tip for their little redheaded waitress. They pedaled back to the Show. Nick grabbed Torturo and kissed him once they were back on the Midway. He bit a little, tasting salty blood where he broke the skin of Torturo's lip.

"Not now, darling. Tempting as you may be, I have to go take care of the animals. And since you're still hungry enough to try eating me, yet again, I suggest you go to the mess tent and continue your lunch."

Nick gave him a smile and headed for the lunch tent. He sat with the twins, letting them gush over him and chatter about how Torturo adored him already. It made him feel guilty. It was tiring being horny all the time, especially for Torturo. He hadn't had much practice at it. But he liked what he had seen this morning and wished he had been more amenable to talking at the last stop. He would talk more this time.

After an enormous lunch, Nick headed back to the train car. He heard Torturo in the shower, so decided to surprise him. He stripped down and stretched out on the bed, trying to coax another erection. It came easily. He had to be willing, wanting. He had to make sure Torturo never put him off the train.

After a moment, when the shower made no sounds of slowing, Nick had an idea. He'd heard that the train supplied anything they wanted. With the amount Torturo smoked, Nick had asked for a lighter. It hadn't materialized on the nightstand, so he went looking for it now.

In the top drawer of the nightstand, he found a cedar chest. The box filled his hands, oddly heavy, its top curved like a pirate's chest. He opened it. A number of rings, many of them men's wedding rings with a few class rings—one with familiar insignia, a match for the topaz one Nick wore—lined the bottom. A hair ribbon and a decorative comb joined a pair of hoop earrings and mother of pearl cufflinks. Nick looked over the class ring then picked up a bullet that lay tangled in the mess.

He turned the bullet in his fingers, still naked, when the bathroom door opened. He looked up and suddenly had no problem remembering why he wanted to get hard a few moments ago.

Torturo stood there, just hanging up the towel, stark naked. Nick stared—the odd bits and bobs in his hands forgotten—taking in the pierced eyebrows and nipples, the foreskin rings, the scrotal ladder, and the half-hard cock twitching his direction. He wanted to touch the smooth, strong chest and feel those large hands all over him.

"What a lovely sight to come home to." Torturo came to the bed and kissed Nick, then tugged at his new ring.

Nick just looked up and kissed him, very hard from the sight of his handsome man. "Hello, darling. Ready for some wickedness?"

"Always ready, if you're being wicked. What would you know of such things, my repressed, closeted, sad little invert who doesn't even listen to secular music?" Torturo noticed the box in his hands. "That isn't for you, darling. Put it back, please."

Nick took in Torturo's expression, something between frightened and angry, and put the bullet away. "What is it?"

"It's mine." Torturo slid under the blankets and turned his face to the wall.

"Not unless your name is Cynthia M. Wishom and you're a senior at Raymore-Peculiar. Is there something I should know?" he teased, but the words fell flat.

Torturo rolled back over, not the Pain King at all, just a beautiful man in his late twenties with too much pain in his eyes. He seemed to be considering something.

Nick kissed him, a bare brush of lips. "Jacob? Please?"

"They're the Show's now. That's all that's left of them. It's the only grave they'll know. So put it away." He closed the lid for Nick. "The Phantasmagoria does not run solely on dimes and quarters and magic. It runs on blood and souls." He kissed Nick. "You'll understand more in time."

Nick turned his automatic scowl at being dismissed into a flirty smile. He tucked the box away. He would have to think more on this. "You asked what I would know of wickedness," he said. "Try this." He kissed Torturo deeply, feeling the barbells in his tongue, and then trailed the kisses down Torturo's neck to nip hard at the sensitive spot behind his ear. "Can I do whatever I want?" Nick grinned up at him from where he knelt. "Because if that's the case, I'm going to lick and kiss every hole in your body." He got to his feet and startled when Torturo kissed him.

"I like the way your mind works." Torturo smiled at him.

"I just want to make you happy." Nick kissed the first hole in Torturo's earlobe.

"You do make me happy." He sighed as Nick brushed his tongue over the inside of his ear and then kissed him. "Darling boy. You do know how to make a dull Thursday pass." Torturo cuddled him in to lay side by side, Torturo smoking and Nick just resting on his chest, sucking one of his long, thick fingers, trying not to think how it would feel inside him.

*   *   *

Friday went off without a hitch and Nick, as always, was high on the crowd and the give and take of drawing them in and building a tip for the shows. After the last show, he flung himself at Torturo, kissing him hard and rubbing against him.

"I think work turns you on more than I do." Torturo laughed as they made their way to the Backyard.

Nick laughed with him. "Never." He kissed Torturo again, his need and love warming the cool November night.

CHAPTER 10

WORKING

The harvest yellow and orange gave way to the red and green of a Christmas carnival in Miller City, Ohio. That iced into blue and white for a Winter Fling in Clinton, Connecticut. Valentine's Day, with pink and red lights on all the rides and a Tunnel of Love for the dark ride, found them in Tustin, Michigan, with only a few brave souls enduring the ten degree weather.

March found them in the rapidly greening Jonesboro, Arkansas, where the green and pink lights of the Spring Break Carnival mingled with the first colors of the delta. At the next stop, Nick liked the pink and yellow and purple of the Easter carnival.

With the arrival of spring, Torturo took the horse out for long rides on Thursdays after the Show posters were up. Nick, terrified of horses since the kindergarten field trip to the zoo, when he'd been stepped on by a pony, gritted his teeth and asked to be taken along. Torturo rode bareback, holding on with his knees. Nick rode behind him, his face buried between Torturo's shoulder blades, his arms tight around Torturo's waist. They would ride at a walk and a trot and sometimes a gallop. Nick clung the tightest during the gallops. The one time Torturo had jumped a fence, Nick had actually screamed and been promptly embarrassed.

With summer came the red and yellow lights for June, followed by red, white and blue color scheme for July. August and September had the same generics as June. Nick felt a bit nostalgic as Labor Day passed into Halloween. The Ferris wheel turned. The seasons turned.

The Show never changed. The patter seldom changed. He had found his rhythm, at least while he worked. And even off-duty had gotten better. Torturo was always ready for sex, at least after he'd sated the first devouring hunger after awakening. Nick found he could manage two or three erections, but after that, he didn't want to climax for the rest of the weekend. They adjusted.

The working days rolled by, one blending into another, distinguished only by the color of the lights and the designs on his clothing. Nick found, if not peace and love, at least contentment and satisfaction. He liked waking next to Jacob, making love, working and then ravishing his lover in the spill of the crowd's energy.

Labor Day 1987 found them in Shuqualak, Mississippi. This particular Monday afternoon, Nick ducked into the car after the two o'clock, which he never did. He stopped inside the doorway in stared in shock.

Torturo knelt on the bed atop a very attractive boy, his big hands pale around the youth's dark throat. With each squeeze, the young man thrust up against Torturo. Nick watched in horror as his lover closed his fists, choking the life out of the man.

Still naked, Torturo left the bunk and noticed Nick. He pulled Nick aside as the streams of memory began swarming in every door and window, encasing the man in a silvery cocoon. Nick could only gape as the bed swallowed the cocoon whole. He saw Torturo clutching something and pried his lover's fingers open.

A little oval medal, showing the Virgin Mary standing on a crescent moon, lay in his palm. Nick picked it up and looked at the back. A small red pebble with the legend "Exindumentis" were on the back. Torturo closed his fingers over it again and then laid it carefully in his grave box, his face sad.

Nick, unable to tolerate his presence another moment, fled the car. He wandered down the Midway, aimlessly, ignoring the clowns and boothmen that greeted him. He hesitated at the gate, but since it was day, he walked off the lot and onto MC Nees Street. He ignored the cars and walked south, away from the field at the north end of Nees, down through the barren blocks of Oak, Center, and Pine. After he crossed Highway 21, the street dead-ended again. He made his way back to the highway and followed Mulberry north past all the closed little stores.

From a storefront church, he heard singing, like no hymn he'd ever encountered. He read the door which said, "Song Service, Monday, 5 P.M." Nick lingered on the sidewalk, listening to the deep southern voices slurring through words, with the accents in the wrong places, a piano that sounded more like it belonged in a barroom than a church and the claps on the wrong beats. It moved him and disturbed him both until he had to wander in.

There was not a white face in the church. Taken aback, Nick sank into a chair in the empty back row, hoping to not be noticed. He knew the words, "Come unto me and I will give you rest." Rest sounded wonderful. But the upbeat piano and the firm conviction with which the worshippers sang let him know there would be no rest for him. As they finished and remained standing for the prayer, he slipped out the door.

The sun hung low and hot in the September sky and he hesitated. He could wait here. Stay out of the Show until after sundown and see what happened. Maybe he could get work here and find a way home. Rest. Finally rest from the endless desires that had consumed him, with his consent, since the day he came aboard.

He sat on a bench, the Phantasmagoria's music still faint in his ears. Even at this distance, he could see that the roustabouts had the Wheel partially disassembled. As the Mississippi sun bore down on his neck, he watched them take down another eighth.

Come home, Nicholas, sounded in his head. He shook his head to clear his ears. *Come home. It's time to go.*

His feet almost unwilling, Nick ambled back to the grounds. The French voice in his head, Clovis, he realized after a moment's confusion, kept talking. He did not go at once to Torturo's car, but lingered, watching the games booths being struck. Finally, just as Clovis began yelling at him and the train built up its head of steam, he vaulted aboard, making it as far as the sofa before collapsing into hibernation, ignoring Jacob's outstretched, imploring arms.

*   *   *

When they awoke in October, the horse had gone. Jacob had said it was always that way, that the dying ones just vanished during the hibernation. Nick watched worriedly as he didn't even bother with coffee that morning, just drank brandy.

By afternoon, he'd graduated to straight whiskey, still in the tea jar, but with no tea mixed in. Nick avoided the piercing tent. When Torturo gave him the look of the big eyes and the hopeful mouth, Nick couldn't refuse him anything and Nick had too much to do to be swept into bed for half the day. Since Torturo seemed disinclined to go out and put up posters, Nick took Marv with him.

The magician turned out to be very good company. They got everything settled in town and rode back to the Show. Torturo turned and left the mess tent when they came in together. Nick braced himself for ugliness, but Jacob never came to the car that night. The next morning, Friday, Nick worked on some adjustments to his costume. It was usually fine, but he liked things to fit a little more snugly. Torturo sat, drinking and watching him. When Nick glanced up as he reached for the next sleeve garter, Torturo flashed him the puppy-dog look. Nick swallowed his sigh and leaned across the table to kiss him.

"I know what you want." Nick gave him a sly, sexy smile that he wasn't sure he felt. He was still waiting for the blow-up over Marv. He hoped he could head it off.

"Oh how far you've come since I met you. So tell me, what do I want right now?"

Nick reeled off the list of the usual suspects. "Coffee, booze, another cigarette and my ass straight up for you."

Torturo nodded and finished his cigarette and opened the next bottle of whiskey, his second already. The amount worried Nick more than anything. Torturo got unpredictable when he drank. "Close. Very close."

Nick lit the next one for him and stripped. He hadn't dressed yet this morning, wrapping up instead in a blue bathrobe.

"I want your mouth." Torturo dragged on the cigarette and unzipped.

Nick went between his knees before the words were entirely out of his mouth. He sucked Torturo straight down, without a word or extra motion. He'd had plenty of practice giving good head, so he put it all to work. Easy, by the numbers, a lick here, a flick there, a brief period of letting Torturo fuck his face and then soft bites all along the shaft. He had to make up for enjoying Marv's company. The moan from above him told him he was doing it right, as always.

Torturo came without much delay, which was nice, and stroked his hair. "What's wrong, pet?" Nick hadn't swallowed yet and shook his head. He wasn't sure he wanted to swallow. "Even a poorly paid whore would have more enthusiasm."

Nick definitely didn't want to swallow now. He spat the mouthful of semen on the floor at Torturo's feet. "Then it's a good thing you aren't paying me, isn't it?" He got up, threw his robe back on and went back to tightening the elastic in his sleeve garters. He wasn't going to give an inch. Let Torturo play stupid mind games and drag out his punishment. He had work to do.

Torturo leaned across the table and patted his cheek. "Don't worry, darling. I'll have your ass after the Show and give you what you really wanted." The patting turned into a slap.

Nick never looked up from his needle. "Doesn't matter what I want, sir. You want it. So you'll have it." He hated the submissive sound in his voice, but the response was almost automatic. Abuse made him want to crawl into himself and say nothing but "yes" and "anything you want" until Jacob stopped.

"And what do you want, right now?" Torturo's voice had gone dangerously soft and his hand hadn't left Nick's face. Nick fought to hold steady and not show his fear.

"Nothing." He bit off the thread and set the garter aside.

"Always easy. I like that." He slapped Nick again, rattling his teeth.

Nick didn't flinch. He simply got up, disengaging. "I'm going to take a shower." He ignored Torturo's glare and went. He lingered in the water, not sure how he could repair this. He knew his lover was hurting, grieving, and he couldn't help. He couldn't let Jacob beat him while drinking, but he could be loving and careful.

He came out to find Torturo dozing in the chair, the new bottle empty on the floor beside him. Nick dressed and went out to check the Midway before the Show opened. On his way back, an hour later, he stopped by the mess tent. He came back with food for them.

"Lunch," he whispered, kissing Torturo's temple. "And then showtime."

"Already?" Torturo, still half-asleep, reached for him, pulling him down. Nick went willingly into his lap and kissed his whole face.

"Nice nap?" Nick asked.

"Mmm." Torturo pulled him and Nick kissed him deep and sweet, letting him linger as long as he liked. The affection was better than the drunken fight and hitting. Torturo pulled away with a laugh when Nick's stomach growled.

"Eat." His eyes got large as Nick reached over and took a slice of apple and bit into it, then bent, brushing it against his lips. He bit off his share.

"We don't have time to play a lot," Nick said. "Showtime in an hour." He gave Torturo a last kiss and climbed off his lap. They ate in companionable silence.

The crowds were small for October and no one bought much. Nick remembered seeing most of the town boarded up when they'd gone in to put up posters. All the tips were small but the adult show barely had a dozen people come in. The lack of audience threw him and by evening his patter became hesitant and unsure.

He stayed silent as they climbed back aboard. Torturo started drinking at once which was not unusual, except that he usually poured it into his coffee in the evening.

"What was wrong with you out there?"

Nick shook his head, disturbed. His lover looked ready to abandon the day's sobriety. "I don't know. The energy wasn't there. The words wouldn't come out right tonight."

Torturo slapped him, confirming Nick's fear. It would be one of those nights. "It's the same words every night. Like my act is the same every night."

Nick opened his mouth, a hot retort on his lips. He thought the better of it and closed it. He sat down, took the whiskey away from Torturo and poured himself a drink, his first since college. No reason to be good now. None whatsoever. He had been deluded at first by his desires, now he walked into damnation with his eyes open. He gulped it, feeling the old familiar burn. Without a word, he stripped and went to kiss Torturo.

"Fuck me," he demanded. He could see his words inflaming the Pain King and he elaborated. "Shove into my ass. Make it hurt." He took another drink, only to have Torturo claim his lips as soon as the glass had left them.

"Even better like this," Torturo whispered and pushed him onto the bunk. Nick lay flat on his back, not kissing, and drew his knees back with a pained groan. A sneer curled his lip, but he erased it.

"Still angry at me, then." Torturo reached for the lubricant.

"Not at you. Never at you," Nick whispered. He pulled Torturo down for a rough kiss. "Yes, completely right like this. Dry-fuck me like the little bitch I am." He had never said such words in front of Torturo and saw the effect they were having.

Amazement on his face, his arousal desperately hard, Torturo slammed into him, dry, wrenching a scream from Nick. He pounded hard and Nick kept begging for more in words so filthy he couldn't believe he knew them, even through his tears and yelps. It didn't take long for Torturo to come. He stayed on top, looking down at Nick as if he barely knew this man.

"I should put booze in you more often. You can be mad at me if you want. I can take it."

Nick shook his head. "Why would I be mad at you? You are what you are. You act as you've always acted."

Torturo grinned and pulled out, letting Nick flex his legs. "Despicable."

Nick nodded. "I am. You're only you. You drink, you smoke, you fuck, and you charm the living daylights out of the rubes. It's what you do and what you're good at."

Torturo sat up and went for the whiskey, then thrust another glass at him. "I think I'm going to get you drunk. It will be interesting to see what the real Nick Harper is like."

Nick swilled the glass down. "Good. Maybe I can arrange to stumble in front of the train as it leaves." He knew when he saw Torturo's face that he had finally stepped over the line. Through the booze, he remembered that suicide by train had been Torturo's original plan and his great fear that Nick would attempt it. The rage and fear he saw there made him shake.

"Out. Get out." Torturo yanked him from the bunk, slapping him forehand and backhand. "I'm sick of your self-pity. I'm sick of your sheep's face and sad eyes. I don't give a damn where you go, but get the hell out of my car!" He shoved Nick through the door, barely giving him time to grab his robe.

*　　*　　*

Torturo slammed the door and slumped against it for a moment, breathing hard. He slammed both fists back into it and shoved away. The circle remained unbroken.

He flung himself on the bunk. His father, him and Nicholas, a poisoned abusive circle of three. All his life had revolved in threes. He had known to come with the Show because of Alice and Dinah, their three legs, the two girls making a three with him.

Three rows of peach trees stood behind a privy in his mind. One row made of two and a newly filled hole and the little old gray wooden building starting the fourth row. He wondered if they were even still there after all this time.

Sixty years, twenty threes, lay between the peach trees and the train and now he had his Nick. He was no better than his father had been, taking the unwilling who feigned desire.

But Nick had taunted him tonight and he had truly lost his temper for the first time since the barn on that hot August day.

Unlike his father, Nick had survived his anger. Torturo breathed slowly, tempted to reach for the whiskey and knowing it wouldn't help. Maybe the circle could be broken after all.

*   *   *

Nick wrapped the robe around himself and sat on the bench in the Backyard. He knew it was no longer possible for him to leave. It never really had been. He still had a twenty in his billfold and his ID. But there would be no home and no job and no life if he went. His credit card had probably been canceled for nonpayment so he had no way to get home. He was stuck.

He was sick of it all. The things he did with Jacob revolted him now, when they'd excited him back in August. His mind had been given over to perversity. No matter what refinements Jacob invented for their bed, Nick met his desire and often surpassed it.

He had rings in both nipples now, a large sapphire in his right earlobe, and for Valentine's, it had been a reverse Prince Albert. He shifted in the chair and stuck his hands in his pockets. Out of habit, he rotated the ring that went into his urethra and out the top of his cock. The silver ring and blue bead matched his frenum ladder, the series of five barbells that ran along the bottom of his cock.

It seemed they could not stop without Torturo breaking out the piercing kit. What frightened Nick most was the way the mere sight of that kit made his gut twist with arousal and his cock go hard. The last time, he'd almost come around the needle embedded in his cock.

He didn't need much coaxing anymore, at least not at first. Just having Jacob in the same room made him hot. He did his best to be aroused all the time when his lover was around. He'd learned the best ways to keep his erection and his fellatio skills had improved tremendously. But he never went down to rim Jacob or took a mouthful of his come without suppressing a shudder at the wickedness of the act.

He dozed off in one of the big Adirondack chairs. Strange thoughts, words that were not his own, had grown stronger as they impinged on his thoughts and now insinuated themselves into his dreams. It was the same voice that had coaxed him into the adult show the first night, the same that spoke to him in all situations.

Had it happened back in Peculiar, he would have called it the Holy Spirit. Now he knew, despite suspicions of blossoming schizophrenia, it was just the voice of the Phantasmagoria. But the rational part of his mind said it had to be insanity. He ignored the rational part, drowning it with arousal and blunting it with work.

He ate breakfast and sat in the Backyard, waiting for something. He wasn't sure what. He listened to the Show, and now the voice had a name. He barely noticed Hannah when she sat on the bench across from him.

"Nick, you should go see Jacob."

"I don't want to. We're fighting." The words sounded petulant even to him.

"That's not good." Hannah smoothed her mustache a bit. "He does love you, you know."

"Bullshit," Nick snapped. Hannah scowled as he continued. "He's a psychopath and an abuser. He's a man. There is no love in him."

"You're wrong, Nick," she said, then swallowed hard as Torturo came up behind Nick and laid a hand on his shoulder.

"Just because there's none in you doesn't mean we're all the same," he said, bending to kiss Nick's ear.

"You can't love something that doesn't love you back."

Hannah, seeing that a long-standing argument was taking up again, slipped off to her own car.

Torturo sat down behind Nick on the bench in the Backyard. "You can. But it's painful."

Nick twisted out of his arms. "It's stupid to even try." He turned to face Torturo, finding this went better when the other wasn't nuzzling him.

"It can't be helped." The plaintive yearning in the words tugged at Nick, but he just frowned.

"Of course it can. Love is just emotions and actions. Actions can be stopped and emotions are nothing more than muddy, deceptive thinking."

"I like my emotions. I don't want to be cold like you. You are as divorced from emotion as I am from pain. Physical pain, anyway," Torturo amended.

Nick's frown deepened at the reminder that he caused a lot of emotional pain.

"I'm not cold," Nick protested. "I'm just aware that feelings are deceptions."

Torturo smirked a little and stroked Nick's hair. "I live with you. I know you're cold."

Nick stood up and walked toward the train car. "We can change that," he fired over his shoulder.

"We have to," Torturo agreed as he followed Nick.

Nick marched inside, took a carpetbag from the closet and started throwing his personal effects into it. "All right." He took a single blanket from the cupboard and draped it over the top.

"You can't leave, you know." Torturo sat down and started lighting his pipe for something to do. Nick saw the fury just under the blasé surface.

"No, but you don't have to live with me, either. I'm cold. I'm lousy in bed. And all I do is hurt you." He headed out the door.

Torturo set the pipe aside and caught him, sweeping him into a kiss that threatened to melt Nick's knees, one that went straight to his groin and made his cock twitch. He bit Torturo instead of kissing back. He had to do this, had to make the break now.

"Nicholas..." Torturo wiped the blood away, staining the immaculate linen of his handkerchief.

Nick searched for the words that would make it final. "Go fuck yourself. I'm sure you're capable of it. I've got some space in one of the cars. I'll see you around." He marched out with no real idea of where he planned to go.

*   *   *

Nick made himself comfortable on the pallet he'd done up in the prop car, between the case of pickup ducks and the locker of BB guns. It didn't feel right to sleep without Torturo wrapped around him. The vaguely mildewed vinyl smell of the ducks made him miss Torturo's aftershave even more. No. He wasn't going back and that was final.

The train lurched and he felt the heaviness of the hibernation steal over him. As was their habit, he waited to feel the soft kiss on his ear and the hard cock lying along the crack of his ass.

The train rolled and sleep swallowed him, with neither sensation.

*   *   *

Nick awoke, rolling over for the first kiss of the new stop, and bumped his nose on the BB gun locker.

The pain aggravated him, but he put the feelings away from him. No sense being angry at a piece of metal. Better to be angry at himself for seeking the sinful behavior.

He dressed and went for breakfast. He arrived first at the mess tent and ate rapidly and hugely, wanting to be gone before the others arrived.

When Torturo wandered in, wearing only his pajama bottoms and robe, Nick bussed his tray although he was still hungry. He wouldn't be tempted. He ducked into the Pain King's empty car to shower and dress, then collected his posters and free passes from the front gate.

Nick went through all the usual Thursday work, alone. He found it silent and lonely, the damp November chill even deeper with no Jacob at his elbow to tease him or help him with a poster that was too high.

He set his jaw and caught a late lunch, hoping to miss anyone he could. The voice in his head wouldn't stop. It told him to go home, go back and hope Jacob would take him in. He ignored it and canvassed the Midway, making sure everything was in order.

The games gleamed, perfectly set up. The food vendors whistled as they prepared for the next day's crowd. Nick watched two of the dwarf clowns blow up balloons and the candy butcher arrange her tray.

He barely noticed when Stitches came up behind him.

"Another fight, Nick?"

Nick jumped. "Break-up. For good, I hope."

"It sure doesn't seem to be doing you any good, kiddo. I haven't seen a face that long since Stretch, the India Rubber Man, got his chin caught in the taffy puller."

"Who asked you?" Nick snapped.

"Nobody. Hey, Nick, kid, just take it easy." Stitches looked over the bunting and Nick realized he'd shredded it instead of hanging it. "Go get your ashes hauled. You'll feel better."

"Go to hell," Nick grumbled. "Oh, wait, this is hell," he added and stalked off.

Even the crowds the next day didn't improve his mood. After a very boring evening, thrown on his own slim resources, and the stress of ducking his lover—former lover, he kept reminding himself with rapidly shrinking conviction—Nick found that talking the crowd in annoyed him, too. He hated them all, stupid sheep, vacant thrill seekers needing God more than stimulation, and poor people throwing their money away.

He wanted to rail at them all, tell them to go to work, go to church

128

and save their money.

That stop was an index of the next. The green and red of the Christmas carnival seemed to sink Nick even deeper into his melancholy. He'd seen Torturo stomping through the Show, looking scruffy and unkempt, a most unusual appearance for the natty man. He saw Jacob drinking more through the weekend.

Nick ignored it all, from the chill in the air to the Christmas carols the Show played over the loudspeaker. They were quits. He didn't care about Jacob or how much the man drank. He just wanted to work until the train took him somewhere close to home. He'd jump ship then and walk if he had to. He had no reason to stay, no reason to keep loving a murderer.

CHAPTER 11

TOPSY-TURVY

Jacob half-woke and rolled over. The train had stopped and someone pounded on the door of his coach. He cradled his aching head and opened one eye. A hangover? Preposterous. He'd slept for a month, it should be gone by now. But the pounding continued and made his eyes ache.

"Come in. It's not locked!" he yelled, regretting it.

A petite girl in an oversized parka barreled through the door and shut it against the chilly wind that followed her. "Jacob," she said, making his name a sigh of relief. She came to where he hadn't even sat up. "Jacob, what is going on?" Big gray eyes with streaks of deep cobalt implored him, and pillowy lips quivered, needing to be kissed, not two feet from his own.

At a loss for words, Jacob just laughed and pulled the girl down into the kiss she seemed to be inviting him to take. "Good morning, Nicholas." He smiled when he let her up. "It must be the sixth."

"I haven't seen a paper," Nick snapped. "I woke up and went to the donniker only to find myself sitting down. What is going on?"

"January sixth, Nicholas. It's the Feast of Fools, a day where everything is opposite. Most of the Show will be changed, I expect." He smiled. "That will be nice. The twins make very handsome men."

"It didn't do this last January," Nick protested as Jacob sat up and started dressing.

"Only on leap years, darling," Jacob said absently, looking over the changes in his lover as he dressed. Nick was shorter now, with longer hair. He'd opened his coat and Jacob put his pants on backward as he stared at Nick's breasts. They were lovely, making a cleavage that invited his hands and tongue under the rather abbreviated talker's costume. He was ready to fuck her pretty brains out and say screw the Show.

Jacob sorted out his pants and bent in for another kiss, feeling her marvelous breasts. "Come to bed," he whispered, shoving her coat off her shoulders and letting it drop to the floor.

"Jacob, I'm starving," Nick complained. He stood up and wrapped his arms around Jacob's neck, which had the salutary effect of pressing those breasts against Jacob's chest. He pulled Jacob down for a kiss that left them rubbing against each other and Nick gasping at the feel of Jacob's hard cock against his belly. "After breakfast, I want to make love to you until one of us has to go to work," Nick said.

"Of course, darling girl." Jacob slipped into his coat and held Nick's. Nick gave him a funny look and put it on. Jacob held the door for his lady and smiled when she tucked a small hand into his massive one. He did wonder that Nick wasn't more disappointed at being trapped in a female body, given his bizarre religious ideas. But he expected to enjoy himself thoroughly.

*   *   *

Nick let Jacob lead him to the mess tent. He tried not to clutch Jacob's arm tighter as they stepped in. He let out the breath he held. Almost everyone had changed as he had. A tall black woman ate next to a shorter man with brown hair. A handsome Indian man in a turban ate with Mingxia, who had not changed.

He'd awakened groggier than usual. The prop car had been less comfortable and when he rolled onto his side a warm, heavy weight had settled on his arm. He'd opened his eyes and managed not to yell. The breasts had been the least of it. The missing morning erection and the soft slickness between his thighs had been bad enough. But the jolt of electric pleasure that shot through him when he touched the area, exploring the new hair and missing his cock, had left him shaking.

His first thought had been Jacob. He needed his friend and lover like he'd never needed the man before. He wanted to be reassured everything would be all right. The thought of Jacob as a woman had been almost too much to bear. The relief he'd felt at the very male voice telling him to come in had left him sagging against the train car.

Now, he clung to Jacob's arm, the solid warmth of his lover reassuring him. He let go only to get a tray. They were heavy this morning and when the cook added a huge white plate loaded with food, Nick had to shift his grip.

He ate, ravenous as usual, but stayed very close to Jacob. The morning was cold and his lover was warm. The twins joined them.

"Patched it up, did we, Nicky?" Alice asked, her usual sweet soprano a pleasant baritone. She twirled the new handlebar mustache she wore.

Dinah smoothed her own and teased, "Wait'll you see what we have for you tonight, Tortie, love."

Jacob kissed them both, never taking his arm from around Nick. "Hello, loves."

Alice pouted, an incongruous expression on the strongly masculine face. "You're still a boy. Oh boo."

Dinah nipped his neck. "I was looking forward to seeing how sweet and soft your cunny was."

Jacob gave them a rueful smile and shake of his head. "Sorry to disappoint. But my ass is open for investigation."

Nick shivered, wondering what that act would feel like in his new body, wondering what making love to the twins would be like. He suspected if he offered, he would find out in short order.

Dinah returned his smile with a wicked grin, and Alice chucked Jacob under the chin with a thick finger. "Think you can fit two into that fast-talking mouth of yours tonight?"

"While I'm fucking my girl, maybe." He squeezed Nick a little closer.

Nick protested the crudeness and the suggestion. "Oh hey, wait, I'm not getting on that stage. I work the outside stage."

Jacob cupped Nick's breast and thumbed the nipple, which sent shivers all over him and made the space between his legs plump up and ache. "Are you sure you are tonight?"

Nick tried not to let his voice tremble or show any nerves. "I can still do my job."

"All right, we'll enjoy the usual. And afterward, you're all mine, precious." He tipped Nick's face up. Nick anticipated him and kissed him sweetly. The very smell of Jacob aroused him. It was all right. Loving Jacob was safe this stop and he planned to take full advantage of this chance.

Nick felt much better after eating, calmer, more composed and very distinctly horny. He let Jacob lead him back to the railcar. The day had warmed up some and paper had said temperatures in the fifties. He hoped the work clothes wouldn't been too revealing.

Once inside, Jacob swept him up for more kisses. "Beautiful," he whispered against Nick's throat. "So soft. I miss you, my darling one. Show me?" His hands eased off the coat and opened Nick's shirt before Nick could protest.

Nick watched as the breasts sprang free, tipped with a puffy pale pink nipple that looked nothing like his own tan ones. The rings remained the same. He helped shed his clothes, loving the gentleness of Jacob's touch.

He breathed in sharply as Jacob found his nipples again. They went red and hard, standing up at the first brush of his thumb.

"Adorable." Jacob nipped them lightly which made Nick's knees grow weak. "Like ripe little cherries." He slid a hand under Nick's waistband and fingered the wet softness. "Are you cherry everywhere, little love?"

Nick shoved his hand down Jacob's pants and grasped his cock. "Find out, lover." He felt Jacob shudder at that.

"Oh yes."

Nick stepped out of his pants and stood naked and female before his lover. "Do you like what you see?"

"Like?" Torturo grinned as he shed his clothes. Nick got comfortable on the berth, knowing what that look meant. "I love it."

Nick braced, but the pounce was gentle. Clearly, his lover was a different sort when it came to women. A nebulous thought seeped into his mind and he shoved the idea away. He was male. But with Jacob between his thighs, licking over the hot, slick skin of his twat, Nick had trouble remembering that. He screamed when Jacob closed his lips around the little node that felt as if it were going to pulsate right off his skin.

He lay, limp and wrung out, wondering how women endured sex if they felt their orgasms through their whole bodies and had dozens every session. Then Jacob eased into him, spreading the inner walls wide with his cock, and Nick sighed.

"Everything all right, darling?" Jacob whispered. He kissed Nick, his mouth and face wet with Nick's juices. Nick tried not to flinch, then found himself licking for more of the salty, smoky flavor. His own flavor, so different from when he came from a blow job.

"Fine," Nick managed. He pulled Jacob down for more kisses as they moved, Nick's body seeming to know exactly how to meet Jacob's every thrust. Three more orgasms rocked him before Jacob finished. The thought occurred to him a few minutes later when Jacob rolled off and drew him in. "What if I get pregnant this weekend? Will the Show leave me female?"

Jacob just grinned. "No woman with the Show has gotten pregnant in my memory. Rest easy, sweet girl. There will be no little ones." He kissed Nick and got up, stretching. "There's work to do. Be ready when I get back. Go see the twins for makeup. I fear if you apply it, you'll look like Buttons or worse." He pulled on a flannel shirt and overalls without underwear and stepped into the rubber boots he used to work the animal car in winter.

Nick watched him go and tried to coax his body into moving so he could have a bath.

* * *

His first clue that Jacob had returned to the car was laughter from over his shoulder. He dropped the hair he'd been trying to pin up in a bun.

"What's so funny, huh? I'm not used to this much hair and I have to look professional for the Show."

Jacob kissed the back of his neck and loomed in the mirror behind him. "You're adorable."

Nick stared a moment, looking at the perfect couple he saw reflected, and then turned for a kiss.

He lingered as long as he could then said, "Jacob, love, we have to go into town. Go get cleaned up. We'll pick this up when we come back."

"Yes, we will." He dropped the overalls and shed the shirt. Nick knew he would be hard. Torturo did not disappoint when he undid his pants.

Nick nibbled Jacob's neck. "Earlier was wonderful. I...never mind."

Jacob didn't let go. "What?"

Nick squirmed. "Come on. Work now, play later." He patted Jacob's crotch. "You'll keep." He headed out to see the twins while Jacob settled into a bath.

As he walked, he heard Clovis speaking of the desire he could not name, even to himself. He was a man, dammit all. There was never a question in his mind. But as a woman, he could love Jacob, with no reservations, no bad religion hurting him.

He resolved to think more about it.

Nick returned about half an hour later to find Jacob waiting for him with a smile on his face.

"Beautiful girl," Jacob said and bent in for a kiss. "There is something I would like to do today. Would you take a ride with me before we go into town?" Nick burrowed closer under his arm and let Jacob lead him to the Ferris wheel.

"Oh no. I hate those. Around and around, and way, way up? I'll be sick for sure."

Jacob laughed. "It's slow, and you can close your eyes and just snuggle with me." He squeezed Nick again, blocking some of the cold north wind. They arrived at the foot of the wheel as the operator finished giving it an empty spin.

"Gonna be my tester today, Mr. Torturo?" the man asked.

"Once around, Jack, for me and my girl," Jacob said, settling himself in one car. Nick hesitated. Jacob laid one arm across the back of the seat and beckoned. Nick stepped up on the platform. In a voice pitched only for Nick's ears, Jacob said, "Snuggle with your husband?"

Nick blinked. "Husband?"

"Once around, you two lovebirds?" asked Jack. "You lucky dog, Mr. Torturo. She's gorgeous. Congratulations."

"It's how we marry," Jacob said. Nick blinked twice more and one tear froze on its way down his cheek.

"Yes." Nick sat down and let Jacob snuggle him in close. He closed his eyes and rested in the warm, familiar embrace as the wheel creaked around them.

*   *   *

The weekend passed in a blur of work and sex. When they weren't on stage, Jacob made love to him. Nick thought they would tire, but each orgasm burned hotter than the last and each lovemaking led to more pleasure until Nick lay exhausted and blissful, wondering if his spine had managed to explode from all the sensation.

He rose from Jacob's bed on Sunday evening, pulling on the female costume over his breasts for the last time. Jacob watched, giving Nick the puppy dog face. Nick hesitated in the door of the car. "Jacob, may I stay?"

"Of course." Jacob turned from where he had just stripped. He set the silk pajamas aside and opened his arms with a smile. "Come to bed, darling."

Nick stripped down, sending his earnest wish to the locomotive. He hoped... It didn't matter. He'd find out soon enough. He curled up in Jacob's arms, warm and secure, falling into hibernation with a smile on his face.

*   *   *

The wish did not come true or perhaps it did. Nick was never sure afterward. He woke male, a morning erection pressed against Jacob's back. He slipped into the bathroom, dressed, and headed for the breakfast tent, guilt choking him.

He was male. A man. And he gone to a man's bed willingly for the last year and a half, before he had woken up and escaped. But the moment his body changed, he had been back in, fucking like a bitch in heat, like a slut. He hated the words but he deserved them.

Thin February snow lay on the ground and he stomped off to breakfast. He spent the stop avoiding Torturo. The Show was small and it wasn't easy. Jene offered him a place if he needed it, but he didn't trust the hermaphrodite either.

The crowds were small most of the weekend. Clovis had chosen a poor stop. Nick built the tips as well as he could. He could not resist standing in the back and watching the show. Besides the tent was warm and the outside stage was cold.

The minimal crowds had irritated everyone and the seven o'clock Sunday show came none too soon for Nick. So much for Valentine's being a day of love and affection. He had adjudicated three quarrels between the twins, one degenerating to hair-pulling. He'd found two lost props that Marv had yelled at Hannah over. Jene and Wolfgang had fought so loudly and fiercely that Marv and Jacob had both been needed to quiet that one. Nick really hoped he hadn't heard the wolf-howl or seen Jacob leading a wolf back to the train by a leash made out of his belt. Hypertrichosis, he reminded himself. Wolfgang had a simple medical condition. There were no werewolves.

He stood in the back, watching the last show before the last adult show. The twins sang, but he saw Alice pull Dinah's hair on the last refrain, making her go sharp. Dinah slapped Alice on stage as soon as they finished the song. The audience, cold and less amused than they thought they should be, cheered for a catfight.

The other acts went just as badly. Mingxia dropped the fishbowl on her nose, breaking both and soaking herself in water and blood. Marvello and Hannah bungled the suspension trick. Jene set their mustache afire. One of Nagina's snakes escaped, causing a minor panic. Nagina herself hissed at Elijah and made as if to bite him when he picked it up, accidentally—Nick hoped it was an accident—crushing it in his huge fingers.

The crowd hooted and jeered. Nick could scarcely bear to watch Torturo. The crowd was notably unimpressed by a bed of nails or the razorblades. Some of the young men took to heckling him. When he lifted the weights with his pierced nipples one yelled, "Yeah, reinforced, I bet."

They taunted him during the knife-ladder and the needles, too. He geeked the chicken and spattered half the front row with blood. The boys in the back laughed.

"Yeah, nice effect. You got a hand pump for the blood?"

"No, nor for this." Torturo picked up the cleaver. "Come on up here, boys." Nick held his breath. Jacob always finished the act with the chicken.

The three young toughs, none older than twenty, strutted up to the front, preening like banty roosters. Torturo greeted them, shaking hands.

He held up his left hand and slapped each one lightly on the cheek. "Real hand, yes? You feel it?" He flexed all the fingers.

Before anyone could breathe, he slammed his hand onto the table where he kept his supplies, scooped up a cleaver that Nick had never seen before and brought it down with a crunch and thud.

Nick's stomach lurched when he realized that yes, Jacob had hit his hand. He looked and saw Jacob holding up his left hand, blood spurting over the hoods from where his index finger had been.

The tent went fuzzy and Nick didn't remember anything until he woke up on the berth of the train car. Jacob combed his hair, scowling at his reflection. Nick counted the fingers. All ten but the frown boded ill.

He scooted off the berth and ducked underneath, ignoring the dust. He folded into the back corner and hoped the quilt would cover him. Jacob would be in a mood and that was never good. He stayed put until it was time to go talk the adult show in.

*   *   *

Jacob sat and scowled at the whiskey bottle. He'd loved Nick as a girl, but had insisted Clovis give him the man back. He wondered if he'd made a real mistake.. He wondered if his first mistake had been killing Sin and keeping Nick instead of the opposite. He took another drink.

"Tortie, love, you better get to the Midway!" Alice yelled as the twins barged into his railcar without knocking. They were half into each other's coats, their hats in wild disarray. Their eyes darted this way and that as they stood, panting, in his door.

"It's Nick, he's... OH!" Dinah gasped, pale enough that her very light freckles stood out.

Torturo shoved a pair of chairs under them. "What?" he demanded. "He's what?"

Nick's voice came over the Show loudspeakers. He should have been beginning his pitch to draw the crowds for the last show. Instead, he inveighed the crowd, "Go home, you fools. Fold that hard earned money and put it back in your pockets. You don't want to be here, wasting it, wasting your time."

Torturo's jaw dropped. He barreled out the door, only dimly aware he was wearing nothing but trousers and undershirt, running on bare feet that felt no stick nor stone, to silence Nick.

"Take your children home and read to them," Nick's amplified voice continued, sounding disgusted and pitying. Torturo hated that sound. "Don't stand and gawk at people born different than you."

Torturo shoved Stitches and Buttons aside and charged up the stairs to seize Nick by the collar. He ripped the throat mic from Nick's shirt, tossed it to Marvello, and hustled Nick off the stage to applause and some wolf-whistles from the ladies in the audience.

"Do we get to see him in the show?" one asked.

Torturo barely heard Marvello reassure her they would indeed get to see the Pain King before going into his pitch.

"Let go of me!" Nick squirmed in his hands. "I want them gone. I want this nightmare over. No, Jene doesn't get to butcher their victim tonight!" he added with extra viciousness.

Torturo never relented his hold, no matter how hard Nick fought. The short man was no match for him physically. He shoved Nick into the car and slammed the door.

"What are you doing?" Torturo leaned against the door, breathing through clenched teeth, opening and closing his fists. It was all he could do not to clobber Nick.

Nick sat on the bench and rubbed the back of his neck where Torturo had gripped it. "Telling the truth and ending this. No customers means no show. No show no murder. No murder means Clovis dies and so do we all."

"But we don't want to die." Torturo heard his fear bleeding through his voice.

Nick sighed and looked at his hands and the floor. "It's time. It's past time. You know that."

"That is not your decision, Nicholas. Not yours. Understand that?" He came closer, still frightened, still tempted to knock sense into his lover by main force.

Nick looked up. "Jacob, how old are you? It's been two years and I still look twenty-five. It is time. Clovis says so."

Finally, he did hit Nick, stepping into the sharp, open-handed slap. It snapped Nick's head to the right. "Not. Yours!" he growled, his voice low and dangerous.

Nick gave him an infuriating smirk. "No, it's Clovis's. And I'm carrying it out."

Torturo grabbed Nick by the shoulders. "You can't destroy us. We won't let you."

The smirk never left Nick's face. "You can't stop me." He twisted out of Torturo's hands, ducked between the bigger man's legs and scrambled for the door.

Before Nick could get it open, Torturo grabbed him and tossed him bodily onto the bed. He straddled Nick's chest, holding him down, as he shackled Nick to the wall. Nick lay there, breathing hard and glaring at him.

Torturo stood up and went to the wardrobe. He changed into his costume with an air of practiced calm. None of the fury seemed left in his face. "I have a show to do."

Nick rattled the manacles. "Let me out of here. There won't be a show. They've all left. Clovis is in my head, laughing. He's laughing at you, Jacob."

Torturo gave him the one-sided smile that had charmed audiences out of their pants for sixty years. "Shut up, Nicholas." He went to do the show. Nick's bitter laughter followed him out of the car and carried down the Midway after him.

The adult show drew impossibly huge crowds. Nick's ranting had touched something in the folks and they had paid their money in droves. Jacob had been on and barged back into the car still high from the crowd. The nagging worry that he would have to kill Nick tonight for the good of the show had almost vanished.

From behind the curtain, Jacob had kept half an ear on what the people were saying before he went on.

"Yeah, really bloody. Better'n the movies."

"He cut off his own finger on stage!"

"You gotta see this. And now there's sex in it, too."

He found Nick dozing on the bed, his face buried in the pillow. Nick woke when he came in, startling and then immediately trying to hide the tear streaks on his cheeks.

"Wake up, sleepyhead," Torturo cried jovially.

Nick's eyes snapped open and he screamed.

*   *   *

Nick woke up badly, horrified by the sight before him. He tried to stammer out something but words failed him. Jacob wore only a light robe, much too thin for winter weather and soaked through with blood until dime-sized drops fell from the hem at every fourth step. The usual amount from the adult show never amounted to more than a cup or so.

"What did you do tonight?" he finally gasped. "You're a bloody mess."

Jacob smirked and Nick tensed automatically. That look never boded well. "I brought you a present, darling. In fact, you missed it. I dedicated my whole act to you." His face went hard. "Hold up your hands."

Nick knew better than to disobey when that voice commanded him. He cupped his chained hands over his face and braced for something awful.

Jacob spread a piece of very soft leather with metal rings in over his hands. Then two blood-covered oval lumps of meat landed in his palms, a thin cord trailing from each. Nick stared. When he looked up, Jacob smirked more and spread the robe, showing most of the blood was concentrated at his crotch. Nick realized what he held and offered them back, counting backward from a hundred to stop himself from throwing up. The hair on the leather tickled his palms.

"Keep them. They're yours. It's what you wanted, right?" Jacob unlocked his chains. "Make a wallet or something."

Nick just stared at that, not comprehending the statement. Finally, he decided to carry on. He got the toothpaste glass from the bathroom and a wet cloth. After a second's thought, he ran some water in the glass before dropping the testicles in. He set it and the scrotum on the table and came back to the bed with the cloth.

Jacob just gave him an amused look. "Thought so."

Nick shook his head. "I have no idea what you're talking about. You'll want those when it's time to regenerate. Let me clean you up before you hibernate. You're really nasty." He stroked the cloth gently over the highest of the splashed blood, the stuff on Jacob's forehead.

"I won't be bothering you anymore. And that's what you want. A eunuch like yourself." Jacob yawned.

Nick ignored the words and kept washing, working his way down. He got up to rinse the cloth and get a basin of water. Jacob showed no pain, even when Nick washed the cut skin where his scrotum had been, clearing away the clotted blood. He gave a soft, tired moan of pleasure when Nick washed his cock.

Brisk and efficient as a nurse, Nick cleared away the bloody water in the basin. He heard the train sound the warning whistle as he came back to the side of the bed. He grabbed his coat from the hook.

"If I run, I can make the prop car," he said, sliding his arms into the sleeves.

Jacob grabbed his arm and pulled him off balance, making him sprawl over the bunk. "Come to bed. I'm perfectly safe."

Nick shed his coat and kicked off his shoes. He shifted until he got comfortable and let the hibernation take him.

*   *   *

He managed to duck Jacob most of the March stop. But in April, as the trees were greening and the daffodils blowing, he drew up short at the Friday afternoon announcement over the loudspeaker.

"Tonight, the eight o'clock Ten-in-One will be replaced by a live Passion Play. There will be no adult show. There will be another Passion Play tomorrow night and a special Sunrise Service on Easter."

Nick flinched at the notion. He knew the show held a hymn-sing and revival service every Sunday morning, but he'd never worked up the nerve to go. He just knew Elijah would throw him out because of

Jacob. He gave the idea of a Passion Play some thought. He wasn't sure how they could stage it, since they had very few normal looking people among the crew. The hideous thought occurred to him that it would be a real crucifixion and Jacob would be starring.

He dismissed this as blasphemous and started building the four o'clock tip.

Eight o'clock found him in his usual spot at the back of the Ten-in-One tent, a little nervous. Giant white scrims had been set up everywhere. The old familiar story began, half rear-projection, half live-action. Elijah addressed the council of the Pharisees as the high priest. The others were all just motion pictures, but his timing was so impeccable, Nick could almost believe they were real. Jene, looking all male, led in the donkey colt to recorded cheers of a throng projected on the scrims at the front.

Nick winced. Jacob indeed rode on the donkey. The performance was going to include a real beating and a real crucifixion and the crowd was going to ooh and ah over the realism and never know they'd actually seen true torture.

Marv blustered and boomed across his balcony, commanding as Pontius Pilate. Nick watched each blow of the whip lay Jacob's back open. The twins, as Mary and Martha, clung to Mingxia, dressed in red as Mary Magdalene, and wept. The blood flowed until Nick was sure Jacob couldn't take any more. When Jacob winced at a blow, he knew his normally impervious lover had actually felt something.

The tent went dark and Elijah's voice, deep as thunder, narrated the next events. Nick didn't recognize the Roman who beat Jacob as he staggered under the weight of the huge wooden cross on his back. Then he realized it must be Wolfgang, without the fur. The Phantasmagoria had gone all out for this show.

One of the women in the audience sobbed when a splash of blood hit her face and she smelled the bitter iron of it instead of the sticky sweetness of corn syrup. "It's real," ran through the crowd at lightning speed.

Wolfgang and Jene, both in full Roman armor, wrestled the cross to the ground and spread Jacob atop it. Nick couldn't watch. From the gasps in the crowd and a thud, he knew others found it just as hard. The sound of the crudely forged iron nails breaking skin and tendon and small foot bones before thudding into wood sickened Nick. Jene's nasty laughter filled his mouth with bile. He fled backstage, sure he was going to be sick or faint.

The crucifixion went on for an eternity. Jacob bled and writhed and cried out. Through the scrim, Nick could see him pushing himself up enough to gasp for air. Finally, he choked and dropped limp, the crown of thorns spattering the front row with more blood. Jene and Wolfgang took him down, none too careful, and handed his body to the twins and Mingxia who carried it to the part of the set designated as the tomb. They washed him and wrapped him in white cloth and with some help, got the rock in front of the entrance.

Nick came to the back of the tomb set and helped Jacob sit up, unwrapping his head in the process. He handed over a glass of water. Gently, he lifted the thorns off, puncturing one finger as he did.

"Jacob, are you going to be all right?" He poured another glass of water. After losing that much blood, blood which still seeped through the white cloth, Jacob would need a lot of fluids.

"I'm always fine." The cold suspicion in Jacob's eyes hurt, but Nick knew he deserved it.

He bent in and kissed one of the shallower cuts, the one at Jacob's temple. "There is no adult show tonight. Come on back to the car and let me take care of you." He offered a hand and picked up a heavy robe with the other. Jacob stood, exhaustion pouring off of him like the blood. Nick wrapped him in the robe and helped him back to the railcar.

Once inside, he sat Jacob on the sofa and poured more water, adding a shot of whiskey to this one. "Drink," he said. He ducked into the head and came back with the basin and cloth he'd used in February. He realized as he got the robe and linens off, that Jacob's balls had not yet regenerated.

The girls had washed him, but Jacob had bled again on the walk over. This worried Nick. By now, he should be scabbed over, if not healed entirely.

He washed extra carefully around Jacob's forehead and scalp where the cruel thorns had bitten deep under Jene's crueler pressing. He unwrapped the linen from Jacob's hands and cleaned them, the nail prints in the wrists giving him an odd, twisty sensation in his stomach.

He'd felt the same knots as a kid, during the gorier parts of fairy tales or looking at the pictures in his mother's family Bible; old, full color illustrations of the people dying in the Flood while the Ark sailed serenely on, of Salome presenting the head of John the Baptist to her mother and yes, of the Crucifixion. It was the same odd tingle he had always gotten saying the Apostle's Creed at the words "Crucified, dead and buried." He knew exactly what he wanted to do.

"Jacob...love. May I stay?"

The hope in his lover's eyes almost burned. "Please stay."

Nick turned Jacob's hands palm up, washed away the blood and kissed the center of each. Jacob stroked his face, running a light thumb along his cheekbone. Nick took a deep breath and tongued the nail prints in Jacob's wrists. He looked up with a shudder, terrified he'd overstepped himself.

Jacob pulled him up for a kiss. Nick met him, the taste of blood in his mouth—*holy blood*, his mind whispered—his passions higher than they'd been for months. He finished stripping away the robe and cloth.

Carefully, Nick washed his lover's back. The whip welts had closed and no longer poured out Jacob's life. He washed the blood from Jacob's legs and feet, kissing those holes, too.

Finally, he started cleaning the cut in Jacob's side. Unable to help himself, he slipped four fingers into it, flat, as he imagined Doubting Thomas doing on that long ago day in Jerusalem.

"What do you need, my love?" he whispered.

Jacob opened one eye as if the eyelid weighed as much as the whole world. The exhaustion had not passed, but seemed to grow deeper. Nick wondered if Jacob would survive the next night's show.

"Need to be fucked," he rasped.

Nick had been expecting something like that. "Can I be gentle? I'm afraid of hurting you." He hadn't yet taken his fingers from the wound in Jacob's side.

"You can't hurt me physically. Fuck me the way it feels best for you. I'll enjoy it."

Nick kissed him, sweetly, devotedly and helped him to his feet. "Come to bed then." As they made the four long steps from sofa to bed, he asked, "You sure you don't want some food or something?"

Jacob shook his head. "No. Not hungry."

Nick eased him onto his side in the bed with many soft kisses. Jacob moved a little stiffly but didn't appear to be in any pain. His back had closed entirely. The nail holes had healed like piercings. Nick curled in behind him and kissed the top curve of his perfect ass, shuddering at the intimacy.

So wrong. So wicked. Deepest blasphemy. He ignored his thoughts and dragged his tongue up the cleft of Jacob's ass, teasing as Jacob loved best. The big man shifted, spreading as much as he could in that position. Nick pushed the upper cheek out of the way and shoved his tongue against Jacob's hole, pressing as deeply as he could on the first stroke.

None of his own badness mattered. Jacob needed him. He licked and probed, feeling the tight crinkle around the tip of his tongue and then he added a finger and licked around it.

"Oh, Nicholas." Jacob moaned and the sound was sacred music, a baritone drone that did not fade as Nick took a final lick and slid up behind him.

He eased into Jacob's body, unable to stop himself from bringing his hand up to slip his fingers back into the side wound. He moved slowly and easily to the music in his head, music he suspected Clovis of playing for him, making love as he enjoyed best. After a few strokes, Jacob began pushing back, trying to hasten him.

Nick kept the pace steady until the hymn finished and sped only slightly for the second one. Jacob kept pushing back, wanting more. "Shhh, love." That song finished and the third sounded like "Onward Christian Soldiers," so Nick settled in for a nice hard pounding.

"Yes...yes..." Jacob begged, demanding more.

Nick slid his fingers out of the rapidly healing wound and wrapped them around Jacob's cock which stood, almost pulsating with need. He stroked in time with his own movement, his fingers firm and sure. Jacob met his every stroke and came with a shout, hot jets shooting over Nick's fingers.

He climaxed with a small cry that might have been "amen," but he muffled it against Jacob's shoulder. He curled around his large lover and kissed the last fading scrape on Jacob's temple.

"Rest, love, or you'll never be able to do this tomorrow."

*   *   *

They woke late, nearly nine. Nick insisted on checking Jacob all over during the bath, making sure he was once more hale and intact. He kissed the quiescent head of Jacob's cock and ran his tongue over the newly regenerated balls.

"I said you'd need them." He smiled up.

Jacob beamed down at him.

"Indeed. But I need breakfast more. We slept very late."

The day passed in a flurry of work and meals. Nick's smile never wavered. He heard the music in his head all day, reassuring him. All the sexiest hymns, mostly Fanny J. Crosby stuff, played between his ears. He knew he'd done the right thing at last.

After the crowd was seated for the Passion Play, he made his way back to the car. "Everything's all right, yes everything's fine, and I want you to sleep well tonight." His choice of songs shocked him, since *Jesus Christ Superstar* was pure heresy.

Nick found the noose waiting for him. He stepped onto the chair and stuck his head through, knowing this, too, was exactly the right thing to do. "Let the world turn without you tonight." He stepped off the chair into black pain and pounding ears and endless sleep.

CHAPTER 12

DEATH SHOW

Nick wandered the empty Midway, under the pink and yellow lights of the Easter carnival, not sure how or when he'd left the car. The rides rusted, half assembled, their metal frames looking long-forgotten. Fungus grew on the wooden frames of the booths, the boards gray with age and rot, warped by rain and snow. The canvas hung in tatters. Nothing moved. No canvas flapped in an errant breeze. The place was as dead as he'd ever seen it.

His steps carried him, inexorably, to the Ten-in-One. He pushed aside the flap, the heavy mildewed canvas nearly choking him with its stench, and went in. Not knowing why, he settled on the splinter-ridden board bench of the front row.

He started when a man appeared beside him. The newcomer looked tired and wan. A thin mustache lent his sharp ferret-like face its only distinction. The blue uniform that looked more like a toy soldier's than any military uniform Nick knew hung about his gaunt frame.

"Good evening, Nicholas." Nick knew that faint French accent.

"Hello, Clovis." He looked around. "Jacob must have cut me down."

"No, my dear. You are quite dead. That's why you're here." Clovis gave him a look of amusement. "We all are, you see. But only you and I know it." Nick stared. Clovis gestured at the stage. "Watch, *mon cher*. Watch and see. Myself first."

Nick saw what looked like the colorful onion domes of Moscow appear on the backdrop. Clovis's voice filled the tent. "In October of 1812, Napoleon and the Grande Army began their retreat from Russia. We were the last unit to leave the city, well behind the others, fighting a rear guard action. We tarried a day. When the Phantasmagoria arrived, its wagons hung with heavy drapes and the lead one all enclosed, even the driver's box, we cheered. There had been no amusements, save what we could make on our own. We paid what few poor coins we had and went. Some of my companions planned to kill the horses and oxen for food, but most of us were as hungry in our souls as in our bellies."

Snow flew around the stage in dazzling flecks of light. "My comrades cheered the dancers and jugglers and fire-eaters. I...heard a restless call in my mind. I went into the closed wagon of the animals. I never saw my comrades again. Hui Ping, the driver, told me of the Show. I tended the props and pitched the tent for many years, but never became a part of the Show. Then, Hui Ping called me to the lead wagon and I entered."

Nick stared. "What then?"

"I knew the truth. My comrades and I had frozen to death in Moscow. We did not cover our emperor's retreat. I was the new driver. And so, I have been, across every continent and conveyance, wagon and railroad, boat and oxcart, I am Clovis, Driver of the Phantasmagoria." He touched Nick's forehead. "As you will be, Nicholas."

Nick stared some more. The Russia winter vanished from the stage, to be replaced by high summer and burning buildings. Nick didn't know the city just from looking at it.

"Saturday, August fourteenth, 1965," Clovis said. "Los Angeles, the Watts district. The Phantasmagoria was there."

"Watts? You caused the Watts riots?"

Clovis laughed. "No, that we cannot take credit for. But, we entertained at risk of our own lives or not-lives."

Nick watched a tall black man in a beret and jacket move through the Phantasmagoria, anger stamped permanently on his handsome features. He paused to watch the bearded lady ram a metal skewer through the Pain King's tongue. "Marvello?"

"Marvin Jackson in his life. He met a bad end."

Nick watched the magician set a police car on fire with a Molotov cocktail, only to go down in a hail of bullets. The next night, Marvello performed with Hannah for the first time and the Marvello the Magician banner appeared on one wall of the tent.

The scene shifted to the Midway again. A pretty lady in a striped coat-dress and pumps walked along on her man's arm. Nick didn't have to look too hard to see the bruises on her wrists. She watched Torturo with fascination until her man yanked her away and nearly hauled her back to the blocky, sharp-lined Buick. Nick knew it for a 1958 LeSabre.

They went into a little frame house on a quiet street. It was, of course, immaculate. He couldn't hear the words, but the man yelled at Hannah the whole time she fixed dinner. He had worked himself up into a scarlet-faced frenzy by the time she put it on the table.

Hannah ducked the first slap, but he caught her around the throat and picked up the frying pan.

Nick looked away. Clovis nudged him. He saw Hannah lying at the man's feet, her skull smashed. Her husband dragged her to the backyard and buried her in the dark. Then he packed her bags and bought a bus ticket out of town, putting the bags on the bus.

"Hannah went home to mother, permanently," Clovis said as Nick watched her come aboard in Jacob's car just as he had and wake with a beard and mustache. The poster for Hannah the Bearded Lady hung next to Marvello.

Nick shuddered. The affair with Jacob had ended when she met Marv. The old grudges got carried a long time in a show this small.

He watched as the scene shifted to the jungle, lush and thick. An elaborate temple told him he could only be in India. A pile of wood lay outside the temple as for a bonfire. As he watched, a procession bearing a dead man to the pile wended its way into the clearing. A woman in a gold sari, weighed down with jewelry, bracelets and anklets, earrings, necklaces and a nose ring, walked beside the bier, her face empty.

"Indukala and her late husband," Clovis whispered. "She's been Nagina for more than a hundred and thirty years now."

Sentries posted around the clearing gave the signal. The bearers set the bier on the pyre. Indukala picked her way daintily up the logjam to embrace her dead husband. Nick gasped when the mourners set the pyre alight with her still there. Indukala tried bravely not to scream.

The "Nagina, the Punjab Snake Goddess" banner unfurled in the smoke as the scene faded.

Nick shuddered. "Please," he begged.

"What, my dear?"

"Enough. Did everyone die a horrible death?"

Clovis just smiled wanly. "Nicholas, all death is horrible, whether violent or not. Violent death feeds the Show better. Now watch, it's Elijah's turn."

Nick turned his unwilling face back to the stage and looked into hell. Smoke and fire, screams of men dying and horses in pain, and the bark of cannon-fire assailed him. Two men, one in blue and one in gray, struggled hand to hand, their rifles cast aside and wicked knives gleaming.

"Phillipi, Virginia, June third, 1861. We'd just finished the end of the May Carnival and were still packing up. The rumors of war had me confused, but we welcomed the soldiers in their pretty gray uniforms. The battle, later called Chancellorsville, cut us off from moving for a few days. We welcomed the ones in blue after the battle."

Nick watched the soldiers stare at the freaks, play games and ride horse and steam powered rides. One man who must have been nearly seven feet tall, caught his eye. The fair dissolved into the battlefield again and he watched Elijah move through the fray, shooting and stabbing, his great size making him a target. He took three bullets and kept coming, breaking the blue lines. Bullets six and seven didn't stop him, but the cannonball that cut him in half did.

Nick shuddered again as "Elijah, the Carolina Giant" unrolled down the wall next to Nagina's. He knew Tabitha came next.

The windswept valley under a lonely mountain had snow a foot deep, but the horse pulled the sledge toward a snug little cabin nestled under the pines at the base of the mountain. A pretty laughing woman kissed her husband and gathered the packages out of the sleigh. He held her close and dangled a bit of mistletoe over her face before kissing her again.

He led the horse toward the barn while she went indoors. Nick saw something large, hairy and shapeless at the corner of the barn. As the man passed into the door, it touched him with one massive paw and melted into shadow.

"What was that?" he asked. "A bear would have eaten him."

"A wendigo, Nicholas. You will see soon enough. There are more monsters than the Phantasmagoria in the world. Or there were in the 1870s."

The scene shifted to inside the cabin. Tabitha opened a package and put on a new apron. She put the other under a little pine tree decorated with popcorn strings that sat in one corner. Then she set a big black iron cauldron on the fire and threw in a few potatoes from a bin.

Her husband came in and kissed her hello. He took off his coat and sat. When Tabitha served his bowl of soup, he stabbed her hand with his fork, pinning it to the table.

Nick watched him kiss her as she screamed, then lick down her neck as if tasting her. He yanked open her dress and took a large bite out of one of her breasts. Tabitha screamed until he used his bowie knife across her neck. Then he picked up the cleaver.

Nick shut his eyes and listened to the *chunk-chunk* of the heavy blade. When he opened them, Tabitha's head sat in a dish opposite her husband and her legs roasted on a spit. The man stuffed her torso into a barrel of pickles. The scene faded as the husband skewered one breast and toasted it over the fire like a marshmallow.

The banner for Tabitha the One Cubit Woman appeared next to Elijah's.

The tombstones leaned and loomed in the ancient graveyard. The old church thrust a spindly steeple at the sky. Overhead, biplanes droned against the low gray clouds. The hairy man buried his face in the ground. He covered his head with one hand against the noise and scrabbled at the earth with the other.

He had presence of mind enough to hide in a crypt as a funeral bore a single small wooden casket into the churchyard. As the priest spoke, two men dug out a shallow hole and lowered the little box into it. A weeping woman allowed herself to be escorted out.

Clovis sighed. "Alsace, 1917. It was beautiful before the war."

The hairy man came out of the crypt and dug up the coffin with his bare hands. A soldier lay inside, although Nick would have said the coffin looked too short. The man sniffed him over and lifted one arm, licking his lips.

A shot rang through the gathering gloom. Several soldiers came to the wall. Their leader shot the hairy man in the face. They checked the coffin and Nick saw their comrade had lost his legs. They closed it and buried him deeper.

They hauled the body of the poor, mad ghoul to the crossroads and buried it there, burying the head at one a little farther down the way.

Wolfgang's banner rolled out of the blackness above.

The merciless sun bore down on the workers in the fields, who sweated despite their loose clothing and broad shady hats. Far off, over the endless rice field, Nick saw the tents of the Phantasmagoria. One woman, very pregnant, staggered and leaned on her hoe. Two friends helped her to the shade and brought water.

When the baby was born, a man came over and looked at it. He spat in the dirt, seized the newborn by her ankles and strode to an irrigation ditch, the woman wailing behind him. Nick watched him throw the child into the waist-deep ditch and watch it sink.

"Mingxia the Acrobat," the next banner read.

The next city could be none other than London. On a grimy street corner, a pair of pretty redheaded girls held onto each other and solicited the gentlemen leaving the Phantasmagoria. One opened her shawl and Nick caught a glimpse of bared breasts, their nipples joined by a thin gold chain, above a corset.

A handsome man in an opera cape and top hat solicited their favors. They led him down an alleyway, through several twists and turns, past rat-infested garbage heaps. In a secluded doorway, one of the twins raised her skirt, showing a great deal of red pubic hair. The man kissed her sister and ran a gloved hand into the triangle of hair.

The scalpel across the exposed one's throat stopped any scream and it flashed across her sister's just as fast. Nick watched as the Surgeon of Whitechapel set to work on their bodies, flinging odd bits of organs to the rats who thronged at the smell of the blood.

He tucked his bloody gloves and scalpel away and left at a measured pace. The rats feasted.

Alice and Dinah, the Siamese Twins, joined at the hip, joined the other banners.

A man and a woman, dressed in black turtlenecks despite the summer heat, made their way to a car and kissed passionately before heading home from the Show to a little apartment with lots of pillows on the floor and a very large hookah in the corner.

Jean sat down and started writing. Gene kissed her neck and she smiled at him. They checked the clock and stripped each other with many kisses and caresses. Jean left her half-finished poem on the pillow and got out a length of silky rope. They threw it over a beam in the ceiling, tied slipknots in the ends and slipped their heads into the resulting nooses. Nick shivered in memory.

They faced each other and Jean wrapped her legs around Gene's waist, taking him in as he stepped off the low table. They fucked in slow motion, their faces going red and then purple. When Jean passed out, Gene worked frantically to free her.

Their friends, also wearing black turtlenecks, barged in to find them stiffening in midair, still in mid-sex.

The banner for Jene, a Wonder of Science, rolled out of the dark.

Nick held his breath. He knew what the last act had to be, what it always was during the Show. He took in the white frame farmhouse, the chicken run and garden and the peach orchard. He saw the little burying ground not far from the barn.

Jacob, younger than Nick knew him, strode across the yard from the burying ground with an adolescent's gangly stride. He went into the house.

The gloom and disrepair saddened Nick. The faded woman on the equally faded sofa opened her eyes. "Jacob."

Nick startled. The others had been silent.

"Mama, shush. You're dead. Jesus told me."

"Jacob, I am not dead." There was anger in her thin voice.

"Just hush, Mama, and lie quiet like is decent. I've dug you a nice grave right where you always wanted it, under the big elm." He stepped out and brought in a wooden coffin, which he set on the high table before her.

She struggled onto one elbow as Jacob lifted her into the box. Nick could see the effort cost her most of her energy. "Jacob!" she wailed.

He washed her face and hands as if she had said nothing. He brushed her hair with tenderest care. "Now lie still or you'll muss it. Can't go to heaven with mussed hair, Mama. And St. Peter's waiting on you special. He told me while I was digging."

She pushed up against the lowering lid, screaming. But her invalid's strength was no match for a hard-working youth's. He nailed the lid down and eased the box to the floor, then took up two long ropes and pulled it.

Mrs. Plum screamed all the way across the yard and as he lowered her into the grave. Jacob stood beside it, praying over her. He sang a hymn as he shoveled the dirt back in. As the first clods landed on the coffin's lid, a frenzy of hammering broke out from inside it.

The grave was mostly still empty when the sheriff's truck pulled into the drive. He strode over to where Jacob stood by the grave.

"Mama finally pass, son?" he asked.

Jacob nodded. "Died while I was gathering eggs. I dug the grave just where she wanted it."

A single thin, hoarse scream came up out of the grave. The sheriff startled and jumped down in it.

"Hold on, ma'am, I'll get you out."

"Sheriff, she's dead. Jesus told me so."

"Boy, tain't no dead woman never screamed so." He grabbed the ropes that Jacob had used to lower the coffin and hauled it back up. Mrs. Plum lay quiet and still, her pale face contorted when he pried the lid off. "Ma'am, Miss Catherine, are you all right?"

She breathed shallowly and looked up at the sheriff. "No. Take care of Jacob. He's a good boy, but he ain't right." She let out a rattling breath and the sheriff shivered.

He turned and cuffed Jacob to the tree. "Son, you done killed your mama. Around here, we don't care to bother the judge for that kind of thing." He left and returned in an hour with six men.

They buried Catherine Plum next to her three dead sons. Then they turned their attention to Jacob. One made a noose out of the coffin ropes and threw it over a branch of the elm. Jacob just smiled as they got him to his feet and tossed it over his head.

Nick didn't watch the rest. It explained everything. Jacob had been schizophrenic, with religious delusions. No wonder he couldn't abide Nick's faith.

Clovis smiled sadly at Nick. "Now you know it all. You see, the Show does not make us immortal. It simply prolongs us. And I am growing weak. I shall have enough to change you into what you will need to be. But there is one last scene. You have seen it but do not remember."

Nick stared up at the big cab-over Freightliner barreling down on him where he sat. He threw his arms up automatically and it passed, without even a wind to mark it. "That…" he stammered at Clovis, "that was me, dead in the ambulance."

Clovis nodded and faded.

Nick found himself alone under the April stars, a weight on his left shoulder. He looked and saw his arm had changed. A metal prosthetic of brass and gears had replaced the flesh. He could still feel the blood pumping through the metal. When he tapped his fingertips against his thigh, he felt that, too.

He headed back for the train, exhausted and unhappy with the new knowledge. Ignorance was bliss and he envied the others who didn't know they were dead.

How would he explain all this to Jacob?

*   *   *

Nick didn't have to explain. He awoke to pain. A shooting pain racked his ribs as if someone had hit him. He knew at once what was going on. Despite the pains, which manifested themselves at frequent intervals, he struggled into his clothes and left the empty car.

He charged through the Backyard, heading for the Engine. A hard blow to his shoulder rocked him and another to his belly knocked the wind out of him, dropping him to sit on the ground with a *whoof*. Nick gasped for a moment, got back to his feet and continued.

He saw Torturo hurling rocks at the Engine and shouting at Clovis. When his lover pegged one through the window, a gash opened on Nick's own forehead and blood streamed into his eye and down his face.

"Jacob!" he yelled. "Stop!"

"Shut up, Nicholas." Torturo launched another rock, sending it clanging off the rounded side. "Fuck you, Clovis!"

"Jac—" Nick hit the ground with another *whoof*. He sat gasping, holding his belly, blood soaking the collar and front of his shirt.

Torturo dropped the rock he held and came to Nick, confusion all over his face. "What? What happened to you?"

"You did." Nick peeled away the bloody shirt to show large purple bruises blooming all over his body, including a bright red spot on his belly from the last rock. "I'm just lucky the one that broke the window didn't take my eye out. It was sharp."

Torturo looked between the Engine and Nick for a long minute. Then he reached down and pulled Nick to his feet, gathering him in close.

"I'll be okay," Nick said. "Maybe we should get me cleaned up before the rubes show? The Sunrise Service should just be letting out."

Jacob nodded and led him back to the car. "Sit, darling," he said, easing Nick to the sofa. Nick took the opportunity to steal a kiss of his cheek. Jacob ducked out and came back with a basin of warm water. He washed the blood off of Nick's chest and neck and face, working his way gently to the original wound. It had closed over.

"I'm sorry, Nicholas."

"It's all right. You didn't know. You lost your temper over my arm, right?"

Jacob nodded and rubbed some balm on the bruises, his fingers light. "I did. I wanted to hurt Clovis, not you. He lied! You're to be mine, not his."

"Jacob, love, I am yours." Nick kissed him again, on the mouth, making it sweet and welcoming as well as grateful.

"Yes, but for how long?"

Nick had no answer, so he sat back and let Jacob treat his bruises.

CHAPTER 13

CHANGES

On the warm June morning, Nick watched as Torturo fed the animals. Nick had increased his sweetness and care-taking to demonstrate his change of heart. He started lighting Jacob's cigarettes, using a vintage Zippo he'd found in the drawer. It always stayed full. He made sure to be affectionate, kisses and little touches, the occasional wink, little things to let Jacob know he was seen and thought of throughout Nick's day.

But Jacob had not reciprocated, horrified at the prosthetic arm. He had not come to bed during the May stop. Now, he wouldn't even look at Nick. All Nick's affection hadn't helped. Jacob's temper had grown increasingly shorter with each day they were awake. He hadn't forgiven Nick for the suicide and he still drank. Nick, while not back to the soft submission of his first days, remained quieter than normal and much more attentive. Things were changing. He was changing and it wasn't time to hit his love with those.

He looked up to see Torturo scowling down at him, the first time the big man had looked at him for the whole stop. "What are you hiding this time, Nicholas?"

Nick looked up at him, quite puzzled. "Nothing."

"That's not what Precious says." He buffed the unicorn's horn until it shone golden. "She still hasn't made up to you. You know she can't abide liars and hypocrites." He finished grooming the little beast and she whickered at him, then tossed her mane at Nick and pranced off to where the cyclops bull had already begun stealing her breakfast. Jacob dropped to sit beside Nick on the hay bale, his arm going around Nick almost automatically and his hand caressing Nick's arm.

Nick looked at the floor. "I'm sorry," he whispered. "I can't tell you yet, because I don't know myself."

He glanced up to see Jacob, Torturo no longer, just Jacob—his lover whom he loved, despite all the preaching of his youth—looking at him, his face sad and his eyes large. Nick's lip quivered at the puppy-dog look but he plunged on.

"I wish…" He looked away.

Jacob stroked his hair. Nick smiled at the touch, but it faded. "What do you wish, Nicholas?"

"I wish I could throw myself into your arms, love you and cling. But I can't tell you what I don't even know." Nick looked back at him, his eyes brimming. He took a deep breath. The Show gave him the words and he confessed in a steady voice, "I've been hearing the Show in my head. Not just sometimes, all the time. Clovis has been talking to me."

Jacob startled, pushing Nick away. "Nobody knows the Engineer's name, except me." Nick heard the strain in his voice. He wondered how many times they would have this conversation. Clovis apparently had tampered with Jacob's memories again, making him forget Nick knew of the Engineer.

"I know it. I saw him."

Jacob looked shocked at that.

"When I was…well…dead," Nick said. "I saw him and talked to him. And he told me things as well as changing me. When I get my own car…" He covered his face and sat back down. "Jacob, you don't want to know, really."

"What?" He rose and moved away slowly and Nick realized he had never really seen his lover afraid. Now, the big man looked terrified. Nick wasn't sure what had caused the fear.

Nick looked up at him and hesitated. He debated whether he should tell Jacob now or wait. He flexed the metal fingers of his left hand. Now seemed like the time for it. "When I get my own, it's the locomotive, and I'll never be human again."

"Don't be ridiculous." Torturo backed away. "Stop, Nicholas. Just. Stay here. I'm going."

Nick continued as if his lover's sputtering wasn't happening.

"Clovis is dying. He says he only has a few more years left."

The look on Torturo's face told Nick to shut up at once or they would only hurt more. "Enough. Not another word about it." He made for the exit, leaving everything behind.

Nick wrapped his arms around Torturo, stopping him again. "I love you. I always have, even when I claimed I couldn't. And I would give anything in the world to be able to stay with you."

Torturo extricated himself from Nick's arms. "Don't cling, Nicholas." There was no venom in his voice, only the fear. "Think it over and decide what is happening. Tell me after the hibernation. I'm sleeping elsewhere until the next stop." Torturo turned away, his voice cold. Nick knew he was done listening. The news had been too much.

Nick nodded. "With the others who love you. Understandable." As Torturo gathered his hat, Nick added, "You don't leave the Show, hear?"

"I can't."

"You can, but it'll be very unpleasant."

"No. I'm too old. I will die."

Nick glared a little more at Torturo's back. As Torturo lifted the tent flap, Nick added, "Tell the girls hello for me."

They spent the stop apart, barely seeing each other, save at showtime. Through the grapevine, Nick learned that Jacob was sleeping on a bed of straw in the animal car and cleaning up while Nick was out of the carriage. He ached for his lover, but knew Jacob would deal with his pain and then return.

*　　*　　*

At the Fourth of July stop, Nick caught Torturo before breakfast. They grumbled at each other and Nick hauled him to the mess tent.

"The girls said you never came to them." He ordered Torturo's eggs, but not his own half dozen. They carried the trays to the table, Nick's holding only coffee. Jacob ate without looking up, shoveling the food in mechanically as if not really tasting it. Nick stopped his hand in mid-bite. In the same newfound commanding voice, he said, "Jacob. I know what I want."

"So you've said. Repeatedly." There was no heart beneath the sneer. The words were tired, not angry.

"I want whatever will make you happiest. If you could see it clear to giving me a chance and taking me as I am, I'd like to be your Nick.

For as long as I can." He lowered his voice. "Right now, there's a very large Jacob-shaped hole in the middle of me."

"You hate me. You hate the sex. What are you thinking?" The words were old and rote. Jacob had said them before, but now they stung Nick to the core.

"I love you. I enjoy the sex. But I can't perform as often as you want me to." He raised his shirt. On his chest, ribbed tubing entered and exited his flesh like snakes. "I'm still changing, Jacob."

Torturo stared a long time, until Nick closed his shirt. He stood up, picking up his tray. "Be proud of yourself, Nicholas. You've done the impossible. You've hurt the Pain King."

"It would only hurt more if I didn't tell you."

Torturo took his tray and went to sit with the twins. A twinge of jealousy surprised Nick as the girls fussed over Jacob. He watched them stroke his lover and soothe him and made a decision. Nick picked up his own tray and went to where they sat.

"You can keep going, Nicky," Alice said.

Torturo ignored him and that hurt most of all. "So, I'm not good enough now that I'm a freak, too, is that it?" Nick snarled, shocked at his own anger.

All three of them startled at the words. The girls had never heard such venom out of Nick. Torturo resumed kissing Dinah.

"Nicky, don't be bitchy. Go eat and let our poor darling alone. You've done quite enough damage for one morning." Alice glared.

Nick found it a wise decision to go eat by himself. He watched them all through his toast.

Jene, a late riser, came in for their breakfast. They saw Torturo sitting with the twins, glumly staring into coffee he didn't even have his flask along for. "Dissension in the family?" They smirked knowingly as they passed.

Torturo sighed, but Alice, with legendary redheaded temper, snapped, "What I told our Nicky goes for you, too, Jene."

Jene smirked again and went to sit with Nick. Nick had never really been comfortable around the hermaphrodite and the sight of both hands working to feed different sides of the mouth always disconcerted him. Nick kept his eyes on his own cup, not talking to Jene and no longer looking down the table.

Jene smiled. "Have you had enough of him? Would you like to come spend some time with Wolfy and me? We have room."

Nick just hid behind his soup-bowl sized mug. He ignored Jene and tried eavesdropping on Jacob and the twins. After a moment, their words came to him clearly, but with a metallic undertone, as if over a speaker or radio.

He heard Torturo say, "My mistakes."

Dinah shushed him. "Hush. Nicky is not a mistake. If I heard right, he does love you, he just doesn't know the words."

Torturo shook his head. "Love doesn't need words."

Alice kissed his cheek. "And yet you get so temperamental when you don't hear the ones you want." She kissed his ear. "Listen with your heart, not your ears."

Torturo looked over to where Nick drank his coffee and steadfastly ignored Jene. Nick saw him looking and gave him a small smile.

"He'll kill you, you know. He hurts us all, eventually. Only the sluts keep going back for more."

Fed up with Jene, Nick stood up. "Just shut up. I know you hate him. But let me be. I have work to do." He cleared up and tromped out to supervise the Midway set-up.

Torturo smiled as Jene flounced out in the opposite direction.

*   *   *

He was smiling more broadly as they returned from the usual Thursday rounds. Nick had been steady and affectionate and he could see it was genuine today. Jacob watched Nick park his bike and hurry out to see to the Midway. Maybe he could live with Nick changing, as long as Nick loved him.

He parked his own bicycle and stretched out in the hot July sun of deep southern Georgia for a lazy afternoon drink and a smoke. He looked up as a familiar voice addressed him.

"So, you've clubbed him into submission. Did you actually hit him or just brutalize him in bed? Do you still use your teeth too much when you're giving head?"

Torturo tipped his gray fedora up and looked at Jene. "That's right, you never liked rough play. But I didn't think my fellatio technique would be reason to call the whole thing off."

Jene rolled their eyes. "I wouldn't know. You were the one who laughed, tousled his hair, kissed her cheek and said, 'See ya around, dollface.' Not even a backward ride on the Ferris wheel to make it formal."

Torturo took another drink and sneered. "Break my heart, why don't you? It's never a good day when you decide to stalk me. Why do you bother?"

"That's why. My broken hearts. And because you're a bigger bitch than I'll ever be."

Torturo shook his head and tsked. "Nasty, nasty."

"And a bigger prick than I'll ever have," Jene added and smirked as Torturo squirmed. "I got eight inches, remember. Besides, Wolfy is good to me."

Torturo turned his back. "I wish you two much happiness, then."

"Good luck beating your boy into shape. I can't wait to see how else he changes." Jene's tone left no doubt they were gloating.

"The Show surely will make him a masterpiece. As we all have become."

Jene snickered. "Yeah, you're a piece of work. We're well shut of you. And, Plum, we don't mind rough play. It's when you stopped playing and stayed rough. You're an abusive drunk and your Nicky deserves better. Don't kill him before he gets changed. We can't afford another tits-up like Pocahontas."

Torturo flipped a still-lit cigarette butt in Jene's direction. "You certainly do enjoy a little abuse, yourself. So long as you're dishing it out."

She smirked and he shrugged. "Bad habit. Small show."

"Believe me, I know."

"Besides, Wolfy's practicing and the twins are, as usual, masturbating."

"Perhaps I should go watch." He stood up. "It has to be better company than this."

Jene smirked again. "I'm sure they'd let you join. That's why they do it so often, you know." As Torturo walked away, they added, "We remember. We all remember Memorial Day and that townie boy you took out of turn. Go eat, lunch or the sluts. And keep that in mind."

Torturo stalked off to the twins' car. He smiled at the sight that awaited him in the car.

The twins lay naked on the bunk, wrapped in each other's arms, Alice kissing Dinah, with two slim fingers between her sister's legs. Dinah returned the wet kisses and her own fingers rolled Alice's tight nipples. Torturo knocked on the wall.

Both of them smiled as they looked up and saw him. "Hello, darling. Come to play?" they chorused.

He started undoing his necktie. "Of course."

162

They watched him strip and beckoned him over. Alice kissed him as Dinah smoothed his hair.

"Bad day?" Dinah asked before she kissed him.

He joined them in their bunk. "Terrible." The girls draped themselves over top of him.

Dinah sucked on one of his nipples, playing with the piercings. Alice nibbled his earlobe. "Jene again?" Alice asked.

"Yes," Torturo answered shortly. He buried his face in their long red hair. "Make me forget, darlings. Please. Help me forget all of it."

Alice responded by scooting Dinah over and taking Torturo in, letting him move carefully within her. Dinah lay beside them, kissing them both. He came and Alice slid off, pulling Dinah over for her turn.

Dinah went down on him, swallowing him up, then pulling back to nibble. Alice joined her and they reveled in Torturo's pleased moans. Alice let Dinah have the taste of his orgasm and together they slid up to kiss and stoke him. Alice slipped her fingers between Dinah's legs, rubbing her as the three of them kissed.

A discreet knock at the door, followed by Nick's voice calling, "Showtime in an hour, folks," made them pull away. When Nick added, "May I come in?" Torturo looked at the twins. They nodded.

"Of course, sweet. Come in."

*   *   *

Nick tried to keep his face blank at seeing his lover and the twins lying naked and well-fucked on the bunk. He didn't succeed, as miserable jealousy followed by desire trailed over his features. He came and knelt beside the bunk and bent into the human tangle to kiss Torturo.

"Hello, girls," he added and looked surprised when first Alice and then Dinah kissed him. Torturo seized him by the back of his head and kissed him with a hard, hungry mouth. Nick looked up, very surprised. "They didn't satisfy?"

Dinah smiled at him. "Oh, we did. He just loves you. That's the difference." She and Alice made matching mock-pouts.

Torturo smiled. "Listen to the truth, Nicholas."

Nick laughed and kissed him again. "Like you don't get it up for them twice a night."

"And four times for you. I'll be getting old before my time with all of this exertion."

Nick wrapped his arms around Torturo's neck, kissed his ear and whispered, "I do know you love me. I love you, too."

"Aww, he's sweet," Alice said. Dinah leaned out and kissed Nick's cheek.

"Time for a show. For all of us." The girls moved off and Torturo stood up to dress. Nick was ready for work in his summer uniform, the flags and fireworks dancing around the band of his boater hat. "Jene's really cheesed off."

"I couldn't care less."

Nick shrugged. "Small show. It's gonna be uncomfortable. I wonder if Jean is PMSing." It was a running joke. He knew the women of the Show did not cycle, nor did they conceive, no matter how many lovers they took.

Torturo smirked. "Jean is always PMSing."

Nick sighed. "Or maybe you should inspire Wolfy to do his marital duty more often?"

"Hell, I don't blame him." Torturo stood up and reached for his clothes. Nick planted a possessive kiss on the tip of his cock. The twins reached over and petted Nick's hair.

"It'd be…interesting. I mean, them having both." He looked at the twins. "Sorry ladies, I'm being rude."

"No problem, dear. Jene has enjoyed our charms on occasion." Alice kissed his cheek and bounced one of Dinah's breasts in her hand.

Dinah smacked Alice's hand away. "They keep us both happy." She kissed Nick's other cheek. "Unfortunately, it didn't work out well."

Nick squirmed under the attention. Finally he decided the best course was the boldest. He wrapped one arm around each girl and kissed first Dinah and then Alice.

Torturo, now fully dressed, goosed Nick, making him jump and squeeze the twins. "Jene never works out well. Take it as a lesson, darling." He took in Nick kissing the girls. "The Show really has been working on you."

Nick released the girls and rubbed his bottom, in exaggerated pain. "Hey! I'll get you for that." Nick stood up and grabbed Torturo by the lapels, the metal arm much stronger than the flesh one had been, and slammed him into the wall of the carriage. The twins gasped and Jacob looked shocked. Nick mirrored his shock and then both men were laughing.

"You're going to go do your show, then I'm going to spank your ass so hard you have stand to do your piercings," Nick hissed, in his best villainous style, not sure where the words were coming from, but suspecting Clovis. Torturo moaned and bent to kiss him, but Nick dodged his mouth, biting his lower lip a little. "Then after the second show, I'm going to fist you. And after the third, I'm going to pour kerosene up your ass and light it to make you fart fire."

"A bit much punishment, don't you think, Nicky? Like hanging someone for stealing a loaf of bread," Alice said as she and Dinah went for their closet.

Torturo nuzzled his neck. "Did I mention I love you?"

Nick thought, trying to come up with more threats, which he now knew Torturo loved. "They did. You didn't. And for that omission…hmm, I'll think of something." Torturo got his puppy-dog look and Nick shoved him backward again, making him rap his head on the paneling. "Maybe I'll punish you brutally." Torturo shivered in his hands. "Make you sleep on the floor and not talk to you or touch you for two stops."

The good humor went out of Torturo's face. "Now that's real punishment."

"I think we overdid, Dinah," Alice whispered. Dinah turned them and held up two dresses.

"So happy German songs or sad Irish ones, darling boys?" she asked, trying to distract them.

"I like the Irish one better. Looks better with your hair," Nick said, picking up Torturo's tie and adding a slipknot to it.

Torturo ducked his head through the loop. "My vote's for Irish, too." Nick cut off his sentence by yanking the cloth tight.

"Later, ladies," Nick said, as he hauled Torturo out on the makeshift leash. Once inside their car, he kissed Torturo again and twisted his nipple rings. "We don't have time for a real fight or for sex." He went to the drawer and pulled out a padlock, before shoving Torturo's pants down around his knees and locking the foreskin rings to a guiche tunnel Torturo had recently added. "Mine. When you need it come to me, dammit! You never thought I might want to get laid, too?"

Torturo went to his knees as Nick yanked his tie into a choking noose. Nick dropped the ends of the leash and kissed him.

"I love you. I'm loyal to you. And you fuck around at every chance, even when I'm available. You know what, you're sleeping alone for the next three stops. I can take it. Prove to me you can. And, the padlock stays on except for the adult show." Nick jammed his boater down on his head and stalked out to go to work.

* * *

Torturo stayed on his knees thinking, wondering what had gotten into Nick and whether this would be a permanent change. He wasn't sure Clovis was improving his boy for the better. If the changed turned out to be permanent, he could find his ways around it and enjoy the new roughness. But if Nick condemned him to celibacy...the very thought made him shudder. The Phantasmagoria had not just given him amazing regeneration and pain tolerance, it had left him horny all the time. He recovered from orgasm faster than any male he knew and craved the next one immediately.

Consumed with his thoughts, he slurred through the monologue of the afternoon matinee and almost got booed by a teenage heckler. Nick caught him as he came offstage.

"Backstage. Now!" Nick's confidence made Torturo's knees weak.

But he put on a show of boredom. "What now?" Nick slapped him. Torturo stared, wondering who this aggressive little man was. Nick had never committed physical violence before today. He definitely did not like the personality or body changes in his lover.

"Now I have to work four times as hard to get crowds in." Nick's hand flew again, rattling Torturo's teeth. "Get with the program!"

Torturo slapped him back that time. He saw Nick grit his teeth and his blue eyes went cold.

"Just get out there and work like you're supposed to," Nick growled.

Torturo seized Nick by the shoulders and kissed him hard for that. He wanted this man. His cock pulled at the lock that bound it to his balls. Nick jerked away from the kiss.

"You have a booth to run. And I have a crowd to cajole into seeing that Torturo the Pain King is not a washed-up drunk who'd be better off in a geek pit instead of on stage."

"Someday, they'll be right," Torturo said, turning his face away.

Nick slapped him again. "They aren't right. Don't you dare believe it." Torturo hung his head. Nick's voice softened as he added. "Now go to work. And please? Do it right?" The hand along Jacob's face, soft and gentle, spoke volumes.

"I promise."

Nick kissed him, gently, sweetly, but leaving no doubt that the balance of power had shifted in the relationship, abruptly and definitely.

"I love you," Torturo said.

"And I love you. I'm a jealous jerk sometimes." Nick stole a fast kiss.

"I'd better go. Before I can't keep my hands off you."

Nick gave a nasty smirk. "Not like you can do anything. The anticipation of the day I let you out will keep you good." He slammed Torturo into the side of the train and kissed him very hard, putting some teeth behind it, until Torturo moaned under the onslaught and thrust futilely at him.

"Now anticipate." Nick hurried off to start building the tip for the next show.

Jene stepped out of the car and Torturo looked up from wiping the blood off his face. "Well, doesn't he just adore you? That's a side to our darling Nicky we haven't seen before." They got very close and Jean reached out to wipe a blood droplet off his lip. She tasted it slowly. Gene smirked. "Looks like a mutual abuse set-up to us, Plum. Enjoy him. Oh, and we told him all about that boy in Pocahontas. What was he, fifteen?"

"Go fuck yourself," Torturo sneered.

"Of course, our darling. Wolfy loves to watch."

*   *   *

The changes seemed permanent. Nick strutted down the Midway as if he owned it, giving orders to everyone from Torturo down to the newest clown in a tone that said he expected immediate compliance. He tested all the rides personally and sampled the wares of each food booth, making sure the quality remained high.

For the first time in his life, Nick had found a place to be himself. The only problem was that he wasn't sure he was himself. He suspected a fair chunk of the new personality wasn't him at all, but Clovis and the other drivers. He had dreams sometimes of battles in China against the Ming Dynasty or of making astrolabes in medieval Persia.

It didn't matter, really. He had work to do and Jacob to love. He had a mechanical arm that still had all the sensations of a flesh one. He had to be careful. During one ride test he'd left dents in the safety bar of the Ferris wheel by gripping it too tightly.

They were in South Carolina when Billy, Nick's relief talker, defected. While most carnivals ran three talkers, each talking an hour and resting for two, Nick found his throat would now sustain two hours of talking and one hour of rest.

Billy had met a little woman, barely four feet tall, who worked at the local grocery store. She'd flirted with him. He'd flirted with her. On Sunday night, he'd taken her arm and walked off the grounds with only a tip of his straw boater to Nick.

"Hope he's happy," said Bonzo, whose sad-sack hobo makeup belied the hope in his expression.

"How long has been with the Show?" Nick asked.

"About ten years."

Nick nodded. The little lady would get an ugly surprise soon enough, but at least he wouldn't age and crumble into nothingness before she got him to the car.

Now the Show had a problem. Nick needed the back-up, so he started checking the crowds. Any time he saw a likely talker, or heard a good, clear voice from the Midway, he would summon that person up on stage and run them through the teaser part of the show. They had no luck finding anyone.

The personality change was permanent but the mechanical changes, after the arm and the tubing, seemed to have stopped. Nick gave a silent sigh of relief every time he thought about it. He wasn't hungry anymore. He hoped Clovis didn't do anything too radical.

The endless series of holiday weekends rolled away. Jacob kept drinking. Nick avoided the car on Labor Day so Jacob could refuel the train. He understood it all now.

It was crisp Halloween, in the mid 1990s. Nick had almost given up keeping track of the year. Jacob fiddled with the end of the jewelry displays and Nick sprawled in the piercing chair. The Midway was all set, chores were done, and the gate would open in an hour.

"Jacob?" He could smell the whiskey on Jacob and figured it for the second bottle of the day. Enough to be very relaxed, not enough to spark his lover's hair-trigger temper. The sun-tea jar still sat in the tent, but Nick knew it held mostly whiskey and almost no tea these days.

"Hmmm?" Jacob sounded mellow. He set the last of the captive bead ring boxes in place.

"I need you to listen to something."

"A patter?"

"My insides. There's something weird going on."

Torturo's tread was heavy, but not lumbering, so Nick knew he'd had just enough. Torturo pressed Nick to lie back in the chair and laid his ear against Nick's chest and then his stomach.

"Strange…"

"Nothing. I haven't been hungry for at least two stops. But now, I think my heart stopped. All I hear is a ticking sort of sound."

"But you're still warm." Torturo felt his hands.

"And I'm still horny," Nick added with a grin, licking his lover's neck. "I know, I know. Only an hour until showtime. But you're all set up. Wanna steal some time?"

Jacob smiled at him and helped him out of the chair. "You know me so well."

*   *   *

They lay together afterward, Jacob's head pillowed on Nick's chest, listening. There were no bowel sounds, no gurgling and grumbling. And, worst of all, Nick had no heartbeat. Jacob heard a faint *tick-tock, tick-tock,* but not the steady *lub-dub* he had fallen asleep to so many times. He had nightmares during his naps, and sometimes during hibernation now, a new and unpleasant development. But Nick was always there to clutch closer and hear his soft breathing and listen to his heart. Now, it would be no better than sleeping with an alarm clock.

The first bars of the background music began over the loudspeakers. They dressed hastily to go about their days. Nick took a last kiss, smiling up at him. Jacob bit down his anger and went to work.

The ticking preyed on his mind. He turned it over and over as he worked in the piercing booth. A steady stream passed under his needle this stop, eyebrows and noses and lips. A few tongues and a couple had requested private sessions. Still, the thrill of putting needles through willing flesh did not drown the *tick-tock* that ran through his brain.

He managed all the shows, encouraged by the crowd's enthusiasm for all things brutal and bloody. They had cheered everything from the razor-blades to the chicken, the fire for the twins and the weights on his cock. He had done the wiener roast stunt again, for the first time in years. While no one had bitten it, several people, male and female had tasted him.

But he had come to a conclusion as a pretty redhaired boy licked his cock with too much intent for a public show. He was done. He couldn't feel the pain, hadn't since he'd picked a fight with a roustabout over the care of the horses. But he was tired of it all. Of the torture, of the crowds, of the Show. Nick didn't love him, couldn't possibly now that he truly had no heart.

"Tick-tock," he snarled as he closed down the piercing tent. "Tickgoddamned-tock."

His mind made up, he started for the gate. From behind him, he heard Nick call his name, but he ignored it.

Torturo had never realized the Midway was so long, or so dark. It seemed that every other streetlight had burned out, the jolly orange jack-o-lantern bulbs shattered in rusty twisted sockets. The intact ones guttered dimly, the light barely reaching the ground.

He caught Nick's reflection in the shattered glass of the mirror maze and recoiled at the skinless horror, as he had the other times he'd seen it. A shadow that was not his chased along the ground as he heard Nick running to catch up. A third and fourth skittered along booth fronts and concession stands. He'd seen these before, too. He paused for a moment near the ragged shell of the duck booth, ignoring the mildew-covered ducks and the bleached skeleton propped against one rotting timber. He closed his eyes and took three breaths, pressing the heels of his hands to his eye sockets.

When he looked, all the streetlights were lit and Tony gave him a friendly wave as he dried off a green rubber duck with bolts in its neck before packing it away. Nick was intact, as always, and followed almost on his heels as he reached the exit turnstile.

Torturo took another deep breath, steeling himself. No matter what Nicholas did, he was going out that gate.

Nick set his hand on the exit turnstile after the last rube had left, barring his way. "Go get aboard. Clovis will leave without you." Nick gave him what was supposed to be a jaunty smile but looked miserable and scared.

"Let him leave."

Nick shook his head. "No, go on, get aboard."

Jacob, not feeling anything like Torturo now, stepped closer and took Nick's hand. "Let's do it."

Nick swallowed hard. "If I walk out that gate, I'll be thirty-eight and I'll be holding a dead man's hand."

Jacob shrugged. "Eighty-nine's not necessarily dead. And you can't love me anymore. This solves all of it."

Nick pulled his hand away. "I don't want you dead. I do love you."

Jacob shook his head. "Nicholas, let me go. You have no heart. I know I've said it many times, but I listened to your chest tick like a damned alarmed clock this afternoon. What can you possibly be loving me with? Your liver?"

Nick shook his head in negation. "With all my mind and all my actions, with every touch and word. Isn't that enough? The heart is just a pump for blood." He caught Jacob's wrist.

"It's over." Jacob made two steps before Nick dug in his heels, pulling backward toward the train. The third step, into the turnstile, took even more effort. He smiled when he felt Nick let go. He glanced back and saw the man on his knees. Turning the smile into something more like a smirk, Torturo stepped out of the gate.

Jacob stood outside the Phantasmagoria after dark for the first time in almost seventy years. He expected the accumulated weight of his true age to crash in upon him at any second. All he felt was Nick's hand, like a steel band closing on his wrist. Without hesitation, Nick yanked him back through the turnstile, heedless of bruises or snagged piercings.

The force of the yank took Jacob off guard. He recovered to find himself flat on his back, inside the Midway, with Nick sitting on his chest. Tears streaked Nick's face.

"It's time to go. Let's get aboard."

Jacob just closed his eyes. He was consigned to immortality with a lover who had no heart. The kiss shocked him, sending electrical waves from his mouth throughout his body. Nick hadn't kissed him with that much real hunger since their first night.

Tears dripped onto Jacob's face and he reached up and caught one before it rolled off of Nick's nose. Nick smiled, even through the tears. "We've spent thirteen years together. I'm not giving you up this easily."

Torturo shook his head. "We both hurt. Why don't we end it? Now. Both of us."

Nick shook his head in response. "Because it won't end for me. You can leave and turn to dust, but I have to live out there as an old man, with no skills, no job and no life. Or, I'll end up old and unemployed, trying to care for my ancient lover. If I don't die of being half clockwork."

Torturo stroked away another tear before it could land on him. "Then stay here without me. The Show will always love you. And you won't have me to trouble you anymore."

Nick just kissed him again. "We'd better hurry. The wheel is down and most of the rest is loaded." He got up and helped Jacob to his feet. They headed to the train, Jacob casting one last longing look at the gate as Nick half-dragged him.

Nick stood in the door of Jacob's car and kissed him. The train lurched once. Jacob grabbed him and pulled him in. They tumbled backward and ended up with Nick atop him again.

"Hi." Nick gave him a sheepish little grin. Nick got off him and they shut the door against the rapidly fading world outside. He stripped and crawled into the bunk beside Jacob, burying his nose in Jacob's neck. Jacob tipped his face up.

"I do love you," Nick said. He stretched up for a kiss.

The hibernation swept them in before the kiss finished.

*   *   *

Jacob woke and stretched, listening to the alarming creaking of his joints. When he sat up, his back ached. His knees snapped when he stood up. Nick rolled over, groping for him with his flesh arm.

"Wake up, my lazy darling." He bent down and kissed Nick.

Nick opened one eye, then both flew open and he stared. "Jacob? Have you seen a mirror?"

Almost dreading to look, Jacob shook his head. Nick sat up and kissed him. That, at least, reassured him he hadn't turned into some nightmare ancient, even as creaky as he felt.

The mirror was still a nasty shock. Lines marked his forehead and the corners of his eyes. His mustache grew thicker now, but didn't cover the lines around his mouth. His clean jawline looked heavy and gray streaked his temples.

Nick kissed the gray hair. "Very distinguished."

Jacob felt the lines, almost not believing he had gotten off so lightly, while the rest of him bemoaned his lost beauty. "Ten? Fifteen years maybe?"

"Sexy," Nick kissed his neck and cheek. "I'd say forties." He looked up, his lips parted and his eyes hopeful. "Kiss me?"

Reassured of Nick's affection, Jacob took the offered kiss, slowly and sweetly. That much hadn't changed. Nick still fit into his arms, against his body and under his lips properly. He sat down and drew Nick onto his lap.

"Maybe I should grow a beard to cover up some of the aging problem."

Nick smiled. "Only you think it's a problem. But a beard would make you look devilishly sexy."

"Someone as vain as I am aging that much in a few seconds? It's a big problem." Jacob fingered his forehead again.

"I tried to stop you. I still have you and you're still handsome." Jacob gave him a sweet look and Nick stole a kiss. "And that, Jacob, is all that matters, you vain old fool." He kissed Jacob again, to show there was no malice in the words.

"Can you blame me? I have to seduce everyone at the show. Every night." He sighed and glanced at the mirror.

Nick kissed his nose. "But now you look like a rake who is capable of doing so and knows all of the world and its wantonness."

Jacob raised an eyebrow, suspecting flattery. "Really, darling?"

"Oh yes. The man I met was a beautiful young man, angelically fair, with habits far too old for him, and a wicked desire he didn't seem old enough to understand. But now..." Nick broke off for another kiss, this one hotter than ever. "Now the pipe fits you. The age gives you sensuality and perversion only adds to your charm."

Jacob smiled broadly. "Perversion...I like that. Thank you." He nuzzled Nick's hair a bit. "I have to continue to be the horrid man that made your ex-fiancée slap me, of course."

Nick barely heard. He startled Jacob with a hard kiss, his tongue filling Jacob's mouth, his hands demanding on flesh that was softer now than when they had gone to bed. Jacob crushed Nick to him, feeling his cock wake under the onslaught his lover's mouth on his.

Nick gave him a grin as they parted. "I don't know why, but I'm crazy hot for you this morning."

Jacob shook his head. The brief stirring from the kiss had not been enough to wake him fully. His stomach rumbled too loudly. "Perhaps after breakfast and chores." They dressed and as they stepped out of the car, he looked at Nick very seriously. "I am sorry I trapped you aboard. It was very selfish of me."

Nick kissed his cheek. "You were right. There was nothing left for me." He ducked under Jacob's arm for the walk to the mess tent.

"You could be married with children right now. Your oldest would be just turning into a teenager."

"I'd have been miserable. If word got around about the show, we'd be social pariahs, probably kicked out of church, which would have killed Lisa. If we'd moved, I'd have always remembered. If I had gotten out of the train after sex, do you know how much more miserable I'd have been? A lifetime of kissing a woman who didn't arouse me, fired only by memories of the man who did."

Jacob looked pained and forced the words out. "There are other men."

"I wouldn't," Nick said confidently, then crumbled. "Or I would have, only to destroy myself and her in the process."

Jacob squeezed him tighter. "So I decided your life and get to keep you instead."

Nick looked thoughtful. "I broke her heart, but she probably got over it and married someone better for her. And I got you. I'm yours and that Ferris wheel ride's about all the marriage I'll ever get...or want."

"Did you ever think of calling her?" Jacob asked as he loaded his breakfast tray. Nick only took coffee.

Nick's face went shifty and he hesitated as if planning what to say. "After thirteen years, what is there to say? Oh hi, hon. Sorry to skip town like that, but you're better off without me anyway because I'm gay?" The humor came out forced and harsh, as if Nick himself didn't believe the words. Nick sat down and drank some coffee.

Jacob swallowed a mouthful of eggs. He ate more slowly than usual, his fingers feeling stiff. Nick did not eat. They finished and headed to the animal car. Jacob took off his shirt as usual. Nick ran his fingers over the soft spots of his chest and stomach that hadn't been there before. He kissed one nipple.

"Nicholas, stop that or I'll never get done." Torturo peeked out for a moment behind Jacob's eyes. "Demanding, distracting little thing."

Nick laughed and the sound made Jacob glad. He set about pitching the hay and making sure the animals were fed. Nick checked the animals over for illness or signs of trouble.

Jacob dropped the pitchfork when he saw Nick buffing Precious's horn. She rubbed up under his chin and he brushed out her white coat before buffing her hooves. He knew now that Nick had told the truth about everything. He'd learned early that Precious couldn't abide frauds or liars. It had taken her some time to make up to him. In thirteen years, Nick had never touched the beast.

He mopped his face with his shirt, the November day warm. Nick finished with Precious and went to get some water. He trailed light fingers over some of the softer places in Jacob's once-firm abdomen, and finished by tweaking a nipple as he passed.

Jacob gave his lover a grin. "Is that a hint to hurry?"

Nick finished filling the poultry watering jar, screwed the pan on the top and flipped it over. "Yeah. Your little trip changed you."

Jacob caught his breath, more winded than he should have been from pitching hay. "So I'm noticing."

Nick set out the water bowls and hung the hose in the cyclops bull's trough. He splashed a bit of water at Jacob and snickered when he jumped. Jacob got a wicked grin and tossed a forkful of hay his direction, landing it atop Nick's head.

Nick sputtered and shook the hay out of his face. "You looked overheated."

Jacob hung up the fork and loomed over him before wrestling him down onto a bale of straw. Nick yanked him down for a hard fast kiss, much to his surprise.

"You haven't been this hot for me in years." He smiled as Nick kissed him again, with a wet and open tongue.

"No, and I'm sorry for that. Sometimes, you almost have to lose something good before you appreciate it." He kissed Jacob again. "Not going to lose you."

CHAPTER 14

MICHAEL

The Show continued. They continued. A few new lines, a few more gray hairs turned up with each stop. Jacob fretted, but Nick found him irresistibly sexy.

The search for a replacement talker consumed Nick. Clovis kept telling him to hurry. But one after another, the towns came and went, with no one of distinction until they hit California. In a little coastal town, a handsome blond youth with pretty eyes listened attentively and responded to Nick's flirt.

Nick beckoned him up on stage without asking his name. The Phantasmagoria whispered to him, the quiet, slightly French voice telling him that Michael would be perfect. "Come on up here, sir, I need your help for this next bit." He gestured.

"Me?"

"You, Michael." Nick smiled. Michael climbed up the steps at the front of the stage, smiling, but Nick could see the uncertainty on his face. "All right, all I need you to do is hold this." He handed Michael a large placard with the words "The Phantasmagoria Ten-in-One" on it in old-fashioned circus lettering.

"Just keep watching him, folks, and you'll see something amazing. But now, take a look at Hannah. Hannah, Hannah from Indiana, the bearded lady. Come on out here and let the folks see your pretty face, Hannah darlin'." Nick let his Missouri country accent go a little more hick. He raised his voice, projecting it over the Midway. "We're gonna have us a free show right here, ladies and gents, that's right, absolutely free, right here and now! Gonna bring out Hannah the Bearded Lady, Marvello the Master of Illusion. You've heard the folks talking and now you can see them for yourself."

He took a quick breath as Hannah paraded out, in her heels and fishnets and bodysuit-tux. "Hannah from Indiana, folks, isn't she gorgeous? All woman and the sexiest mouth in the world, but with special grooming needs. Give her 'stache a twirl there, Michael, let her take you 'round the world. It's all real, folks, and all the others are alive on the inside!"

Nick smiled as Michael twirled the end of Hannah's mustache and showed the crowd it was indeed growing out of her face and not glued on.

"Now like I said, Hannah's a special lady and it takes a special man to understand her." Marvello came out on cue, with a flourish of his red satin lined cape. "As you can see, folks, they have the same taste. Marvello the Master of Illusion. Inside you can see him saw lovely Hannah in half, make a woman out of a corpse and lots more. All right, folks, don't quit watching our friend here." The squeaking of wheels as Hannah helped Marv wheel out the guillotine made Nick quiet for a minute. "Marvello the magician is going to cut off our helper's head and then I'll have Michael tell you all about it!" Nick announced as Hannah and Marvello set up the trick.

Michael laughed nervously. "I don't know, man…"

Marvello, his face grave and implacable, beckoned him. "Come."

Michael laughed a little more and approached the garish red and gold-painted execution device.

"Trust us," Hannah said loudly. "He does it to me six times a day." She held the neck stocks open and Michael laid his head in.

Marvello laughed. "Of course, I should add my birth name is Henry… Although I am no king." He gave a booming laugh and dropped the blade. Michael jumped as it rattled home.

Marvello raised the blade and Nick helped Michael out. "A big hand for our helper, Michael, folks." The crowd applauded wildly and Michael looked from side to side. "Don't nod too much there," Nick warned him. "I don't want to have to chase your head like I did the last guy's. The clowns got it and played soccer with it before I could catch up." He pulled an exaggerated face. "Messy."

Michael laughed. "That's too cool. Thanks."

Nick gave a quick pass with his hand and produced a free pass seemingly from thin air. Marvello had taught him basic palming. "For being a real sport." As Michael took it, he whispered, well away from the mic, "See me after the show."

Michael's eyebrows went up. "I'll be there." Nick could hear the arousal in his voice.

"Watch your step there. A little more applause, folks, because he was such a sport."

Nick waited for Michael after the show, sitting off to the side of the Ten-in-One tent. Michael looked a bit dazed by the whole show, but came right up and invaded Nick's personal space.

Nick got himself some breathing room. "You did great. I want to ask you to stick around while I'm getting the crowd for the next show. How are you at public speaking?"

Michael grinned. "Not bad. I've won a few awards in debate club, if that counts."

Nick matched it. "Okay, we're going to plant you in the crowd and do it just like we did. Marv will do the guillotine thing and then I'll have you tell the folks a little about the show."

Michael nodded. "All right. Got a cheat sheet or something so I don't forget the names?"

"You don't have to remember the names so much. Hannah and Marvello are really the only ones who come out. If you get stuck, glance at the posters."

"Okay."

"Great. Just drift back this way when I start talking again, okay?"

"All right."

"Sorry about eating up your day at the carnival like this. Is your wife going to be a problem?" Nick looked concerned.

Michael shrugged and tossed his sun-bleached hair. "Don't have a wife. And I liked it. It was fun."

Nick cocked his head. "No wife? Got a girl?" He lowered his voice a little. "A boy?"

"Nope."

"Ah, free and unattached." Nick leaned in close, then gave him a wink. "See ya later."

After the last all-ages show started, Nick took Michael to sit at the lemonade stand. "You did great. Can you come back tomorrow?" Nick did a pass and produced a free ticket. "I want you to talk the four P.M. crowd into the matinee."

Michael looked flustered. "Uh, yeah, sure." He took the ticket, but Nick didn't let go.

"How do you feel about running away and joining the carnival?" Nick whispered, leaning in close enough that his breath blew over Michael's lips. He watched Michael shiver a little. He was so in for it after this if Jacob saw them, but he had to get Michael back to the Show and he could tell Michael wanted him.

Michael stole a quick kiss, yanked the ticket away and almost fled. From behind him, Nick heard Torturo's laugh chasing Michael down the Midway. He tensed a little, but the big hand that landed on his hair only ruffled it.

"Working hard to get a new talker, aren't you, darling?" Torturo teased. He bent down and kissed Nick, slow and deep as if trying to take the taste of Michael out of Nick's mouth.

*   *   *

Michael came as soon as they opened, bright and early at noon. Stitches showed him over to where Nick was lecturing the newest concessionaire about the proper crispness of elephant ears.

"More damn cinnamon, too!" Nick barked and the pretty cook just cowered.

"Nick? I have your talker," Stitches said. "Let me handle this and you give him some help."

"Thanks." Nick relaxed and smiled at Stitches. After a second, he turned back to the cook, looking more kindly. "Keep at it, Joy. You'll do fine. Stitches here knows how elephant ears should be, so he's going to help you out." He shook Michael's hand. "Come on. I'm going to have you dress the part and try building the tips today."

He led Michael to the Backyard and then aboard the train. Jacob was nowhere to be seen. Nick scowled. He'd hoped his lover would be home, just to avoid the appearance of impropriety. Although—he stole a glance at Michael as he went to the closet—he wouldn't mind being a little improper with the surfer.

He rummaged in the closet and found a Memorial Day suit, in a size too large for him and too small for Jacob. He handed the crisp white shirt and the striped tan pants with their red suspenders to Michael. He kept the tie, sleeve garters and hat with their red and white carnations. "Try these. Looking right comes with the part. Bathroom's through there. Hold your breath and you might be able to turn around."

Michael ducked into the head to change. Nick set the accessories on the table and poured himself a drink from Jacob's bottle.

"This is awesome," Michael said through the door.

"It really is. You know, I used to sell cars? Selling the Show isn't much different."

At that moment, Torturo sauntered in, finishing a last drag on a cigarette. He flipped the butt out the open door and saw Nick.

Nick stood up at once and slipped close to him. Torturo immediately folded him close for a kiss. "Hello, darling. I found our new talker. He's going to try building the tips today. He's," Nick turned in time to see Michael come out, "changing in the head."

Michael stopped short at the sight of the big man. "Uhhh…Torturo."

"So I see, Nicky. He's very pretty when he's guilty."

Nick smiled at Michael from the circle of Torturo's arms. "Told you I lived with my man. You look great, Michael. Be at the stage at twenty 'til." He kissed the bottom of Torturo's chin. "The husband and I need some grown-up time." He winked at Michael.

Torturo sent Michael a glare. "Yes, scram."

Michael shut the door behind him and Nick turned back to kiss Torturo. "He's exactly what the Show wants."

"How do you know this?" Nick heard the flat deadly warning in his lover's voice.

"Clovis told me."

At that, Torturo growled.

"Jacob, stop it. I've been hearing Clovis for over a year now and you know it. We've needed another talker since Billy nipped off with that girl in South Carolina and you know that, too."

"Why him?" Torturo's arms closed possessively over Nick.

"Why not him? He's a good public speaker and he's good looking."

"And you got the hots for him." Torturo spun Nick around and bit his neck.

Nick tried to make it a joke. "If you said blow him, I wouldn't protest."

Torturo shoved him away and Nick landed hard on the bunk. "You've probably already done it anyway."

Nick knew this mood and hated it. Jacob had gotten more bad-tempered as he aged. The loss of his youthful good looks seemed to anger him more than anything Nick could say or do. Every one of his dissipations showed now. Nick realized with a shock how old his lover looked. The wrinkles in his forehead never quite smoothed and one cheek had a seam that didn't fade entirely when he relaxed.

Nick sighed. "If I say nothing, you'll think I have. If I say I haven't, you'll punish me both for doing it and for lying. So I can't win." Nick rose from the bunk and came to Torturo, then pressed him down into a chair, kissing him and straddling him. He sighed. "Hurt me however you're going to and get it over with."

Torturo kissed him for a moment and then said, "You've been into my whiskey. Pour me a drink, too."

Nick got up and did. He handed it over, checked his tie and set his hat on at a rakish angle. "Jacob, I have a tip to build. I have to go."

When he bent in for a kiss, Torturo threw the drink in his face. Nick choked, wiped his eyes and sputtered.

"Great! Just great! Now everyone's going to think I've acquired your drinking habits!" He yanked Torturo's folded silk handkerchief from his breast pocket and mopped the whiskey off his face. He flung it back and stalked for the door, eyes burning.

Torturo just laughed.

"You are such a bastard sometimes." Nick slammed the door behind him, not quite cutting off Torturo's words.

"I really am."

Nick went to work and spent the day taking Michael through the basics. Now and then, he saw Torturo watching them. He was careful to stay professional.

Michael could talk. There was no doubt in Nick's mind after the four o'clock. When Michael did the six, Nick was very pleased at the crowd he drew, nearly cleaning the Midway.

After the last of the crowd was in the tent, Nick sat on the edge of his stage and tipped his boater back. "Most impressive. How much do you like it?"

"I love it." Michael's eyes glowed and his face shone. Nick could tell he was about to get kissed and drew back a little.

"How would you like a very permanent gig with us?" He hadn't talked to Torturo or the twins. Clovis said Michael was the right man and that was enough for Nick.

"Always wanted to join the circus. This is almost as good."

Nick laughed. "Another Toby Tyler. If I said we were on the lookout for a new talker to spell me, would you like to ride along?"

"Hell yeah!" Michael practically bounced at the idea.

"We leave tonight. Come aboard the train before it goes. It's the ride of a lifetime, I promise you. I joined up Labor Day of '85."

Michael did a double-take. "Dude, you musta been six. Well, yeah. Count me in."

"The food's always good. The uniforms come with the gig and as for sex…" Nick chuckled. "Just be sure to negotiate which strap-on you'll let Dinah use. She favors the spiked one."

"Now that's not my thing."

Nick shrugged. "The twins have everyone at some point." He looked very seriously at Michael. "I'm taken."

"I think I'll stick to the pretty guests, then."

Nick grinned. "Go for it. My man does them as he likes."

Michael gave him a look. "Do you?"

"Not interested. I'm his. And he's the best." Nick tapped his pierced ear and stuck out his tongue to show the barbell.

"Niiice." Michael sounded actually impressed and a little horny.

"I've got a couple more, but I'm not showing you. He's the jealous type. Welcome aboard, Michael. Go home, get anything you want. We won't be back." Nick stuck out his hand and Michael shook.

As Michael headed down the Midway to go pack, still wearing his talker uniform, Nick felt the small hairs on his neck stand up.

"I do the hiring," Torturo growled over the back of his neck. For such a large man, his lover moved very silently when he wanted.

Nick spun and looked at him. "Based on what? A little tickle in the back of your brain that says, 'Get him now?' Because that's what I based it on."

"You overstepped." Torturo's voice had a low, dangerous quality Nick had never heard before.

Nick bristled. "I followed the orders of the Phantasmagoria. And that is bigger than you, or the twins or me, all put together." When Torturo glared at him, Nick glared right back. Torturo dropped his eyes first, but only because he took a drink from his ever-present flask.

"I'll see you after the adult show." Torturo made this sound more like a threat.

Nick kissed him and went to start working on that crowd.

*   *   *

Nick was waiting in the train car when Torturo came in. The Pain King was late and smelled of brandy and the twins. The roustabouts had struck most of the carnival already.

"Just in time, love." Nick stretched. He'd stripped when he came in. "Good show tonight. Be good to be on the road, though."

Torturo took another swig from his flask and Nick could smell the girls had refilled it with brandy. "Surprised you're not joining him in his car."

Nick looked puzzled. He had indeed seen the new talker's car when he boarded. "Why would I? I'm yours."

Torturo loomed over the bunk. "You've got a thing for blonds, don't you?"

"Only you." Nick looked up at him and drew him down for a kiss. "I took him because Clovis said." Nick sat up when Torturo pulled away. "You're being a jealous jerk and I'm going to get hurt again for whatever imagined thing you think I've done. Do whatever it is you're going to and clear the air."

"I'm going to make sure your eyes never stray again." Torturo went to the drawer and rummaged.

Nick listened to the voice of the Show and said absently. "If that's what you need to do, Jacob. I love you. Make me good." It had been his mantra during the early punishments and he saw Torturo stiffen at it now.

"On the bed, Nicholas, lock yourself in."

Nick went, still listening. Clovis said everything would be fine.

"Doesn't your belief say that if your eyes cause you to sin, you should pluck them out?" Torturo said in a soft, dangerous voice.

Nick lay clutching the manacles, trying to come up with a rational argument.

::Let him,:: soothed the voice in his head, the same one that had told him to hire Michael. *::Let him take them. All will be well. I am doing great things with you, Nicholas, and this is one more step.::*

Nick shuddered and breathed deeply. Torturo came to him, holding a grapefruit spoon. Nick knew all the contents of all the cabinets and knew they didn't have any grapefruit spoons. Oddly, that fact relaxed him even more.

Nick smiled up. "Make me good," he repeated. He made his eyes stay open and wide.

Torturo struck quickly, a flash of silver at his right eye and then deep, searing pain. Nick had a brief instant of seeing a single blue eye on the spoon before Torturo dropped it into a bowl. He bit his tongue to keep from screaming at the pain that seared his face from his eye socket.

183

It took a minute for him to open his eyes again. The warm wash of blood down the right side of his face nauseated him.

"Please?" he said.

"What?"

"Smile for me? Let it be the last thing I ever see." Nick took a small breath. "Please, Jacob?"

Torturo smiled, sweet and loving. "I love you, Nicholas." He bent in for a kiss. He was still smiling as he brought the spoon down on the left.

CHAPTER 15

NEEDLES

The next stop found Nick's eyes healed. The empty sockets had closed cleanly and Torturo set a pair of round glasses on his nose.

"I wear my sunglasses at night," Nick sang. He'd never sung in front of Torturo and he was shocked to find he knew the words to a rock song. He must have picked it up from the bobsleds. He reached out, groping until he found Torturo. "Jacob, please? Help me get to my coffee?"

"Of course." Torturo was sweetly attentive throughout the meal, helping Nick find his way around. The layout of the Phantasmagoria never changed. Nick counted off the paces to the mess tent and then down the Midway. "I'll get you a cane, darling," Jacob promised.

He left Nick's side only once, excusing himself to the donniker. When he returned, he pressed the grip of a cane into Nick's hand.

"You fished it out of the donny?" Nick asked.

"Yeah, someone had used it for a plunger," Torturo teased.

"Gross." Nick pretended to be disgusted but moved into Torturo's arms for a kiss. He let Torturo lead him through the Midway, tapping his way along, but mounted the steps of his platform himself.

"I'll go get the posters for the town-work. Your boy can come along."

"Nick?" He heard Michael's voice and felt a hand steady him as he tapped out the edge of the platform.

"Good morning. Ready to be brilliant and show me what an excellent choice the Phantasmagoria made?"

"Uhhh…dude? Your eyes?" Nick could hear the horror in his voice, but he didn't understand it.

"What about them?" Nick cocked his head in Michael's direction.

"Did Torturo do that?" Michael tugged the glasses down Nick's nose and Nick opened his eyelids. He heard the sharp intake of breath from his relief talker.

"Yes," he said, as if it were perfectly normal for a man to cut his lover's eyes out. "He did a very nice job, too."

"Fuck," Michael breathed. "Nick, why?"

"Because my eyes lured me into temptation." Nick pushed his glasses back up and felt the edges of his booth and tried assembling his throat mic by feel alone.

"Shit." Michael wasn't getting over it.

Nick didn't understand at all.

"I think you're having a bigger problem with it than I am. I'm not unhappy. Why are you upset?"

"But your eyes… Dude, you're fucking blind!"

Nick shrugged. "It could be worse. He could have split my tongue."

"I've seen that. That could be kind of sexy. Man, I am so sorry." He laid a hand on Nick's arm.

Nick grabbed his wrist and tugged him closer. "Listen and listen well. I let him do this. I have my reasons. The Show changes us all and my changes are accelerating. Jacob doesn't know he's just a tool to aid them." Nick grinned slowly and drummed his metal fingers on the stage. "You're breathing too fast, Michael. Scared, are you? If you think this is bad, imagine waking up fused to your twin sister, or, worse, to your husband! None of us were born freaks."

Michael pulled away. Nick let him go.

"Do you know what the date is, my dear?" Nick almost flinched. That phrasing was pure Clovis and he would need to remember not to use it around Jacob.

"No."

"It was Memorial Day when we took you aboard. It's somewhere in the middle of June now. Summer dates are closer together." Nick waved off the last statement. "After this, we'll hibernate until July 4th. Then mid-August and Labor Day. Then a nice long nap until Halloween. If you want to leave, I would say do it now. You've only been missing for two weeks." Nick said the words out of pure form.

Michael couldn't leave anymore than the rest of them could. He tried not to think about the nasty surprise Billy's paramour must have gotten the next morning.

"No, I don't want to leave." Michael's voice didn't sound so sure now.

Nick could almost hear him shaking his head and setting his jaw. "Then go get acquainted with some folks. Stitches the clown is a great guy and the best guide you can have. Learn your way around the Midway. And be back here at ten so you can go out to help Jacob and Marv put up posters."

He felt Michael climb down from the platform. He waited there, sunning himself and listening to the Show set up. He should make his way around the Midway and hassle everyone. He ignored Hui Ping and Bagodata, the astrolabe maker, as they pestered him inside his head. This morning, he didn't feel like doing anything. He just wanted to sit in the sun.

*   *   *

Nick only changed a little after losing his eyes. Terrified of being alone in the dark with only the other drivers in his head, he clung more tightly to Torturo, when the Pain King was available. On his own, he learned to navigate in the blackness with a cane and covered his eyeless state with sunglasses when he had to work. He never left the car without one hand tucked into Torturo's arm. Torturo took him out more often than Nick would have liked.

The crowds soon learned that while the talker was blind, the man who ran the till was not and they stopped trying to get in with counterfeit dollars.

One day, he sat on the bunk, trying to learn Braille, when Torturo sat down beside him.

"I think you need some decoration. Visible decoration."

Nick turned his face to Torturo out of habit. "Yes? I have an earring." He shivered when Torturo took his face in his large hands and stroked his thumbs over Nick's sunken eyelids. "Anything you want to do," he whispered.

He heard rattling that he recognized as the piercing kit. Even without the sight of the kit, Nick felt himself getting hard. He smiled, but clutched the edge of the mattress knowing this would hurt.

Torturo swabbed down his eyelids. "A simple gold ring, I think."

187

Nick tried not to shake. "Will this revolt the audiences?"

"You'll have your sunglasses on."

Nick relaxed a little. "So, this is just for us?"

"Yes. It's ours." He kissed Nick, sweetly, lingering in the kiss.

"All right." Nick held very still as Torturo inserted the needle in his lower eyelid and ran it upward and out the upper eyelid. "Hurts," he whimpered.

"I know, darling. Nearly finished."

Nick held still as Torturo put the ring in his eyelids. He could no longer open his eyes. He shivered. "I can't imagine how I must look."

"Beautifully broken." Torturo's kiss, when Nick turned his face up for it, was more passionate than sweet and Nick moaned under it and matched the passion. Needles always left him hot.

"You've broken me," he whispered, which made Torturo kiss him again, harder. He shamelessly rubbed his crotch against the knee Torturo had put between his thighs.

Torturo broke away. "If we keep this up, I won't finish the second."

Nick smiled. "Do it, quickly."

Torturo gave a small chuckle and teased, "Yes, boss."

Nick smiled and felt the needle slide in again. He whimpered more loudly this time, but the piercing was done sooner, since Torturo had learned how much force it took. He shook and his breath escaped in something close to a sob.

"Do I look good?" Nick asked.

"Beautiful, you vain little thing." Torturo stopped the motion of Nick practically humping his leg and freed his cock to stroke him

"Love me," Nick whispered. He squirmed out of his clothing when Torturo pushed him back onto the bed, but his eyebrows went up in surprise when Torturo lubed him and settled down to ride his cock. After a moment, he recovered and pulled Torturo down for a kiss. He played with his lover's piercings by touch alone.

"Hurt me," Torturo said and nibbled his earlobe.

Nick pulled on Torturo's nipple rings, then clamped down with his metal fingers. "I love it when you say that."

*   *   *

On their way to the mess tent, Nick asked, "Do I wear the glasses all the time? Or can I show these off in the mess tent? You do such gorgeous work."

"The Show won't mind. The crowds might, though."

"All right." Nick took off the glasses as they went in. He heard a couple of gasps, but Alice and Dinah kissed him and the rings and fluttered over how pretty they were. No one else said anything. He wore the glasses any time he left the Backyard, if the Show was open. Slowly the crew became accustomed to the look.

Michael found him testing the swings for the ride crew. "That's fucked up, man." He touched Nick's eyelids very gently.

"I take it you don't like them? Because I do."

"I think they're freaky. But hey, if you like them…"

Nick caught Michael's arm and guided him to sit at one of the concession tables. "Michael, how are you doing with the others? Because you seem to have a real problem with Jacob and me."

Michael covered Nick's hands with his. "I don't have a problem with you. I think you take too much shit from that old geezer in a big way."

"Not sure I understand. I let him. If I refused, he wouldn't do it."

"But why do you let him hurt you?" Michael sounded confused and worried.

Nick shrugged. "Why not? I won't tell you how hard the needles make me, or how fast I came when he put those rings in."

"But—God!—he took out your eyes…"

Nick shrugged again. "They needed to go." He sighed, sensing another round of explaining this again.

"I don't know, dude. Sometimes I think you normal guys are the biggest freaks here."

"Trust me." Nick leaned across the table and whispered, "They won't stay gone."

"What?" Michael sounded very confused.

"I said I was changing. Take my pulse." Nick extended his wrist and Michael felt around for a couple of minutes.

"Shit… You either have really deep veins, or you're dead."

Nick smiled, knowing it was the latter. He wondered how Michael had died. A surfing accident? A shark? "We change here."

"I ain't changed yet."

"You might not," Nick conceded. "But I am. Even Jacob doesn't know all of it yet."

"Shit. Is he going to freak?"

Nick nodded. "Probably." He ran a finger over the scar above his eyelid. "He did that when my arm changed."

"You know I'll help you if you need it, right?"

"I know." Nick turned very serious. "Michael, start listening for another talker." He could hear the nervousness in Michael's voice as he agreed and Nick hastened to reassure him. "It's not Jacob who's going to remove me from the Show. Michael, it's very complicated. You'll understand soon."

Michael sighed. "I hope so, because I sure don't get it now. Look, Nick—sorry—I got a weird request."

"Yeah?" Nick's eyebrows went up again.

"Can I kiss you?" Michael leaned in and Nick could feel his breath on his face.

He recoiled almost instinctively. "If you want me, ask Jacob."

Michael gave a bitter laugh. "Yeah, he'll say no."

Nick sighed. "Michael, I like you, but I'm not free to do anything."

"I get it." Michael sounded as if he were moping.

Nick pecked his cheek and tapped off down the Midway to check on the booths. Michael talked in a good crowd for the next two stops, until even Jacob conceded the Show had made a good choice.

CHAPTER 16

SEEING

Memorial Day weekend sprang out clear and blue in Hughes, Arkansas. Nick woke up and realized he didn't need the facilities. Of course he wasn't hungry. And there was something in his eye socket.

He sat up and carefully pulled apart the ring in his left one, only to open his eye on a world he hadn't seen for five summer holidays. He took the right ring out and rolled over to kiss his lover awake.

Torturo sat up and scowled at the new addition to his face. Nick closed his eyes, unhappy that his love didn't seem more pleased.

"What? How?" snarled Jacob, not taking this in before his coffee.

"I didn't do it, lover. I just woke up like this, remember." He touched Torturo's face. "I didn't ask for them. Take them out, if you want."

Torturo shook his head. "If I take them, they'll come back with the next hibernation. The Phantasmagoria thinks you need them."

Nick nodded and got up. He went to the mirror and stared. "I knew they weren't normal eyes." He turned the featureless ovals of deep blue crystal to Torturo. "I can see your thoughts." The words came out in amazed pleasure. Nick wasn't sure he could articulate what he saw. His lover seemed to glow, a little halo of light around him. It changed colors and Nick knew somehow that those were Jacob's moods.

Torturo shot him an odd look. "What am I thinking?"

"That you're pissed and grumpy and confused and a little scared and you really, really want your coffee." That got a smile out of Torturo. Nick reached for his clothes. "Then let's go get you some. The mess tent is probably up."

Torturo caught him and pulled him back for a kiss.

Nick smiled and returned it slowly. "I love you," he said. Torturo didn't dress and didn't let him up. He just kept staring at Nick's eyes. "I'll miss my eyelid rings. I bet they were sexy."

"Your eyes are beautiful now." He kissed Nick again. "Get some coffee…and I'll figure out your next piercing."

"I can watch?" Nick smiled broadly. "You just got turned on thinking about piercing me," he added with a grin. "Your outline went kind of red and spiky."

"Yeah. I always do."

"Mmmm, depending on where you put it, maybe I should suck you while you do." Nick nuzzled in the thick blond hair.

Torturo's moan was soft but his outline went completely spiky. "Did I tell you I loved you today?"

"No. But you showed it." Nick smiled. He dashed out to the mess tent and came back with a carafe of coffee and a plate of food for his lover. He ate nothing, but was cheerful and chatty.

"You're happy today."

"You love me. Isn't that reason enough?"

"Of course it is." Torturo finished his eggs, stole a kiss and went to work on the oatmeal.

Nick went to the mirror and examined his eyes. He pressed around them and gasped when one landed in his hand. He looked at it and shook his head to clear it of the dizziness. He could see the eye in his hand, but the eye in his hand could see his face and the mirror on the other side.

Before he could pop it back in, Torturo's long fingers snatched it from his palm. Nick shut his eyelids to reduce the amount of information his brain had to process.

Torturo breathed on the eye and Nick giggled. When he licked it, Nick shuddered.

"Don't do that, love," Nick begged.

"Why?" Torturo slipped the eye into his mouth.

Nick bolted across the room instantly, his fingers in the hinge of Torturo's jaw. "Give it. Don't you dare swallow it."

"Why?"

"Because not only do you have a funny shaped uvula, I really don't want an up-close-and-personal tour of your gut. Now give it back."

"You're no fun," Torturo pouted. He spat the eye into Nick's waiting hand.

Nick rubbed it gently against the soft flannel of his shirt and eased it back into its socket. "Yuck. You didn't seem to understand. I could feel everything and still see."

"That was the idea, my darling. I was going to get hourly updates on what you saw and see if I could arrange to shit it out on stage."

"You are so gross. Like a little kid with a full diaper who has just discovered poo makes his mom crazy. Dis-gusting."

Torturo laughed and swept Nick into his arms for more kisses. "So I wasn't the last thing you saw after all."

"No, but you were the first I saw afterward." Nick kissed him and ran his hands over Torturo's face out of force of habit. "So handsome. I missed your gorgeous face there in the darkness." He kissed his lover for a long while and then went back to the mirror. "These are amazing." He glanced at Jacob, lying quite contented on the bunk. "And I love when you get that pretty sky blue. It means you're thinking how much you love me."

"My beautiful boy." Nick moved back to sit on the bunk and Torturo drew him close, kissing him, whispering, "My brave gorgeous boy."

"You look better than ever," Nick said.

"Why? Am I in Technicolor now?" Torturo laughed.

"All those years without you, just the memory of your smile." Nick laughed as Torturo rolled him to his back and loomed over him, his aging face aglow with pleasure. "Sexy, handsome man."

CHAPTER 17

LOCOMOTIVE

They were sitting in the car on Friday, avoiding the Midway. Clovis's days were indeed numbered if the state of the Show was any indicator. The paint peeled on the concession trailers. The patched canvas of the booths made Nick ache. And neither of them had wanted to test any of the ramshackle rides, which looked put up by half-asleep crews running on the end of their weed and speed. They could ignore the faded wallpaper and threadbare quilt in their car much more easily.

Nick sat polishing their shoes and Torturo watched him, smiling. Torturo reached for the piercing case. Nick looked up at the rattle and saw the red spikes of arousal in Jacob's aura. The whole Show had auras now. Nick could read some of them but none as well as Jacob's

"Oh no, you don't. If you get that out, I'm going to get all distracted and your boots aren't going to be ready."

Jacob laughed. "What makes you think this needle is for you, my selfish darling?" He took out a small one and ran it slowly through the webbing between his fingers. "I'm just playing. Keep polishing." He leered and then struck a pose. "The Pain King must look his finest."

Nick finished his polishing fast and got up. "Tease." He stretched up for a kiss, but bit Torturo's lip instead.

Torturo laughed again. "Always." He rattled the piercing case and Nick felt his pants tent away from his swelling erection. "You love the bite of the needle, don't you?"

Nick's breathing had gone fast. "The needle…going in…"

"Is better than sex?" Torturo smirked and rolled a thicker needle between his fingers.

Nick shook his head. "No, it's foreplay. It makes my whole body wake up."

"Oh yes," Torturo breathed on his neck and ran the metal over Nick's skin. Nick felt the goose bumps rising.

"When you do it to me, it makes me want more sensation." Nick looked at him earnestly with the blue crystal eyes. "Everywhere. And I know you'll give it to me."

"Always, darling."

Nick winced and unzipped his pants as Torturo ran the needle through the auricle of his ear.

* * *

They lay together afterward, small drops of blood on the pillow. Nick listened to Clovis talking and became aware that his lover was looking at him strangely.

He rolled up on an elbow and ran his fingers over the gray streaks in Jacob's hair. "You don't hear it anymore, do you? The voice of the Show, I mean. You used to. That's how you knew to bring me along."

Torturo shook his head. "No. It didn't choose me. I never heard it like you hear it. Clovis would speak up a little, but mostly it was just nudges toward doing something."

Nick nodded. He looked down at his right hand which had evinced some tubes running the length of his fingers and brass struts along the bones that morning. He flexed it, watching the Swiss-watch precision of its motion. "I hear him all the time. That's why I'm changing." He looked up. "What am I turning into?"

"I don't know." Torturo's voice was soft and unpleasant.

Nick looked at him. "I'm sorry you're all pissed off."

Even more quietly he said, "I'm not."

Nick shook his head and sat up. "You can't lie. I know the look and your aura is all red-streaky." Jacob slid to the floor and knelt before him, hugging him around the waist. Nick stroked his thick blond hair and pressed his head in to his own chest. "Can you hear the clockwork? Tick-tock, tick-tock. Love-you. Love-you."

"Before the end, I will be begging you never to leave. Don't send me away into a world I no longer recognize."

"Never. I would never do that, just as you never left me at any of the stops."

"Not even as vengeance for all the terrible things I did to you?"

"No, darling." Nick kissed him lightly on the forehead. "You never left me, no matter how horrid I was. My own beloved Jacob. My husband. You never did anything I didn't let you do." Torturo only held him tighter at that. "You did very little I didn't beg you for. And I loved you for it."

"You don't anymore?" Jacob raised a stricken face to look at Nick.

"I loved you even when I said I didn't, even when I said I couldn't. I'll never stop. I'll always love you, no matter what I turn into." He took the kiss and smiled. "I love that pale blue you're showing. I know it means you love me. What can I do for you, love?"

Jacob smiled, his brokenness fading into Torturo's confidence once more. "Love me? Hurt me?"

Nick kissed him and opened for his tongue, only to laugh when Torturo pulled him off the bed and onto the floor with him. He bit his lover's mouth again, harder this time and listened to Jacob moan at the taste of blood.

Nick gave a soft, sinister laugh. "You've been a bad boy."

"Very bad," came the agreement accompanied by quickened breath and a hard cock pressing into Nick's belly.

Nick slapped him lightly with the newly enhanced hand, letting him feel it. "What sort of punishment do you need, Jacob? You evil little shit, I ought to ram this up your ass as payback." He closed the metallic fingers over one nipple, scraping the struts over Jacob's chest, and pinched until he felt the metal of the rings starting to dent. He let up and listened to his lover sob.

"Yes…destroy me," he begged.

"Never." Nick bit his neck and licked at the blood. "You taste too good."

"Use the hand. Ruin me."

Nick gave a nasty chuckle and flipped him over. "Gonna fuck you first." It had taken a very long time for him to learn to say that and he'd never forgotten the pounding he'd received the first night he'd asked Jacob to do so. He smiled at the blissful look on Torturo's face and then rimmed him for a moment, trying to get enough lube.

Nick opened his pants, but stopped. He stared at what he had revealed. "Jacob, you better have a look at this before I shove it into you." No arousal or viciousness colored his tone, only shock.

Torturo twisted around to look at what Nick was seeing.

Nick looked down at his erection. Long brass pistons lay along the sides, bolted into the flesh, painlessly. As he watched, they pulsed in and out with tiny jets of steam, stretching his already hard cock a little. A hydraulic hose came out of his groin and fastened into the middle. Another came from the middle on the opposite side and burrowed into the head.

The reverse Prince-Albert made them both stare. The silver ring that entered Nick's urethra and came out behind the corona of his cock had turned into a buzz saw-like gear.

"Okay, it wasn't like that when I got dressed." Nick held his cock gingerly as if afraid it would bite him and touched the metal parts. "It doesn't hurt."

Torturo swallowed hard. "But does it feel good?"

"Doesn't feel bad." He touched the gear and winced as its sharp edge drew blood. "Ouch. That's going to hurt."

"You can't kill me with it." Torturo rolled back onto his stomach and spread his cheeks. Nick didn't miss how hard his lover had gotten.

This time, in deference to the metal, he added plenty of lubrication. He eased in as gently as he could, not liking the feeling of cutting into his lover. When the gear began turning, he screamed in horror as the blood flowed around him. He pulled out at once.

Torturo didn't scream, he just gasped as tears ran down his face. He whimpered a little.

"No, I can't." Nick watched in horror as the blood flowed into the slit of his cock and then through the tubes. "Oh lover." He kissed Jacob's neck and back. "I'll never have you again." He steeled himself to ask. "Or do you want me to do this?"

Torturo swallowed hard and smudged the tears away. His mouth worked a few times and he finally said, "No."

"Then I won't." Nick moved down to suck him.

"What happens when your tongue turns to a razor blade?"

"Then you fuck me." Nick licked at the scrotal ladder.

"How will it change your ass?"

Nick looked up, exasperated. "I don't know. Just love me for the time left us."

Torturo pulled him up for a kiss and they sprang apart as if stung. The gear, silent when Nick touched it, whirred when he came within two inches of Torturo's body. The pistons strained, stretching Nick's cock to bridge the last of the distance between them.

Torturo moved in close again and Nick whined as the pistons stretched him.

"Ouch. Please, it's not comfortable."

Torturo gave him an odd look. "It doesn't like me?" He watched the pistons pull out a little more.

"Oh, it wants you." Nick stepped back. "Ouch! Jacob, please?"

Torturo reached down to stroke the Frankencock and the gear buzzed like an angry bee, jerking sideways to cut him. He laughed.

"Stop that!" Nick pulled several feet away. "That gear hurts me, too."

"What does it want?"

"Your blood," Nick whispered.

Torturo offered his hand again. Nick moved closer so the pistons quit yanking at him. The gear sliced deep into Torturo's hand and the blood spattered all over Nick's cock. Again, it flowed into the slit to pump along the tiny hoses. Both men stared.

"Vampire cock." Torturo winced as it carved out a small chunk of flesh that made a very visible lump in the hose.

Nick moved away. This time, it took about five feet of distance before the pistons stopped trying to reach Torturo. Tears ran down his face as he watched his beloved bandage up his maimed hand.

"What's wrong?"

"It hurt. The modifications are trying to get to you and I only stretch so far."

Torturo nodded. "It thinks it's my time for payback. Perhaps it won't be happy until you complete what you started."

Nick shook his head. "No, no, I won't."

"It can't kill me," Torturo reassured him.

Nick took a breath. "I will only if you want me to." Getting the nod from Torturo, Nick lubed generously and made it hard and fast, trying for the most rapid orgasm of his life. The pistons moved him even more and he wept throughout, from the feel of the buzz saw and the blood.

Jacob was screaming by the end.

Nick pulled out the second he came and moved as far from his lover as he could.

Torturo lay still on the floor, face pale from loss of blood, his lower half scarlet. The last of the blood pumped along the hoses and Nick realized he felt too hot and bloated.

Neither man moved for over an hour.

*   *   *

Nick finally got dressed and went to where his lover lay. Torturo gave him a weak smile. His lips were cool under Nick's.

"Well," he whispered, "I told you to ruin me. Tell it to heal faster?"

"I've been trying." Nick kissed his pale lips again. He held Torturo for a long while and kissed him. "I want to finish the change."

"How will I manage not touching you?"

Nick sighed and turned his face away. He drew his knees up and buried his face in them. Torturo drew him down to lie on the floor and curled around him.

"I don't know." He moaned as the buzz saw started again. "No, oh please, no."

"No," Torturo whispered. "Not just from holding him."

Nick moved away, his shredded pants with the whirring gear and pistons pumping giving lie to that hope. He curled up on the couch. Torturo felt strong enough to climb into the bed, where he fell asleep at once.

They dozed until the twins came knocking.

"Darling boys, we have a show to run!" Alice called through the door.

"No," Torturo moaned.

"Tortie, Nicky, get yourselves out here or we're coming in," Dinah added.

Nick groaned and changed his pants for work. "We're coming, ladies," he called. "Get up, Jacob. Torturo the Pain King has a show to do."

"Torturo can't get up. And Jacob couldn't give a good goddamn about the show right now."

"Well, hell, what are we going to do?"

The twins flung open the door and stared. For the first time, Nick realized how far the blood had spattered. The once-elegant railcar looked like an abattoir.

"What's the hold-up?" Alice demanded.

"The rides are…up." Dinah trailed off as she saw the blood. "What were you boys doing?"

Alice ran one finger into a puddle and licked it.

"Went too far," Torturo managed.

"Obviously. And now our headliner is damaged." Alice scowled at Nick, who tried to look as innocent as possible.

Dinah dragged Alice over for a closer look at Nick. She took in his

199

eyes and hand and the general modifications the Show had made. " Oh Alice…" she whispered.

"Tortie, it may be time," Alice agreed.

"Time?" Torturo slurred. Nick could tell the haze of pain and endorphins had him slower than usual.

"For our sweet Nick to see the Engine."

Torturo shook his head. "No. Not time."

Nick listened to Clovis for a while. "Not just yet." He smiled at the twins. "I will be the Engineer soon enough."

"He's right. I will heal. I should be all right for the matinee."

Nick blew him a kiss and went to work.

"Tortie, he knows. He's taking it well," Alice said.

"We woke up quite astonished to be conjoined," Dinah added. "What did he do to you?"

"He fucked me. His cock has changed, too."

"Into what?" Alice found a couple of cloths and the girls started wiping up the blood, their motions slowing as he described the changes, especially the moving parts. By the time he had told them everything, Alice's hands were down both of their panties and she was frankly masturbating. Dinah slapped Alice's hands out of her drawers.

"If you're not up for the adult show, Tortie, he can do it," Dinah suggested. "Our own sexual automaton."

Pricked with jealousy at this comment, Torturo got to his feet. Both girls reached out hands to steady him.

"I think I can manage," he said gamely. "Without the spiked strap-on tonight though."

Dinah nodded. "All right, just a regular one then?"

"Yes. Just this once." They each kissed his cheek on opposite sides and he hugged them both. "Darlings."

"Our lovely Tortie." They helped him dress for the show. He wasn't bleeding anymore and his color had started coming back.

"You'll do fine," Alice said.

"It's not as if the nails hurt that much," Dinah added.

"No, and just leave Nicholas to me."

Alice giggled. "You're jealous. Leave him or what? Or you'll cut his eyes out again?"

"No. They just pop out anyway." Dinah wrinkled her nose in disgust, but Alice giggled again. "But I may swallow them like I threatened to."

For that, Alice kissed him, deep and hard, with a bite at the end.

Dinah turned her nose up. "Revolting."

Torturo gave her a grin. "I know I am."

"Sexy delightful man," Alice purred.

Nick had reached full ballyhoo when they made it to the shabby Ten-in-One tent. Torturo paused and watched him for a moment. Nick winked and kept working the crowd. Some seemed revolted by his mechanical aspects, while others were fascinated.

*   *   *

The day went slowly. Nick kept an eye on everything, especially Jacob. No Pain King banners hung along the deteriorating Midway. Instead, "Lilith, the Succubus," had taken his place. The posters, new but as faded as the rest of the Phantasmagoria, showed a beautiful, scantily dressed woman with enormous bat wings leering invitingly at the passerby. Jacob was going to be pissed.

Jacob sat in the piercing tent, drinking and watching the crowds. He had no customers. Nick noticed no one even seemed to see the piercing booth. He set his jaw and warned Clovis that he would be keeping Jacob, that Clovis would not devour his lover for the last bits of energy. Clovis said nothing.

Nick talked in the crowd for the adult show and hurried over to Jacob. "Are you still bleeding?" He had to back off to three feet when his cock twitched and the buzz saw started.

Jacob opened one eye from where he napped in the piercing chair. "I think so." He yawned and stretched, creaking. Nick stared. The man he had hurt that morning had looked fifty-ish. Jacob's hair was entirely gray now. Broken veins covered his once-sharp nose and heavy jowls. The clear hazel eyes that had pierced him in the car dealership peered blearily at him.

"You should see Lilith. She's amazing. Clovis did an excellent job on her."

Jacob growled at that. He waved an arm at the rest of the down-at-the-heels show, taking in the creaky rides, shabby costumes and mended canvas. "Worth it for hurting everyone? I can't hibernate, Nicholas. You'll wake up alone."

Nick knew the truth of that statement. His handsome lover, his beloved husband who had never dissolved their informal marriage on that distant Feast of Fools, had become a very old man in the space of an afternoon. It was time.

"No. Come." Nick walked away, back to the train. Instead of the car they had shared for so long, he headed to the locomotive.

* * *

Torturo followed him, his ancient joints protesting. Pain, pain like he had never felt shot out of his knees, eating along his legs with each step. "Nick! Wait."

Nick turned around. In the darkness, his eyes glowed blue. Not a steady blue, but a deep, flickering blue as if fires danced inside him. "It is time. Clovis is dying. It's time for me to take his place."

Torturo shook his head. Surely he could have one more night. Clovis could wait until the end of the stop. He remembered he couldn't even be near Nick now, but he still protested. "Not yet."

Nick stepped as close as his modifications allowed. "We had hoped to wait until the end of the year. But he can't even make the end of this engagement. That's why he made Lilith. That's why we've been so rundown for months. Now. Tonight." His eyes glowed brighter, like oil lamps, like headlights, cutting a blue swath through the night. Nick repeated, in a voice that was no longer only his own but carried a number of other accents and tones, "It is time."

"I can't let you go yet." The admission fell out of Jacob's mouth, not nearly as difficult as he had thought it would be.

Nick reached his hand out. "Come with me." Torturo took it without missing a beat and they walked slowly to the locomotive. "I'll always be with you. Come up into the cab." Nick mounted the steps, pulling his lover behind him. The sealed rear of the Engine stood open.

Torturo stared into the pulsing, fleshy metal nightmare. The brownish-red walls almost breathed as they entered and he felt the spongy floor shudder under their feet. Nick nodded, a small smile on his face. He looked like a man coming home after a long day of work. He led Torturo fully into the cab and stopped before a large chair in the center of the floor. It looked as if it had grown there, all veins and organic curves. The smell of coal and metal, damp flesh and sex made Jacob's head reel. A large cover stood open above the empty chair.

Nick opened his arms and Torturo came into them instantly, kissing him and clutching him, heedless of the buzz saw or pistons. Nick kissed him back, deeply, all the love of their decades together coming through.

"I love you, Jacob." He smoothed the gray hair away with the fleshy pads of his right fingers. His metal arm rested on the chair.

"Don't go." Jacob held him more tightly.

"It's time. If I don't, we all die. You, me, the girls, the whole Show." Nick looked at where Torturo clutched his waist. He moved back to cling to him a little. "I'll always be with you. I'll always love you." He smiled. "You'll hear the Show in your head, I promise. You will wake young and beautiful again,"

Torturo didn't let go. "Nicholas…"

"Jacob. Please." Torturo's fingers unfolded slowly. Nick stepped back. "I love you." He sat down in the chair, which closed over him like a clam shell.

Torturo made one last grab, but too late. In his head he heard, *::I love you, my Jacob.::* Sobs wracked him as he leaned over the Engineer's chair.

::Don't trust me, lover,:: Nick said. *::You have to leave. I can't keep the Engine open any longer. Go back to your car. Lie in the bunk. ::*

Jacob didn't know how to talk to him now, so he just followed the order, walking back slowly, feeling each step as a miserable ache that echoed the empty, Nicholas-shaped hole in the middle of him. Once in the car, Nick spoke up again.

::When you get there, strip. And just talk, as if I am beside you or think, as you used to at Clovis. ::

He undressed and lay back on the bunk. "I need to touch you."

The blanket wrapped around him and the mattress conformed to his body. *::You are. ::* The mattress shifted more and fluidly. It intruded on his anus and molded around his cock. *::I am the train. Anything you touch is me.::* The mattress slid about six inches into him.

Jacob moaned. He ran his hands over the mattress, stroking it as he would Nick. The whole bunk cradled him more closely, moving and making love to him.

::Mmm, that's nice, darlin'. :: Nick's mind-voice laughed as Jacob rubbed against him, frantic and wild. *::I love you and I'll always be as close as the nearest wall.::* He laughed as Jacob came.

Jacob lay, stroking the pillow as if it were Nick's face. "Can I still hurt you?" he asked.

::Yes. Do you want to? Just strike or stab or pierce the walls or the mattress or the counters. I cannot die.::

He smiled. "Then I can still fuck you. Are you content?" he asked, slowly.

::Yes. I have you. I have the Show. And I know what I am now. :: He delivered a mild electrical shock to Torturo's groin. *::And I can still*

hurt you. ::

He gasped. "Oh, yes…" Nick zapped him a couple more times, before adding one to his ass. The mattress sprouted spikes, not as close together as his bed of nails. Jacob gave a blissful smile. "In your control now."

::*Yes, and I can make you hurt so many ways.*:: One of the sharp spikes slipped into Jacob's anus, making him gasp. ::*You've been so bad, thwarting the will of the Phantasmagoria.*::

Jacob cried under the invasion and the pain. "I have."

It went deeper, seeming to grow thicker as it did. ::*And now I can punish you forever.*::

"Oh yes… I deserve it."

::*You do, you foul thing. You clung and you cried and you tried to stop my transcending.*::

A band wrapped around his chest, spikes digging into his nipples and skin. "Only because I love you. Yes…ruin me," he begged as the spike hammered in and out of him.

::*I already did tonight. You are a filthy sinner, barely worthy of my attention. I should punish you by ignoring you.*::

"No, please no. I won't survive."

Nick shuddered around him, a motion that rocked the whole car on its rails. ::*Come for me.*::

The spike moved harder and Jacob rode it desperately. He shot, spattering on the wall. The white fluid vanished, absorbed into the wall. Everything around him softened into soothing comfort. The mattress and blanket no longer tormented him, but cradled him.

::*Beloved Jacob.*::

"I love you."

::*I love you as well. And I will always care for you now. You'll be young again.*:: He rocked the bed gently, trying to lull Torturo to sleep so he could heal before the next day. Jacob stroked the mattress lazily. ::*I do love you. Rest now. Dinah's masturbating with her spiked strap-on, just dreaming of using it. Two more days and then you can sleep within me for a time.*::

"Heaven," Jacob mumbled, already drowsy.

::*Yes. As close as you'll get and all the hell you need to pay for it.*::

EPILOGUE

The crowd thronged through the Midway in the July heat. It wasn't a bad crowd for four on a Friday afternoon. The Ten-in-One had just started when the loudspeakers suddenly blared "Stars and Stripes Forever," the time-honored signal that something was wrong.

Marvello stopped in mid-reach for the guillotine cord. The crowd stared and the power failed. After a moment, a smooth male voice with a Midwestern no-accent came over the loudspeaker.

"This is Nicholas Harper, the Voice of the Phantasmagoria. There is no reason to be alarmed. Our generators are experiencing a brief shutdown." The crowd nodded. They were accustomed to rolling blackouts since the energy riots of the 2090s and the rationing of the 2110s.

Nick continued and, backstage, Torturo smiled at hearing his beloved's voice again. "If all guests will proceed to the exit, we will give you wristbands and show passes for tomorrow. The Phantasmagoria is closed for the day. Please proceed to the exit in an orderly fashion. All crew, please board the train."

The crowd went quietly enough, a couple of children crying as their fun was cut short, only to be mollified with the promise of a return trip tomorrow. Stitches and Bonzo stood at the gate handing out wristbands.

When the last person had left, Stitches yelled at the speaker, "They're all gone, Nick."

"All Show crew will proceed at once to the train. This is an emergency. Do not hesitate, do not retrieve anything. Come now. We have wasted a lot of time avoiding a panic. Sit and secure yourselves. "

Once the Show was aboard, they were thrown into seats and bunks by the lurch of the train taking off.

"My darlings, this next hibernation will be a long one," Nick informed them, his face appearing on every television and smooth surface. "It's war, nuclear war. We will be safe enough in the Between-Time, but I will not awaken you until the world is safe again."

"We understand," everyone said, individually.

"I will care for you. When the fire and dying are through, there will be some people left. And in time, there will be villages again. There has always been a Phantasmagoria. There always will be."

The performers and clowns, roustabouts and concessionaires all lay down. Their blankets covered them of their own accord and each received a caress from the pillow. Torturo kissed his and pressed against the mattress.

"Sleep now, my darlings," Nick whispered, his wheels clicking on the flaming hot, radioactive rails that only half-existed in his reality. Jacob, cradled within him, hibernated until the next stop.

*   *   *

Miguel stepped carefully around the new thing in the square, making sure Rosa's leg didn't catch on the stones. He drew the water from the well and set the jar on the opposite hip before wrapping one arm around his parasitic twin. She lolled in his arm and made her usual burbling noises.

"What is it, Miguel?" asked Pilar, who stepped up with her family's water jug and twitched her tail out of the way.

"I don't know. It looks made. And old. Old like *abuelita's abuelita.*" Miguel prodded it with a stick and a handsome man stood before them. He wore old, old clothes, the kind they only saw in books about the way people were hundreds of years ago, before the Burning. More, he had no deformities, not even a birthmark. There was no one in the village who did not have something.

He smiled with clean, white, perfect teeth. "Hello! I'm Nicholas Harper, Voice of the Phantasmagoria. The Show is coming soon, to your very town! You'll see things you never imagined. Alice and Dinah, the most beautiful women in the world will sing and dance for you." The man vanished and the image of two redheaded northern women appeared. Miguel almost wept. They had to be angels as they moved from opposite sides of the image and met in the middle, kissing cheeks before spinning away, their sweet soprano voices high and clear.

Nick's voice continued. "The Modern Methuselah, Jacob Plum. Born in 1907, yet looks no more than forty." A very good-looking white man, also unblemished, smiled and vanished. "He'll tell you of life in the twentieth century and you can shake his hand."

"Marvello and his lovely assistant Hannah will amaze you with their illusions." A black man and a white woman wearing identical clothing, hers cut much higher, pulled flowers and scarves from each other's hands and ears.

"Nagina the snake charmer and Mingxia the acrobat, both from the mysterious East, reveal the secrets of the Orient to all comers." A pretty Indian woman danced between large snakes, her bangled ankles flashing, and a tiny Chinese woman set a goldfish bowl on her head with her feet.

A tall white man preached, but much more enthusiastically than Pilar had ever seen old Padre Ramón do and his small, pretty wife sang old hymns in English. "Brother Elijah Grant, the Carolina Giant, a giant among men and revival preachers and Sister Tabitha, his wife, will preach an old-fashioned revival and hymn sing."

"Wolfgang, direct descendant of Wolfgang Amadeus Mozart, will amaze you with his talent." A handsome European man played the piano with great flair.

Nick reappeared and gave a smile to the people watching. "All these and other marvels await. They're all alive on the inside. The Phantasmagoria is coming!"

Miguel and Rosa, with Pilar helping support the girl, ran to tell the village.

ABOUT THE AUTHORS

Angelia Sparrow is a librarian-turned-truck-driver who has been writing off and on for over thirty years. She got her first professional writing break in 2004. When not perpetrating romance, she lives quietly in the Mid-South with her husband, four kids and two cats. She enjoys crochet, cooking and gardening.

To learn more about Angelia and her writing, please visit her website at: http://www.angelsparrow.com.

*   *   *

Naomi Brooks, International Woman of Mystery and Stalker of Stockboys, is a retail escapee and technophile residing in Northwest Ohio. She enjoys a life of feline servitude, and is addicted to Netflix, The Sims 2, and World of Warcraft. Her first professional piece appeared in 2006. When she grows up she wants to be Errol Flynn, or Adam Lambert. Whichever.

AMBER QUILL PRESS, LLC
THE GOLD STANDARD IN PUBLISHING

QUALITY BOOKS
IN BOTH PRINT AND ELECTRONIC FORMATS

ACTION/ADVENTURE	SUSPENSE/THRILLER
SCIENCE FICTION	DARK FANTASY
MAINSTREAM	ROMANCE
HORROR	EROTICA
FANTASY	GLBT
WESTERN	MYSTERY
PARANORMAL	HISTORICAL
YOUNG ADULT	NON-FICTION

AMBER QUILL PRESS, LLC
http://www.amberquill.com

Made in the USA
Charleston, SC
13 February 2011